Mistletoe
and
Mr. Right

TWO STORIES OF HOLIDAY ROMANCE

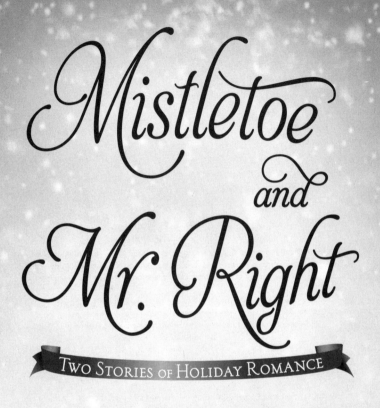

Mistletoe and Mr. Right

TWO STORIES OF HOLIDAY ROMANCE

LYLA PAYNE

BLOOMSBURY

NEW YORK · LONDON · OXFORD · NEW DELHI · SYDNEY

"Mistletoe and Mr. Right" first published as an e-novella in November 2014
by Bloomsbury Spark
Bind-up first published in the United States of America in October 2015
by Bloomsbury USA
www.bloomsbury.com

Bloomsbury is a registered trademark of Bloomsbury Publishing Plc

For information about permission to reproduce selections from this book, write to
Permissions, Bloomsbury USA, 1385 Broadway, New York, New York 10018
Bloomsbury books may be purchased for business or promotional use. For information
on bulk purchases please contact Macmillan Corporate and Premium Sales Department at
specialmarkets@macmillan.com

Library of Congress Cataloging-in-Publication Data
available upon request
ISBN 978-1-61963-927-0 (hardcover) • ISBN 978-1-61963-956-0 (e-book)

Book design by Yelena Safronova
Typeset by Westchester Book Composition
Printed and bound in the U.S.A. by Thomson-Shore Inc., Dexter, Michigan
2 4 6 8 10 9 7 5 3 1

All papers used by Bloomsbury Publishing, Inc., are natural, recyclable products
made from wood grown in well-managed forests. The manufacturing processes
conform to the environmental regulations of the country of origin.

To Mary McCormack and her family, proprietors of the Donour Lodge in Fanore, Ireland, who played wonderful, warm hosts (and tour guide and chef and book recommender!) to my friend and me on our trip last summer. Your enthusiasm and humor and beauty are rivaled only by the Burren itself.

Your little piece of Ireland stole my heart.

Table of Contents

Mistletoe
and
Mr. Right

Chapter

1

All my daydreams of Ireland are colored in greens—lime shades, olive hues, carpets of emerald grass all topped by a stormy sky. The reality disappoints me with far-reaching grays and whites, sprinkles of browns, and the slightest hint of purple on the cliff side, but then again, maybe I held expectations that were too high for December. It wouldn't be the first time in my life that expectations didn't live up to reality.

Nerves dance in my stomach, taking lessons for tangos or fox-trots, maybe hoping to make it big on *So You Think You Can Dance*, and not only because the rain slanting across the windshield of the winner of the Tiniest Rental Car Ever turns difficult travel into a nightmare. The roads in Western Ireland wind and twist, turning back on themselves like a slithering snake, bordered by waist-high stone walls that appear to have grown straight up out of the earth. Boulders so massive they must have been dropped there by giants litter the steep hillsides, adding to the wonder of being in a new country for the first time in my life.

I've never driven on the wrong side of the road before, or from the wrong side of a car, and this is the first time I've driven a stick shift in over four years. More than a few tree branches have fallen victim to my bad American driving since I left the airport in Shannon. With the increasing rain and the fact that I'm not the best driver in the world even in familiar conditions, it seems possible that I may not make it to Fanore alive.

That would put a real damper on my boyfriend's surprise Christmas gift—my unexpected presence at his family's bed-and-breakfast.

I take the last turn toward Brennan's hometown and settle back into the seat, trying my best to relax my death grip on the wheel. The small village—*wee*, from his descriptions—won't appear for at least another thirty miles.

A smile touches my lips at the thought of the last four months with my boyfriend; a smile that's aiming for nostalgia but stretches too thin. Too nervous. The night we met lingers in the back of my mind, like a ghostly handprint, but mostly it reminds me of all the hopes of that fresh beginning.

And how they've started to fade . . .

It had all been perfect. Like a movie, like the way I'd

planned on my life taking that all-important turn toward forever exactly when I'd planned on taking it.

❦

Junior year started a week ago, but we've been too slammed getting through recruitment with Gamma Sigma to enjoy any of it. Semesters begin early for sorority girls, and the first parties never take place until after bids have been passed around to new pledges and we've all managed to assure them we're capable of conducting ourselves like proper ladies.

I'm tired, worn out even though classes have barely started, and inclined to blow off the Lambda party, but my roommate Christina refuses to take no for an answer. As usual.

"Jessica, seriously. Come on. We've been holed up in this house staring at résumés, faking smiles, and eating peanut-butter sandwiches for over two weeks. Let's get out. Smile for real. Maybe even laugh."

"I don't feel like it." I cast a look toward my ethics text-book, the sight of which inspires reconsideration. "What would I even wear?"

"Who cares what you wear? Just get up and put something on." She knocks my feet off my desk and goes to stand in front of the mirror, slathering on thick lip gloss and sticking on fake eyelashes while I drag a simple plum-colored sundress from the closet we share.

"This?"

"Sure. It'll make your eyes pop." She eyes me in the mirror. "Maybe straighten your hair."

I groan, but one look at the dark brown nest atop my head cuts off any formal argument.

We're primped, out our door, and through the door to the party within the hour. The Greek houses at TCU are on-campus dorms, which means no parties, raging or otherwise, so we're being hosted by one of the Lambda brothers at his rental.

It's a standard night, with standard red plastic cups brimming with watery Natty Light from the keg and standard music pumping through their sound system as Chris picks up a drink and leads me into the backyard. The sweltering air sticks my dress to every piece of wet skin, and my hair clings to the nape of my neck. Everyone around me slams their drinks, desperate to get to the point where they don't notice how uncomfortable they are, but the idea of losing control of my mouth or my body has always seemed far worse than enduring the heat of Texas in August. Or anything else, for that matter.

I sip a bottle of water, laughing when the mood hits me, mostly scanning the crowd for this guy Jeremy that I've had a crush on since he played in our charity soccer tournament last year.

Instead, I keep catching grass-green eyes attached to shaggy brown hair and a stupidly handsome face over by the fire pit. I've never seen the guy before, and he doesn't really fit the über-rich, preppy mold of a Lambda, which makes me think he must be new. TCU is too big for me to know everyone, but after three years it's small enough to recognize all of the faces.

"Are you going over there, or what?" Chris slurs, her gaze following mine. "You two have been staring for like, two hours."

I shrug, uncomfortable. "I don't know. I like it better when the guy makes the first move."

"What?" Her eyes pop open in exaggerated shock and she clutches her chest, which is easy to do since it's shoved halfway out of her clingy black top. "Jessica MacFarlane, feminist and go-getter extraordinaire, thinks her ten-year plan is going to come together waiting for a guy to make the first move? Keep dreaming."

I whack her arm but can't help smiling. Chris and I have been close since pledging Gamma Sig together freshman year, but we're total opposites—starting with the fact that she thinks my plan is complete crap.

That said, she has a point. If I'm going to get engaged within a year of college graduation, giving me plenty of time to travel and establish a career before having the first of two children, maybe the time for waiting has passed. I'm already a junior, after all.

Who says guys have to make the first move, anyway?

I smooth my dress, toss my hair, hoping the humidity hasn't turned it into a coonskin cap, and take a deep breath. "Okay. I'm going in."

The walk across the small yard seems to take an eternity,

especially since Handsome sees me coming before I make it halfway there and breaks into a heart-stopping smile.

"I must say, I like being the one who makes someone else walk across a room for once." He greets me with an unbelievable accent, his green eyes fastened to my face. "I'm Brennan. Donnelly."

"Jessica MacFarlane," I manage, my fingers tightening around my sweaty plastic bottle. It pops and his eyebrows go up, his whole face smiling. "That's a great accent. California?"

He laughs, luckily aware I'm joking, and my muscles relax the slightest bit. This isn't so bad.

"Ireland, I'm afraid."

"What are you doing in Texas?"

And so the conversation unfolded, uncovering mundane facts about him and about me, until he loosened up enough to ask for my number before we headed our separate ways. He called after the standard three days, we'd gone to another party together, and that had been that. Nothing special, except for him, and the way he checked every box on my list.

Unlike everyone else in my life, Brennan didn't comment on my not drinking. He didn't think it was weird that I have to have every last detail planned out. He lets me be me, which is great.

Or it *was* great. I frown, pulling my thoughts back to the present as the sign for Fanore pops up on the side of the road. Now, after four months of fun but no clear direction for the future, I'm wondering if Brennan's lack of interest in how I do things translates to a lack of interest in general.

And I'm not getting any younger.

A gust of wind knocks the car sideways and I focus harder, noting that my boyfriend was not joking when he described Fanore as a blip in the road. Maybe four turnoffs angle from the main road, where there are two pubs, a post-office-slash-convenience-store, and a few other storefronts I can't make out through the rivulets streaming down the foggy windshield.

The sign declaring the turn for the THISTLE FARMHOUSE B&B comes out of nowhere. My tires lock and slide when I slam on the brakes in an attempt to navigate the turn, but they manage to keep me on the road. The car slams into dirty, deep puddles of mud along the unpaved road toward the Donnellys' bed-and-breakfast, jarring my teeth and sending vibrations through my limbs. My knuckles are so tight on the wheel my fingers have gone numb, and I force slow breaths out through my nose. We're almost there. Dying on an Irish back road to nowhere before college graduation is not part of the plan.

Cows and sheep graze beside the road, oblivious to the freezing sheets of rain, and if there are fences keeping them safe from my kamikaze driving, they aren't visible at the moment. At least three other bed-and-breakfasts lurk in the mist—one called the White House, and then the Donour Lodge, which has some amazing landscaping. Fanore lies deep in the country, with the crashing ocean and rocky beach on my right and nothing but pastures and homes on the left. The Donnellys' place must be the pretty white farmhouse up ahead.

I squint, trying to guess how much farther, when something white and furry flashes in front of the car.

This time the brakes respond to my frantic stomps, tires working hard to grip the sludge of the road, but they can't prevent the nauseating *thunk* followed by a pathetic *mewl* that challenges the rush of the wind.

Chapter
2

I throw open the door, not bothering to grab an umbrella. Time could be of the essence, though what on God's green earth *I'm* going to do for a mortally injured animal is anyone's guess.

A goat lies under the front bumper, its legs hidden beneath the car. I don't see any blood, but the road is a mess of mud and water that could easily hide whole body parts, so that doesn't mean much.

The goat peers up at me with a bewildered expression and bleats.

At least it's alive.

My chest tightens and my stomach clenches as I squat in the mud, cringing over ruining my best pair of jeans and hating myself for it at the same time. "Oh, I am so sorry. Don't die, okay? Please? I just really can't handle the drama right now."

True to form, my brain handles emergency situations by babbling. To a goat, no less.

Get a grip, Jessica. Think.

Moving the goat could be bad, like jostling a person that's been in an accident. Based on my pop-culture knowledge of life in the country, I'm pretty sure paralyzed animals get bullets to the head as opposed to motorized scooters.

Pouring rain sticks my hair to my forehead, dripping in my eyes and down my cheeks like tears, but I'm far too gone to panic and indecision to care. The fear that I've just murdered a goat aches in my belly, and worse than that, this is going to be my introduction to Brennan's family.

Hi, I'm hoping to be your soggy, psychotic daughter-in-law one day. Love me?

"Well, I never thought I'd see this in a donkey's years," a deep baritone sways from the darkness. It startles a squeak from my throat and I slip in the mud trying to stand up. "Here I've been swearing that old goat wasn't ever going to die."

I make it upright on a second try, tottering on cramped knees while I try to make out the stranger's face through the messy night. He's tall—taller than Brennan by at least a couple of inches—maybe about six foot five, but no one could describe him as skinny. Even bundled up in a thick canvas coat and an askew wool cap, it's no secret this guy takes care of himself. The rain plasters escaped chunks of dark hair against his head, and bright blue eyes reach out and grab me.

They brim with concern and something that resembles contempt, with a side of amusement.

The combination makes me bristle even though I've done what he's accusing me of at the moment. "I don't think I've *killed* her."

Yet.

"Yet," he grunts, echoing my thought as he crouches near the ailing goat.

I grind my teeth together and try my damnedest not to cry. My tears tend to show up most often when I'm frustrated or embarrassed—or one of my well-laid plans has gone awry—as opposed to signaling actual sadness, and there's nothing more annoying than having people offer comfort just when I feel like punching them.

The goat bleats again and my heart twists. My own pitiful problems climb into the backseat. Where they belong, given that they don't include being mowed down by a vehicle that would be mercilessly bullied on the Texas playground of giant trucks and expensive SUVs.

I shouldn't make fun of the thing. If I'd been driving my ancient "Ford Exploder," this goat would be toast.

"Is she going to be okay?" I ask, shuffling up behind the guy and chancing a peek over his shoulder.

He doesn't answer but reaches down, prodding her with one hand and lifting with the other until she gets her legs underneath her and crawls to her feet. The goat gives a quick shake, spraying dirty water all over my jeans and the mystery man's olive-green jacket, then hops off into the grass.

"Is she limping?"

"Probably. She just got ran over by a car." He stands up, using the hem of his jacket to wipe clean the fancy camera hanging around his neck.

I take a deep breath and count to four. Five would have been too many, since the guy has turned to go. "Hey! Thank you. I mean . . . what's your name? I really owe you one."

"No, the *goat* owes me one. I didn't help her for your sake." He shakes his head at me, clearly peeved. Maybe she's his favorite goat or something. "You should be more careful. There are sheep in the road more often than not, and the visibility is shit in this weather."

"I guess that makes it ideal for photography, then?" I snap, unable to stop myself.

The guy—who might be Batman the way he's safeguarding his identity—gives me an appraising look, as though he's just admitted to himself there might be a working brain between my ears. "What are you doing out here, anyway? Don't get many strangers."

I lift my chin. "Not that it's any of your business, but I'm surprising my boyfriend for Christmas."

"So, you just thought you'd pop in, huh? That's a great plan. Guys love that." He grins at me as if he's made a hilarious joke. "Who's your boyfriend?"

I hesitate, because I don't even know why I'm even talking to this stranger. In the rain. To a guy who has just

14

derided my brilliant plan. But ignoring him goes against my Midwestern programming.

"Brennan Donnelly. Do you know him?"

Something flickers across his face—a shadow, gone before its source is revealed. "I know him. Less than two hundred people live in this town, plus I work for the Donnellys."

He works for the Donnellys? That's awkward.

I swipe my bangs back, squinting through the rain. "Oh? So you're not a full-time photographer of nighttime rainstorms, then? I'm not surprised."

Except I am sort of surprised. My thoughts turn, as usual, to trying to solve the puzzle in front of me. Like why a guy who appears to be about my age would work on a farm instead of choosing university or a trade.

Stop. Not everyone is smart enough to realize the value of planning things out in advance.

"You're the one *driving* in this mess, with a plan that's going arseways fast," he shoots back, then closes his eyes as though he's counting to five before sticking out a gloved hand. "I'm Grady Callaghan."

We're both standing out here getting soaked, so I decide against playing the petulant sorority girl and shake his hand before climbing back into the car, reveling in the dry heat pouring from the vents.

Specks of cold rainwater fly off my coat and splatter on the dash. The goat has disappeared into the dark. Through the streaked windshield I watch Grady Callaghan's retreating form follow suit, and I fight off the worry that he might throw an untimely wrench into the spokes of my brilliant plan.

The rest of the two-minute drive to the farmhouse passes without incident, but my neurotic brain won't let go of the idea that Brennan's family is going to find out what just happened and hate me forever. All I can do is hope one surly Grady Callaghan keeps his mouth shut about his goat heroics.

Based on his lack of interest in niceties or friendliness in general, I'm guessing I shouldn't hold my breath, which is a shame because now that the drive is behind me, my plan is otherwise back on track and solid as ever.

If anything has ever looked as good as the warm glow from the white farmhouse's windows, I can't recall it. My nerves return, working on perfecting their cha-cha now, and all the deep breaths in the world aren't going to convince them to take a water break. A glance in the rearview mirror reveals a complete and utter mess—my hair hangs like wet strands of linguini, mascara smudges charcoal half-moons under my eyes, and dirt streaks my forehead and cheeks like pale stripes on a tiger. Add all that to the effects of an eight-hour transatlantic flight, which has graced me with red veins through the whites of my eyes and wrinkled my clothes all to hell, and I can only assume my introduction will be less than stellar. I look more like an overworked hooker who specializes in outdoor sex than a proper girlfriend.

But Brennan will be happy to see me at least.

I pull some face wipes from my toiletry case in the backseat and get rid of the dirt, shed my mud-splattered coat, and pull my hair back into a single braid that immediately starts dripping water on my shoulder. My jeans are still wet and gross, but this is as presentable as it's going to get, so instead of stressing about it I remind myself why I'm here—to find out whether to push in all my chips or fold this relationship now—and race through the rain for the cover of the front porch.

The house, or bed-and-breakfast, stands two stories high, with dingy white siding and stark black shutters. Light spills from the windows and onto the wide wooden porch, warming my blood even though the sharp bite of the wind and rain continue to slap at my back. My hand shakes as I knock on the door, but as with most things, once the task is complete and there's no turning back, most of the fear dances off into the ether.

A middle-aged woman swings open the door, making the pretty wreath of fresh holly bang in the process. She stands at least two inches shorter than my five-foot-seven—she's rounder than I am, too, but not in an unattractive way. Her blue eyes study me with more than a little suspicion as she swipes at a stray chunk of gray-streaked auburn hair.

"Yes?" She demands, looking me up and down with a frown that reveals lines around her mouth.

My tongue sticks to the roof of my mouth because somehow, in all of my daydreams and planning, I hadn't

17

consider what I would do if Brennan didn't answer the door.

"I, um." *Articulate, Jessica.* "Is Brennan home?"

The question pops her eyes open wide, making room for curiosity to join the annoyance. I suppose visitors aren't welcome two days before Christmas, but friends of her son's at least have a chance.

"Yes, he's—"

"Jessica?" Shock nudges my boyfriend's voice a few ticks higher than normal as he peers around the corner of the entryway. My heart still thuds at the sight of him—he really is stupidly handsome, with his mahogany hair, strong jaw that's sporting the right amount of stubble at the moment, and broad shoulders that fill out every last inch of his flannel shirt.

Brennan's stunned expression loses out to dismay, then the same sort of irritation I'd glimpsed on his mother's face a moment ago before settling on a smile that's a little suspect. It's at least ten breaths before he moves toward me to grab me in a hug.

My blood feels icy and slick despite the eventual greeting, but I shove the bad juju down and squeeze him back, deciding my surprise had been enough to make him forget how much fun we'll have during an Irish Christmas. How much fun we always have.

"What are you doing here?" He murmurs against my ear, lips brushing my skin in a way that sends tingles down my spine.

I pull away, light-headed and buoyed by the happy, almost genuine light in his eyes. He's still pale, almost woozy, as though he's seen a ghost—though whether I'm the ghost of Christmas past or present with an option for future remains to be seen.

"Surprise!" I spread my arms with a grin, just like I practiced. "I missed you and didn't have plans for the holidays, and you know I've always wanted to visit Ireland." The whole spiel sounds kind of lame now, much worse than through all of my rounds with the mirror.

Brennan shakes his head and it's impossible to tell whether he's amazed or flabbergasted—in a bad way. The confusion isn't new to us, though, and he recovers nicely, slipping an arm around my waist. "Mam, this is my girlfriend, Jessica. Jessica, this is Maeve Donnelly, my mother."

"It's so nice to meet you," I gush, giving her my best interviewee smile.

She returns it with less enthusiasm, cutting another irritated glance toward her son. "A pleasure, although I must say this comes as a bit of a surprise, since we weren't aware Brennan was dating anyone seriously."

My heart sinks, landing somewhere around my stomach. He never told his parents about me?

I'm saved from the oppressive, choking amount of awkwardness spewing out onto the porch when a man who has to be Brennan's father wanders up, probably to see where all the cold air is coming from. He looks so like my boyfriend—same reddish-brown hair, same grass-green eyes, same freckles. Same easy smile, as though there could never be a reason in the whole world for worry. A teenage girl trails behind him, her arms crossed and curiosity plain on her freckled face.

"We have a guest!" Mr. Donnelly sticks out a hand, greeting me in a rich brogue much harder to understand than his son's. "Colin Donnelly."

"Jessica."

"Nice to meet you, Jessie."

My hand disappears into his weathered one. Calluses that could tell stories of baling hay and clearing land and probably birthing litters for the goat I nearly killed scrape my palm. "It's Jessica, if it's not too much trouble. And likewise."

"I'm Molly," the girl chimes in, pinching Brennan's bicep so hard he yelps. "His sister."

Brennan recovers and looks me over, seeming to notice for the first time that I'm not as put together as I pretty much always am. "You look wrecked, chicken."

"Yeah, it's raining."

"Been pissing like a hellhound all day," Mr. Donnelly nods, nudging his wife out of the way. "Come on in out of the chill, why don't you?"

Warmth and light gush over me, around me, comforting the way I've always imagined a mother's touch. It improves my mood in an instant, especially when Mr. Donnelly swings the door shut on the storm. Being in the house is like being wrapped in cotton.

Catholic markers hang everywhere, along with crucifixes

and little shrines to the Virgin Mary and . . . some other saints that aren't familiar to my untrained eyes. Even though I researched Ireland and its history for days before leaving, my brain refuses to recall facts about the struggles of the people, the reason behind the wars that ripped it in two, or even which country belongs to the United Kingdom. It has something to do with the split of the Catholic and Protestant Churches. Maybe.

What good is being anal if it leaves me at the least opportune moment?

Family pictures and religious sayings decorate the walls, and the former bring a slight smile to my face. Brennan hasn't changed much in the past fifteen years if the photos are any indication. The easy smiles on the family's faces, the way they touch each other without thinking about whether it will be awkward, stab my heart with a sliver of envy. If I took it out and examined it, the real true reason for my plan, for coming here, would glint in my palm, but that's a hundred percent off-limits.

Mrs. Donnelly, apparently recovered from the shock of my arrival, nudges us toward the kitchen. "Come in, come in. We were just about to have an evening snack to warm us up before bed."

A pot of tea steams in a knitted cozy in the center of an ancient oak table, delicate painted cups and saucers set out in a circle. There are tarts and cakes, some cookies— or biscuits, as Brennan calls them—arranged on a pretty Christmas-themed platter.

It's like something off a *Christmas in Ireland* greeting card. All of the charm and intrigue that drew me into Brennan's life fills the room, snuggling around me. The strong, aching desire to know more, to understand enough to be able to at least pretend to be a part of their family, escapes without my permission. I blink back the tears that prick my tired eyes, more sure than ever that coming here was the right move for us.

Slow down, Jessica. You've been here five minutes. You're not allowed to reveal the freak for a few days.

"Sit, dear. Have a biscuit and tell us why you're soaked to the bone." Mrs. Donnelly doesn't take her own advice, bustling around as we all settle in, making sure we have what we need. Her fluttering—and her question—return my nerves to their polished dance floor.

But Mr. Donnelly rescues me for the second time in ten minutes. "Maeve, for the sake of everything holy, please park. You haven't stopped moving since we woke up at four this morning and my blood pressure is soaring."

"Fine." She whacks him with a dish towel, a smile touching her lips as she slides into the seat to his right, on my left. "Please tell us about yourself, Jessica. Brennan is a typical lad in most ways, I'm afraid, which means we've been left clean in the dark about this whole courtship. What's your last name? Where are you from?"

I give Brennan an exasperated look that he misses because he's too busy scooping homemade goodies onto the china in front of him. "Well, my last name is MacFarlane."

Molly chokes on her tea, sputtering as drops of amber liquid hit the holly-embroidered tablecloth and soak in. Mrs. Donnelly hides an expression of dismay, leaving me to assume something—no idea what—is wrong with my last name. Brennan thumps his sister between the shoulder blades a bit harder than necessary and she smacks his arm, their tussle distracting everyone from me, at least for the moment.

"Kids, come on. You've been in the same room for two minutes," Mr. Donnelly admonishes before turning his steady gaze back to me. "Go on, Jessica."

Something about the way he says my full name makes me wonder if he finds my insistence on using it ridiculous, but nothing in his expectant expression backs up my feeling. It's probably my own ears hearing it that way after years of correcting people.

"Well, I grew up in Missouri and I'm majoring in journalism." My neck feels hot from all of the attention, but there's nowhere else to toss it. I kind of asked for it, showing up like this.

"Why are you so dirty?" Molly wrinkles her nose, her cheeks still pink and her hair out of sorts from the choking incident.

She had to remind everyone I hadn't answered that part of the question. Lying went against my code, but telling them I mauled their livestock on the way into town doesn't appeal to me, either. "I, um, had to get out of the car and move a tree branch."

"How did you and Brennan meet?" The teenager peppers me with the next question around a mouthful of what looks like cranberry scone.

"At a frat party," Brennan grunts. "Nothing too special about how it started, I guess."

I wait for him to add something sweet about how it's been special since or how quickly we connected but he doesn't, and the silence twirling through the room goes faster and faster until it's hard to breathe. It's accompanied by the scraping of forks against china, the occasional murmur about snow arriving in time for Christmas morning, and the chiming of a cuckoo clock on the wall.

Mrs. Donnelly looks up at it, then gives me another tired smile. "Well, it's certainly nice to meet you, Jessica."

A yawn stretches her lips wide and inspires one of my own, a reminder that I've been up nearly twenty-four hours. My eyes burn, nothing on my mind now but a sincere hope that she's going to show me to a bedroom.

I'm guessing Catholicism has something to say about Brennan and I sharing a room.

No one moves, and a desperate urge for conversation tugs at my tongue. "I know it's unbearably rude of me, showing up like this two days before Christmas, but I couldn't think of a good gift for Brennan and this seemed right." I try a smile, earning matching nods in return, as though they're a family of bobbleheads. "Anyway, you know us Americans. Unbearably rude is kind of our national slogan."

The joke tumbles flat on its face, and Mrs. Donnelly

reaches over and pats my hand. "It's no trouble, dear. We've missed our boy these past few months, and it'll be refreshing to hear about his time in the States from one of his friends. Not much of a talker, our Brennan."

"That's the truth," I reply, a little miffed that she referred to me as his *friend*. And that he didn't correct her.

She takes me down the hall to my room and then gives me a tour of the guest bathroom before handing over clean towels and bidding me good night. I collapse on my bed as she closes the door, wondering how much to read into my not getting to say a proper good night to my boyfriend before being herded away.

Maybe he'll sneak in to see me in a bit, to tell me how happy he is to see me, how glad I made the three-thousand-mile trip to surprise him, and apologize for being so stoic upon my arrival.

I fall asleep before I can even think about changing clothes, so if Brennan does knock on my door, it falls on deaf ears. Ghosts fill my dreams, but unlike old Ebenezer Scrooge, mine all lurk in the past. My spirits don't have anything nice to say about the future.

Then again, they never do.

Chapter
3

Rays of sun peer through the sheer curtains framing my window before I'm ready, but at least last night's storm has dissipated. My body craves coffee, even knowing it's probably going to be tea from here on out, which is better than nothing when it comes down to a choice between chugging caffeinated tea or suffering withdrawals.

I put on a bra and tug on a pair of jeans, then grab a sweater before peeking out into the hallway. The quiet in the house makes the squeaks of my boots on the hardwood floors sound like cymbals. Even so, I make it out to the front porch without running into anyone else, and I breathe the crisp sea air deep into my lungs.

This morning, Ireland greets me like I imagined—a thick mist drapes the boulder-dotted shoreline like a shawl as sunlight winks off of the crashing gray waves. The rain turned to snow sometime during the night, so there's still no green, but the pristine white blankets covering the hills add the perfect ambiance to the late-December morning. A white Christmas in Ireland. This trip *can't* be a mistake.

The door creaks open behind me and a sleep-tousled Brennan steps up beside me, a colorful, handmade afghan wrapped tight around his shoulders. Pieces of his hair stick up in chunks and there are reddened creases on his cheeks, but when he smiles at me, there's no one more beautiful in the entire world.

"Morning, chicken." His brogue thickens enough when he's sleepy to trip me up, but I've gotten used to the nickname, which weirded me out at first. Apparently it's normal to him.

"Morning." I lean in for a kiss, not caring whether either of us has morning breath. We dispensed with that formality a few weeks after we started sleeping over. He lapses into silence, reigniting my lingering doubts. "Are you mad?"

"About you showing up?" He doesn't look at me at first, choosing to squint toward the sea instead. An eternity passes before he shrugs, turns, and slings an arm around my shoulders. "Nah. I mean, I was pretty surprised and my mam's a planner like you, so she might have a panic attack, but it's good to see you."

"Also we've been together four months now. It's time I met your family."

"And you took the initiative, as usual." He smiles to

soften the judgment in his words, then leans down to kiss the tip of my nose. "How can I get mad at you for being Jessica?"

And that's that. It's so Brennan; he's entirely go-with-the-flow and nothing bothers him. Ever.

Which, honestly, is starting to bother *me*. Because if he doesn't care about anything, what does that say about his attitude toward me or the potential for our relationship?

Chris would roll her eyes and tell me to shut up. That we've only been together four months and we're twenty years old, so who cares if we don't know right now if we'll get married. If it's forever.

I look at my handsome Irish boyfriend who does his best to understand me, and also happens to be dynamite in bed, and decide to listen to her. Try to relax and explore, to revel in the new experience.

"You guys, Mam is going to beat you both if you don't get in here for breakfast," Molly chirps, sticking a head full of frizzy strawberry curls out into the morning. She eyes us. "Are you two being gross or what?"

"Not as gross as your breath," Brennan retorts, tossing me a wink before chasing his sister into the house.

I take one last look around the magnificent scene before heading into the dining room, feeling better about this whole thing. Brennan and I might not be there yet, but I still think a holiday with his family, in his country, will make him realize he wants to hang on to me.

The family gathers around the rough, pitted table, along

with an addition from last night. An elderly man perches on one end, the sun glinting off the age spots on his bald head. He peers up at me through giant owl-like glasses with a skeptical expression, as though maybe I'm a cantaloupe he can't quite decide on buying based on smell.

"This the Scottish girl?" he grunts.

"Granddad, Jaysus!" Molly's cheeks go pink.

At least now it's clear why she choked last night at the mention of my last name.

"I'm not Scottish, I'm American. My father never even mentioned it." Not that I remember much before my ninth birthday, when he died. But it seems like a fair protest.

"You've got the blue eyes and the stature. Can't breed that out." The old man waves a dismissive hand. "You'd probably walk two miles out of your way to pick up a penny, too."

"Dad, seriously." Mr. Donnelly reaches for a piece of flat oatmeal-colored bread. "Knock it off. We're supposed to pretend to like the Scots now, and that guy who stole your girlfriend at university died ten years ago. Give up the fight."

"Ten years too late," he grunts, still giving me a look like he's wondering what crimes—real or imagined—I've committed. "You're pretty, though. So that's something."

Brennan shoots me an apologetic look and pulls out a chair next to the old man. Mortification heats my face even though it's ridiculous to feel embarrassed about my last name. I didn't choose it and it doesn't mean anything—not to what's left of my family, anyhow.

I stick out my hand. "I'm Jessica."

He looks down at my hand, then gives me a gap-toothed smile without shaking it. "Michael Donnelly."

"Can we eat now?" Mrs. Donnelly raises her eyebrows at her family as though daring any of them to say no. "Good."

I join the others in filling my plate with yogurt, granola, fruit, some scrambled eggs, and a sausage patty. Brennan holds out a plate of bread and scones, nudging the thick oatmeal loaf toward me with a finger.

"It's soda bread. A tradition around here."

"Sure." I take a slice and doctor it up with butter and jam, then take a bite. It's delicious, with an interesting flavor and texture that's like bread, but not. "Yum. I like it."

"'Course you like it. Anything's better than haggis and porridge." Granddad says, talking around a mouthful of yogurt.

"What's haggis?" I ask in my best innocent voice.

"Mam makes the best soda bread in town." Brennan informs me, intercepting his grandfather's reply.

"That's a beautiful picture," I comment, nodding toward a black-and-white photograph hanging on the wall. It captures a moment in time—a woman on the beach, her back to the camera as her dark hair blows in the wind, teasing the hem of her dress out toward the crashing gray waves. Mossy rocks frame the scene, a perfect, jagged addition to the fierce image. "Did one of you take it? Or a local photographer?"

"Oh, our farmhand Grady took it—he's always snapping

photos with that camera of his," Mrs. Donnelly adds, an indulgent smile turning up her lips. "Quite good at it, too."

"Huh." It's all I can manage, my mind trying to reconcile the gruff, off-putting guy from last night as the kind of artist who could see the unique beauty in that photo.

"Did anyone see Nanny Goat this morning?" Molly changes the subject, picking at her eggs. "She's got a fierce limp."

My heart pounds to a stop. The silence in the room rushes in my ears like static and the world slows down, as though we're under water. *Shit.*

"I saw her yesterday and she was fine. Feisty as ever." Mrs. Donnelly refreshes my tea, even though I've only sipped twice. "Tried to bite me."

I don't have to say anything. As long as stupid Grady Callaghan keeps his mouth shut they'll never know what happened last night. But the goat could need to see a vet or something; plus if they *do* find out I ran into her, they're going to know I sat here and basically lied to their faces. With only three days to make a good impression, losing time by insulting them will hurt more than admitting my mistake.

"I hit her with the car last night," I mumble. They all stare at me, even Brennan, surprise slacking their jaws. "I mean, I don't know if it was Nanny Goat. But it was *a* goat."

"What? Why didn't you say something when you got here?" Mrs. Donnelly's accusing gaze actually burns.

"He didn't know," I rush on when she turns it on Brennan. "I didn't tell him."

"You should have told us." Mr. Donnelly's not looking so affable now, lines crinkling around his mouth. "She might need to see a vet and getting one out here two days before Christmas isn't going to be easy."

"Come now, Colin. This way we won't have to butcher a turkey for holiday dinner," Granddad chortles, laughing so hard he starts to choke.

"Nanny's going to be fine," the same smooth, baritone brogue from last night interrupts.

I twist around in my wooden chair to find Grady in the doorway from the kitchen, his stocking hat clutched between his bearlike hands. His bright eyes land on me, looking more gray than blue without the glare of the headlights. They're reproachful, as though he's resisting the urge to reprimand me for keeping the whole incident a secret. I fight the urge to roll my eyes, since he's sort of helping me.

"You checked her out?" Mrs. Donnelly looks worried, as though I hit Molly and not a biting goat.

"I saw her last night right after it happened. She was a little stunned. A wee bruise on her left foreleg, nothing more." He casts me another glance, and I do my best to look thankful for his support.

I *am* grateful he stepped in because the family is going to trust his opinion over mine when it comes to a goat, but he doesn't have to be so *ugh* and smug about it.

"I didn't say anything last night because I was embarrassed." My face flames, adding credence to my story. "And Grady said the goat was fine. I should have told you, though."

"Did you get some breakfast, son?" Mrs. Donnelly asks Grady, ignoring my apology.

Her husband returns his attention to breakfast, but a frown pinches his lips, replacing the perpetual almost-smile. Grandpa Donnelly *tsks* in my direction, dancing eyes more than a tad amused. Even though Brennan squeezes my knee under the table he seems out of sorts, at a loss as to whether to defend me.

"I did, ma'am, thank you." Grady smiles at her, as sweet as pie. "I just popped in to say I'm running to town. Does anyone need anything?"

"No. Well, maybe some cranberries?" Mrs. Donnelly nods. "And you're joining us for Christmas dinner, yeah?"

"Sure look it," he replies, nodding.

The nodding makes me think he's answering in the affirmative even though the phrase means nothing to me. Brennan utters it all the time and it seems to be applicable in response to absolutely anything under the sun.

The Donnellys' farmhand clomps back toward the kitchen in his work boots and I feel a tap on my hand. Grandpa Donnelly grins at me again, a conspiratorial glint in his rheumy eyes. "Why don't you go grab a bottle of brandy outta the press? You look like you could use a drop in your tea."

Press? Do they make their own brandy?

I shake my head as Mrs. Donnelly cuts in. "I wouldn't mind, either, dear. I've got a bone-deep chill I can't seem to shake."

33

Here we go with another awkward conversation. "I actually don't drink."

It comes out of my mouth like an apology, one I've been making for a year and a half at school, but it's easier to joke my way out of it when I can use inappropriate euphemisms and profanity.

"You don't *what*?" Grandpa Donnelly squints at me. I'm the potentially bad melon again.

"She doesn't like the way it makes her feel," Brennan explains. He's trying to be helpful, which is sweet, but he's making me sound like a high-maintenance bundle of anxiety.

"Are you, like, that one weird religion? Mormon?" Molly's eyes pop huge, as though a movie star just sat down across from her. "Like John Travolta?"

No matter how hard I kick my feet and claw at the surface, this conversation is going to drown me. "Those are Scientologists. And I'm not Mormon; it's just a personal decision that works for me. I like to feel like myself."

"It's just one drink, girl." Grandpa interrupts. "Even Jesus drank wine!"

"Well, Jesus didn't have to worry about date rape drugs," I quip, wondering at the last minute whether jokes about Jesus are allowed. Personally, I'm sure the guy had a sense of humor, but the Donnellys seem pretty damn serious about the whole shebang.

It shouldn't surprise me that not drinking would be a big deal in Ireland. Brennan drinks with almost every

34

meal—not to the point where he's an alcoholic or I'm worried about it; it's part of his lifestyle.

My choice is a *thing* at college, too, but I care less about impressing those people.

Instead of taking a chance on making things worse by talking, I stuff a giant bite of sausage in my mouth. My tongue works it around, surprised by the texture and flavor—it's not like any regular sausage. The taste isn't bad, exactly, but my stomach isn't sure about keeping it, either.

"What kind of sausage is this?" I ask after managing to swallow the first bite. I'm sorry it was such a big one, although it still tastes better than my foot, and that's been in my mouth pretty much since I arrived.

No one answers right away so I look up to find my boyfriend watching me with a mixture of amusement and worry etched on his handsome features.

Dread mixes with the mystery meat, making me sweat. "What?"

"It's not sausage. It's called black pudding."

"This is pudding?" I prod the dry clump with my fork, trying not to sound like too much of a clueless American. "It doesn't look like pudding."

"That's because it's not made with milk," he explains, his fingers gentle on my leg now.

"What's it made with?"

"Well, some pork fat." He pauses, flicking a glance toward his mother, following that up with a grimace. "But it's mostly curdled pig's blood."

I can't even respond. By the time the words get from my ears to my brain my breakfast is shooting up my esophagus. There's no time to apologize or attempt to look less horror-struck, because I need to *not* throw up on Mrs. Donnelly's dining room table.

Brennan starts to stand but I fling out a hand, shaking my head as hard as I dare. "No. Stay."

I flee outside because it's far closer than my bathroom. Even so, I barely make it to my knees in a fresh patch of snow before refunding my entire breakfast back into the earth. I gag for another couple of minutes, my brain refusing to stop repeating the phrase *curdled pig's blood*.

"You seriously couldn't make it to the jacks?"

I groan, already able to recognize Grady's voice. Largely because it keeps popping up whenever I *don't* want an audience. The glinting sunshine makes my eyes water as I look up to find him towering over me, a grossed-out grimace on his rugged face. "What's a jacks?"

"The toilet? Bathroom, whatever you Americans call it?"

"No, as a matter of fact. I could not make it to the *jacks*." I wipe my chin with a handful of snow and put more in my mouth for a rinse. It's a nasty thing to do in front of someone else, but for some reason it doesn't bother me.

"You got some on your jumper."

That term I know, because like every self-respecting girl, I'm obsessed with *Bridget Jones's Diary*. Although why people in the UK insist on calling sweaters *jumpers* is beyond me. If this is even the UK.

I've got to look that up again.

"Thanks for noticing." Tears gather in my eyes, because pretty much nothing has gone right since my plane touched down in Shannon. Brennan's parents hate me, and worst of all, I can't shake the feeling that he'd rather I hadn't come all this way.

Or maybe it's the sinking feeling of truth—he's not the one.

My tears fall faster, keeping time with the sound of my unraveling plan inching me closer and closer to the kind of uneven life littered with land mines I swore I'd never accept again.

"Aw, come on. It can't be that bad, Jessie."

"It's *Jessica,*" I snap, grinding my teeth and climbing to my feet. He's so much taller than I am that I still have to tilt my head back to look him in the eye, and when I do there's something there that makes my stomach dip and twirl and my heart pick up its pace. Honesty. Appreciation. A touch of eagerness.

It's gone so fast I might have imagined it, but my puzzling reaction to his kindness lingers.

"And it *is* that bad, but it's not your problem."

"No, you're not a Jessica. Jessicas are stuffy, uptight school librarians or mams who manage their stress by mixing pills and wine. You're definitely a Jessie. Or a Jess?"

"I can't thank you enough for the opinions, which you seem to have a wealth of, but you really don't know anything about me." I stalk off toward the house, shivering with wet pants and shaking hands. He shouldn't be able to get to me with so little effort.

"There's no shame in barfing up black pudding, you know! It's not for the weak!" He bellows after me, dissolving into throaty laughter that coats the air like fresh honey.

Responding would only make things worse. Guys like Grady, who amuse themselves far more than they amuse others, never learn. I have enough problems to solve without trying to figure out a guy I'm never going to see again after Christmas. There's certainly no point in acknowledging the way my stomach fluttered when our eyes met. The way it seemed, just for a moment, that we have something in common. How the moment I insisted he didn't know anything about me a small voice in the back of my mind whispered, *Are you sure?*

"Wait." I turn around, shading my eyes from the glaring sun, to find Grady watching me with an indecipherable expression that renews the tremor though my blood. "Um, could you get me a few things at the store?"

"Sure look it," he nods. "Whatcha need? Pregnancy test?"

"You're hilarious. Are you a comedian in addition to being a farmhand and a photographer?"

"Don't forget goat rescuer. Just added that one to my résumé."

"Well, make sure and include professional pain in the ass," I grumble, fighting a smile. I give him a short list of items that have at least the potential to put me back in the Donnellys' good graces. If they like pumpkin pie.

Part of me—a part that scares me, because it's the one that reminds me too much of my parents—wants to stay out here trading barbs with Grady. It's hanging a smile on my face, a lightheartedness in my soul that rebukes the annoyance I want to cling to, but there's no room in my life for unknowns. Anomalies. Everything has a place, a purpose, and flirting with an aimless artsy type halfway around the world doesn't fit.

I sweep away my odd attraction to Grady along with the dusting of snow still clinging to my jumper and step back over the threshold toward my proper future.

The dining room sits empty, most of the dishes and breakfast foods carted off into the kitchen. A peek into the front room reveals Granddad Donnelly in front of a news program. Clinks and the rush of running water from the kitchen draw me in that direction, but the low murmur of voices, one of which belongs to my boyfriend, slows my steps. Maybe eavesdropping isn't the best way to turn this trip around but knowledge is power or whatever.

"Can't you just give her a chance? You haven't gotten to know her at all."

"I don't dislike the girl," Mrs. Donnelly's voice rises above the *clank* of pots being washed. "But how will someone of Scottish descent who doesn't drink fit into this family?"

"We're dating, Mam, not getting married. It's one holiday."

My heart sinks, forcing me to swallow hard.

"You're not a boy, Brennan. Every relationship has to be evaluated this way because it could happen." Her tone softens. "I see the way she looks at you, like you're exactly what she thinks she's been waiting for, and who can blame her? But between the things we've mentioned, plus our religious differences . . . be smart, kid."

"I am, Mam. Don't worry about me."

"I'll never stop," the woman replies, and the smack of a loud kiss waltzes into the hallway.

To hear that Mrs. Donnelly doesn't think I'm a good match for her son, and that Brennan wasn't thinking of me in those terms in the first place, sucks the air out of me like I'm a deflating balloon. I lay flat and sad for a count of five, then I breathe in and clench my fists.

Because damn if Jessica Anne MacFarlane is going to let a few stumbling blocks get in her way.

Instead of confronting him and making an even bigger mess of things, I do my best to make myself useful the rest of the morning—wrapping presents for Brennan's mother, reading quietly in the sunroom while the men go out to butcher a turkey for Christmas dinner and Molly and Mrs. Donnelly head next door to exchange gifts with the neighbors.

The sound of the mudroom door and stomping footsteps from the kitchen make me think Grady's back with the groceries, which will at least give me something to do. I find overflowing bags on the counter and locate the one filled with the makings of a crust, pumpkin filling, and whipping cream.

And a pregnancy test. Hilarious.

I toss it on the counter and unpack the rest of my goods, getting to work. Kneading dough, measuring ingredients, and the soothing motion of the rolling pin ease the tension from my neck and back. The snowy Irish landscape charms me through the farmhouse windows, the scent of cinnamon and cloves races and tumbles around the kitchen, and the warmth of the wood stove mingles with Granddad Donnelly's snores from the other room. It's nice. Like the way family should be, even if they're not mine.

Yet.

The holidays have never meant quite the same thing to me since my parents lost their home the December I was in first grade, but it's hard not to believe this year could be different. That my *life* could be different.

Hope washes over me, and the task of baking a pie is mindless enough to let my thoughts roam over the boxes that still need to be checked off: finish college, get engaged, find a fantastic job at a local news station with tons of potential for moving up the ladder, get married, get the fabulous promotion, start investing, buy a house, have the first kid.

That's the ten-year plan. One that leaves no room for

living on the street, holding a handmade cardboard sign outside the local McDonald's. No chance of an empty belly or an empty cup that never filled up quite enough to afford a Happy Meal.

Regardless of where Brennan's at or what his mother thinks, he's kind and stable and has a good head on his shoulders. Finding the right guy means consistency, and that means never having to be afraid of what each new day will bring.

And I don't think that's too much to ask.

Chapter
4

I shove the pie in the fridge, leaving the whipped cream to chill in a separate container, and go for a walk down to the shoreline. Even though it's not the kind of beach that would draw vacationers by the thousands—no sand, only mossy, ancient boulders—it's beautiful and peaceful, which is, at least in some ways, better. The rocks don't provide much comfort as far as my rear but the crashing of the waves and the sight of the sun dipping toward the horizon manage to infect me with a calm acceptance that's hard for me to come by, normally.

There's still time. This might work out and anyway this is the twenty-first century. Maybe I should think about rewriting my plans so that the engagement and marriage are optional boxes. Doing it now feels a little bit like failing, though, and that makes my skin crawl.

The sun slips lower, splaying out on the waves like

marmalade on toast. I've stayed away long enough, and every bone in my body feels porous and weak, as though ready to collapse. My eyes feel like there's sand underneath the lids as I make my way over the rocks and through the pasture, taking care to avoid giant piles of poo. Wandering cows and sheep pay me no mind on the way—they must not have heard the scary rumors about me from the goats yet— and the Donnellys' dogs regard me with bored expressions.

Brennan meets me outside the house, pulling me into a hug that knocks the wind out of my lungs. "Hey, chicken, I've been looking for you! Mam wants to drive all the way to Ennistymon for some last-minute bits and bobs. It's a fair bit down the road, so we'll probably be gone for dinner, too." He checks his watch. "You're invited, of course, but you'd better get in there and change if you're coming."

"I don't know." I swallow, not even sure why the negative reply comes out of my mouth. "I'm not feeling my best."

"Probably jet lag. It can be rough if you're not used to it." He squeezes me again, dropping a kiss on top of my head. "Go splash some water on your face and get into some dry clothes. See how you feel."

I nod, gathering another kiss before heading down the hall. A *whooshing* breath falls out of me with the click of the door. The sight of the comfortable, quilted bed pulls me forward and onto my face. It smells like lemons and fresh detergent and I roll over on my back, meaning to get right up and change. Pouting and holing up in my room is no way to convince Brennan I'm the fun, energetic, sexy girl of his dreams, but now that I'm horizontal my eyes droop.

There's always the convincing argument that the less time I spend with the Donnellys, the fewer opportunities I'll have to reinsert my foot into my mouth. But I should get dressed and go, if for no reason other than it's my first time in Ireland, and I should see more of it than one dinky town.

And that my plans are inching back on track.

A knock opens my eyes, which are blurry for having been closed only briefly. " 'S open."

Brennan comes in and closes the door behind him, walking over to the bed and flopping next to me. "Did you fall asleep?"

"No." I glance at the clock and realize almost an hour has passed since we parted ways. "Oh. Maybe?"

"You are so adorable when you're all rumpled." He leans in for a kiss, wrapping his arms around me, pulling me tight against his chest.

We deepen the kiss out of habit, out of practice, until my body is on high alert and our tongues are exploring as intently as our hands. Brennan's hand slips under the hem of my sweater and brushes the bare skin of my belly, making me gasp against his mouth. My hands tangle in his hair, tipping his head to give me better access. We're getting carried away when there's a second knock at the door and his mother sticks her head inside without waiting for permission.

No matter how fast we jump apart there's no way she

misses me tugging down my shirt or her son patting his hair back into place. She frowns but doesn't comment, thank goodness. Strike thirty-seven.

"Are you ready?" She directs the question at Brennan but can't help eyeing me, who is clearly *not* dressed for public consumption.

"I am," Brennan says easily, as though embarrassment never entered his mind. "Jessica's not going. Jet lag."

She waits, her mouth working as though she's dying to say something else, until my boyfriend rolls his eyes. "Go, Mam. I'll be out in a minute."

He grins at me, but as hard as I try, I can't return it. This trip just won't right itself.

"Oh, chicken." He cups my jaw between his palms, holding my face steady so there's no way to escape the intensity of his bright gaze. "Mam's feelings won't change mine. She just doesn't know you well enough yet."

"Yeah, but I sprung this on you before you were ready, and all I've done is embarrass myself and make your family think I'm all wrong for you." It all tumbles out at once, a tangle of failures breathing between us.

"But you're *not* all wrong for me," he argues, gentle as he reaches for me again. "They'll get to know you and come to adore all the little quirks about you like I have."

His reassurance doesn't make me feel better, though I can't put my finger on exactly why, and I nudge him away. "You go. Don't keep them waiting. I'll wrap presents and go to bed early, and we'll try again tomorrow."

He kisses me lightly, then folds me in a brief hug. "See you later."

It's not until after he leaves that the reason his pep talk fell flat becomes glaringly obvious—that he considers the things that make me *me* just simple quirks to be overlooked.

I wrap the presents I brought with me—mostly TCU gear and some tea Brennan mentioned his mother adores—and think about climbing back into bed. But as much seclusion and comfort as the quaint room offers, the thought of being stuck until tomorrow morning sounds about as good as being trapped in a coal mine without my iPhone.

Maybe I can find the barn. Check on the stupid goat that got my trip off to such a bang-up start.

First I check on my pie, only to find it missing a tiny sliver. Its maimed state would normally irritate me but instead makes me smile. At least one person in this house appreciates my offering.

It's cold outside; a brisk, swirling wind picks up flakes of snow and whips them into little cyclones of white lace against the star-splattered sky. The crunch of the snow under my boots, the chill of the air as it falls into my lungs and rushes out past my numb lips tug my spirits upward, if only a little.

The landscape remains beautiful at night. Now that I've seen the rocky hills and far-flung ocean during the day, they're easier to make out in the moonlight. Outbuildings appear on the five-acre property, and even though I've never lived outside of a city in my entire life, the barn is the biggest of them and not at all hard to find.

Inside, it's warm, a tad overly so after the crispness of the outdoors. There's a smell that's far less pleasant than the other scents that have regaled me so far, and the hay spread out across the floor and baled in the corners and in the loft doesn't look the cleanest. A few sheep *baa* as they nose the brittle stalks, thick bells on their collars jangling as they shuffle about in an attempt to get comfortable for the night. The Donnellys' sleek dogs lounge by the huge entrance doors, as uninterested in me and my movements as they were when I crossed paths with them earlier today.

The cows must still be out and I don't see any horses. I peer into the empty stalls, standing on my tiptoes, then push open the door to the third one when Nanny Goat's dirty coat catches my eye.

At least I think it's Nanny Goat. This goat is white, with a funny beard and little horns, just like the one under my bumper last night.

A crate is buried under some hay toward the back of the stall and I sit down, pulling a bag of carrots from my pocket. I'm hoping they weren't scheduled for Christmas dinner but it wouldn't be right to check on Nanny Goat without a peace offering for last night's faux pas.

"Hey," I start. The goat looks over at the plastic bag in my hands, slight interest in her black eyes. Sticks of hay hang out of thick lips. "Want some carrots?"

She takes a hesitant step toward me, then another. The slight limp in her foreleg makes me swallow hard, but even though I'm no expert on . . . well, anything that lives on a farm, it doesn't look too terrible. Not bad enough to get her popped, anyway.

I hold out the carrot, determined to wait her out, and it doesn't take long. A giggle escapes as her soft lips brush my fingers. The carrot disappears and she stares at me with blank eyes. They're deep pools, empty but not without simple beauty, and she takes another carrot without asking.

"Hey!" I scold, but then tip my head, reconsidering. "Okay, fine. I hit you with a car, so take as many carrots as you want."

She lets me scratch her behind the ears as she munches more carrots. Her fur is wiry instead of soft but affection stirs for the odd little thing all the same.

"You're not so bad," I observe. "A tad smelly, but it's not much worse than a frat house the morning after a particularly fun after-party."

The goat makes no comment and we sit in the silence for a while, the only sound the grinding of her teeth and the occasional shuffling from the sheep. My mind wanders over my conversation with Brennan earlier tonight. Over everything that's happened since I showed up in Fanore.

I hear the echo of Chris trying to talk me out of this crazy escapade as we got drunk the last night of finals.

"You're going to scare—" Hiccup. "Scare him off," Chris finishes, stumbling into our room.

"If I do, then he wasn't the right guy anyway, right?"

"Haven't you ever been young? Like, just went with the flow? Kicked off your shoes?" She flings one foot out, her flip-flop careening off the mirror and landing on the windowsill.

"Yes."

"No, you haven't."

I kick off a flat, but it only bounces two feet before settling right side up inside the closet where it belongs. Chris cracks up and I frown. "I love you, Christina, but you do not get it."

"Get what? That you're so paranoid you're going to end up like your mother it turns you into a lame lamester who's about to ruin a halfway decent relationship with a totally hot accent? I get that."

"The weird thing is," I tell Nanny Goat, "I don't think I'm missing out on anything. I mean, it's not worth it, flying by the seat of your pants. Not if it means not knowing where I'm going to sleep or where my next meal is coming from, right?" Nanny Goat makes no comment but she does watch me, as though considering what I've said while enjoying her evening snack. Perhaps she has a thing against talking with her mouth full.

"I can still be a world-class news anchor before I turn thirty without a husband, right? Probably even sooner."

I hadn't expected to pick journalism as a major, but it's called to me since my randomly chosen elective freshman year. There's something so stable and reliable about the news, every night at ten.

"I really am sorry about hitting you last night, Nanny.

50

You were probably so scared, those headlights bearing down on you and a crazy American chick behind the wheel." I give her another scratch and this time it seems as though she might enjoy it. "Did that mean ol' Grady at least give you some good drugs for the pain? We could wrap up your leg with some ice and a bandage, at least."

"She'd eat the whole thing inside five minutes." Grady appears at the stall door, a long piece of straw hanging from his full lips. He rests his arms on the top of the wooden slats, blue eyes sparkling like he swallowed the stars.

I ignore the lurch in my breathing. "How long have you been out there?"

"Long enough to know you talk to goats." He smirks. "And I wasn't lurking, I was doing my job."

"Which is what this time? Showing up at inconvenient times?"

He gives me a *look* but the crinkles at the corners of his eyes betray his amusement. "Well, some people would be grateful for the help I gave last night. And this morning. Why'd you bring up the goat incident at breakfast?"

"I *didn't* bring it up. I got backed into a corner."

"This place has nothing but Jessie-sized corners, seems like." Grady winks at me, which is infuriating and familiar and startlingly sexy all at once, then enters the stall without asking. He drops a hand to rub Nanny Goat's head and that pisses me off, too, because she seems to like him far more than she cares for me.

I mean, I'm the one who hit her but I also brought

carrots. She doesn't seem impressed by my glare but Grady's grinning when I look up. "What?"

"Nothing. It's just . . . you know goats are morons, right? She doesn't remember what happened last night, and in ten minutes she'll have forgotten that you snuck her contraband treats." He plops on the crate next to mine, a little too close for comfort.

He seems to know he's a little too close for comfort. Which is the only reason I don't put distance between us. Two can play the intimidation game, and even though that's usually not my knee-jerk response, Grady seems to have a knack for expanding my comfort zone.

"Whatever. Maybe I like talking to goats because they don't talk back."

"Unless you're a couple of pints in, I suppose." He sobers, watching me with a scrutiny that's too intense. "Are you okay, Jessie? Pregnancy test not go well?"

I grit my teeth but refuse to correct him again regarding the nickname. I'm not so much *okay* but Grady Callaghan doesn't seem like the wisest choice of confidante. "I'm fine. No test needed, thank you very much."

As though a girl like me doesn't double up on everything, including protection.

"Hmm." Grady pulls the straw out of his mouth and drops it on the floor, scuffing it into the pile with the worn toe of his boot. "Let me preface this with saying that sticking my nose into other people's business isn't my idea of fun."

"I feel a *but* coming on, so you're welcome to just cut it off there."

"See, if you were half this saucy when dealing with the rest of the clan, they'd have fewer reservations about you bedding their precious boy."

My jaw falls open. "That is none of your business!"

"I know. It's just that this whole thing is painful to watch." He catches my gaze and holds on, nothing about his posture or expression suggesting he's teasing. "And if you think you'd rather be single, why'd you come here?"

He had been lurking for a while if he'd overheard me trying to convince the goat—and myself—that the plan could be altered. Anger bubbles, but it eases to a simmer as quickly. Maybe I'm overlooking a golden opportunity here. Grady knows Brennan. More intel could be the key to turning this whole thing around.

"I'd rather not be single and alone forever," I admit. "So I guess I'm just trying to figure things out."

"Yeah, but you're what, twenty? What's the hurry?"

It disappoints me for some reason, to find out he's just like everyone else, at least in his opinion on this subject. "I'm not the kind of person who leaves things to chance."

"How can falling in love be anything *but* chance?"

Normally, this is where I'd walk away from the conversation. Sigh and accept he doesn't understand and never will, but the open honesty on his face and the frank intensity in his blue eyes convince me he really wants to know the answer. So I forge ahead.

"Falling in love and finding someone to spend your life with are two different things."

"Are they?" He wrinkles his brow. "I mean, I guess I get that in some sense. Like, you might spend weeks in bed with a certain kind of bloke but marry the one whose going to be at work every day and at home every night."

"You make it sound shallow."

"Well, it's just that . . . again, what's the rush? Isn't now the time in your life to spend weeks in bed with the wrong bloke?"

As much as I want to, I'm not ready to talk to Grady about my past. Only one person knows the whole truth about where I come from, why my scholarship to TCU means so much, and the reason behind my determination to be able to take care of myself after graduation, and that's Christina. Brennan only knows bits and pieces because having him look at me and see a sob story instead of a person would ruin everything.

Somehow, I get the feeling Grady wouldn't run, but I just shrug. "I like plans."

He levels me with a serious gaze and our eyes lock. They're fused, stuck in place like someone glued them there, and even though it should be awkward and I should be in a hurry to look away, I don't.

"I like plans, too. But people like the Donnellys—ones who have never had to swerve unexpectedly—don't understand their true value. If you're looking for a way into their family, you've got to relax. Let them see your funny side, your good heart." He nods to Nanny Goat. "Maybe leave out that you'd rather confide in goats than people, though."

Grady ducks my swat with a smile, a genuine one this time. The sparkle in his bright eyes fades to genuine concern that reaches out in tendrils that seem to brush softly against my skin.

It sounds as though he understands what it's like to lose everything because you're not prepared, and the idea that here, halfway around the world, I would meet someone who gets it—really *gets* it—siphons all of the air from my lungs. I want to know how and why, dig around in his brain, root in his soul, but Grady isn't my boyfriend. He's not the one who should be understanding, not the one I should be confiding in—not to mention that a mostly grown man with no career plans and no education doesn't exactly fit my criteria for a serious boyfriend.

Despite the truth of every one of those thoughts, my blood runs too hot at his nearness. At his words. The compliments he gave me and the time he's taking to make me feel better all zing awareness of another human being through me like I've never felt before. I clear my throat, desperate to regain some control. "Thank you. For listening."

"It's my pleasure." He pauses, seeming to consider whether he wants to continue. "Brennan's not a bad guy. If you have concerns, you should talk to him. Give him a little more credit."

"You guys are friends?"

"We both grew up in Fanore and we're the same age, so,

yeah, we've always been friends." He points a finger my direction. "But I said a *little* more credit not a lot. He's still a guy."

"So are you."

"How kind of you to notice, Jess."

I roll my eyes this time. "You're just doing that to get a rise out of me now."

"Doing what?" he asks, all innocent big eyes.

A smile sneaks onto my face despite my exasperation, and silence settles over the barn. Coziness lulls me, creates a buffer between us and the world outside, as though things are possible in here that could never even be spoken out in the cold.

"Why do you want to be a news anchor?" he asks, startling me out of my cocoon. I frown at him, but Grady doesn't even have the good sense to pretend to be sorry for eavesdropping.

"I don't know. It's a steady paycheck, and it's a service people need."

"*Hmm.*" I'm starting to realize that Grady is good at watching, at listening, and he might not realize he's looking at me like I'm an idiot when his brain is focused on gathering information. "But with the Internet and considering that most people *avoid* the news because all it does is remind them of things they can't change, don't you think that's a tad . . . obsolete?"

"Well, when you put it that way." I poke him and he grabs my wrist to thwart the attack. A pop, then a sizzle shoots up my arm, dissolving into a shiver when it hits my armpit.

Grady drops my wrist like it's covered in acid, swallowing hard and shifting on his crate. I'm desperate to break the sudden tension, to bring our level of comfort back to where it was moments ago. My brain function fades to a minimum in the wake of his touch, my tongue stumbling over *ums* and *wells* before finding the rest of my explanation.

"I think you're right. With the way the Internet is changing reporting, people our age and younger are going to go out of their way to avoid the networks. They're slanted. In politician's pockets. News is going to be a grassroots project, probably through social media because of its immediacy. Any network that wants to stay relevant is going to hire more reporters and send them everywhere with their smartphones."

The opinion rolls off my tongue without a second thought because it's something I've thought about often— I even turned in a massive research paper on the subject. If I were a different person, traveling the world and reporting news in real time, no network filter, would be super appealing.

"I can see that. We're *already* seeing it, really, with the way social media sites are where people go to see what's trending by the minute." He nods, his gaze thoughtful but more guarded than it was a moment ago. "But you, Jessie MacFarlane, still want to sit in a studio every night and read someone else's words off one of those things."

"Teleprompter," I supply, feeling attacked. "And I don't

think my getting blown up or working for pennies, never knowing where I'm going to lay my head from one night to the next is going to change the world."

"I think we don't know who or what will change the world." A strange sadness touches his smile. "Our world changes, and then we trace back to the spark. The moment the earth tipped on its axis."

Questions stick in my throat because he's lost in a memory. As someone with deep, private closets of her own, I know better than to force open the door. The idea that this guy I've never met thinks it's possible to change the world—that *I* could change the world—opens up windows in front of my eyes. In my soul.

They let in too much light, too many possibilities, and fear makes me slam them shut.

"Maybe. But I know I'm not brave enough to take on a project like that."

"Not part of the plan?" He gives me a smile, but it hasn't recovered from whatever triggered his melancholy.

"Nope. Afraid not."

Grady's shoulders tense as he reaches out, calloused fingers brushing the back of my hand. My brain insists I jerk it away, that taking comfort from a guy not my boyfriend is wrong, but my body refuses.

"I'm sorry your surprise didn't go off as planned. If it makes you feel any better, the Donnellys aren't going to approve of anyone for Brennan who isn't Katie McBride. So, it's not totally your fault." He pauses, managing a more familiar, teasing smile this time. "Aside from the attempted vehicular goat-slaughter, of course."

"Ha." I pull my hand away under the pretense of straightening my ponytail. "Wait, who is Katie McBride?"

"Brennan's high school sweetheart. First love. Maeve named all six grandkids they were going to give her." A line of wrinkles appears between his eyebrows. "He never mentioned her?"

I'll say one thing about Grady Callaghan. He sure knows how to ruin a moment.

After freeing myself from the comfortable confines of the barn and trekking back across the crusty, cold snow toward the farmhouse, I'm greeted by Donnellys. They tumble out of two cars, and the sight of Brennan and a girl I don't recognize supporting a pale, sweating, barely conscious Mr. Donnelly between them dries up my greeting in my throat.

Chapter
5

Oh my God, what happened?" I'm breathless after sprinting the last several yards to the front porch, following my boyfriend and the mystery girl into the house.

"He had an allergic reaction," Brennan grunts, laying his father on the couch in the living room. "He's going to be fine, just a bit drugged up."

"What? How did that happen?"

The guilt tightening the skin on Brennan's face makes my palms sweat. "Don't freak out, chicken, but my dad's allergic to nutmeg. He thought that pie you left in the fridge was sweet potato, because that's what we eat at Christmas dinner, and snuck a few bites."

I actually feel the blood drain out of my face. "I'm so sorry. I didn't know, I swear!"

"Of course you didn't, dear." There are lines on Mrs. Donnelly's face that weren't there this morning, and even though fatigue still tugs at my eyes, there's no way she looks any better. "It was an accident, pure and simple. We're lucky Katie was there."

Katie?

I turn toward the stranger, a girl around my age with waves of silky black hair flowing from underneath an adorable green knit hat, complete with pink flower on the side. The color of the hat is no match for her eyes, which are the shade of emeralds and just as sparkly. Freckles scatter across her perky nose and the smile that splits her cheeks could probably power this whole damn island.

If this is Katie McBride, the girl is a nightmare. Mine, anyway.

"Oh, right." Brennan clears his throat. "Jessica, this is an old . . . friend. Katie McBride."

"Katie McBride, the hero of the day," Molly chirps after stomping every last flake of snow from her boots and leaving them by the front door.

I look down to find mine leaving puddles on the polished oak floors.

"Stop it, you all. All I did was recognize the issue and get an EpiPen from the first aid kit in my car." A pretty pink blush splashes across her cheeks. She turns an apologetic gaze toward me. "I'm a member of the volunteer fire department, so I always carry one. It was seriously no big deal."

Great. I basically try to murder Mr. Donnelly and Katie McBride steps up to save his life.

"It's lucky you were there," I tell her with what feels like a decent attempt at a smile.

"Wasn't it?" Molly beams. "And she's staying for Christmas!"

Brennan puts an arm around my waist, eyes brimming with an apology he's either not able or willing to verbalize among others. It helps that he at least realizes why this would be uncomfortable for me even though he's never mentioned this girl, ever. "We ran into her in town, and once Molly found out her family is in Africa for the holiday, she insisted—as in, threatened to handcuff her if she said no—that she come back and spend the next couple of days here with us."

"It's so nice to meet you, Jessica," Katie says in a soft voice. "Brennan didn't stop talking about you the whole drive."

"The whole drive? Wow." The smart-ass reply slips out, surprising everyone including me. It's on the tip of my sassy tongue to inform her that this is the first time *I've* heard *her* name but that seems like taking Grady's advice to relax a bit too far. "It's nice to meet you, too."

"I'm freezing my bollocks off. Can one of you mongrels shut the blasted front door?" Grandpa Donnelly snarls, prodding his granddaughter with the rubber end of his cane.

Molly responds, skipping out of the room with a grin on her face. In fact, all of the Donnellys are smiling, and I'm not a selfish enough person to wish a lonely Christmas on Katie. But part of me wonders whether or not inviting her had been the plan all along, derailed by my showing up unannounced.

But there must be a reason Brennan never mentioned her. We've talked about past relationships and he mentioned that he dated a few girls in high school, but when I'd confessed that he's my first real boyfriend he'd allowed me to believe there weren't any serious ex-girlfriend's lurking behind door number two, either.

Mr. Donnelly and his crotchety father shuffle off to bed after hanging up coats and scarves and boots in the foyer and Molly bids us all goodnight at her mother's prodding. It's late—after midnight—and Katie's yawning. I'm past tired, too, but Brennan pulls me aside when his mother slings a fleshy arm around her hero of a guest and sweeps her away.

"I have to tell you something," he says, making a face that says he thinks I'm going to freak out.

"Let me guess. Katie's your gorgeous first love and your parents are still secretly hoping the two of you will work it out, get married, populate the island with beautiful babies, and live happily ever after?"

He eyes me, not sure what to think if his expression is any indication. "Pretty much, yeah. How do you know that?"

"Lucky guess." I sigh at the flash of annoyance on his face. "Grady."

"You two just keep running into each other when I'm

not around, huh?" Brennan gives me a thin smile. "Don't believe everything he says about me."

"But his assessment of your past with Katie is spot on?"

"Yes and no. It's true my parents love her and things were serious for a while. But we were kids, Jessica. People grow up. Apart. Move on. You know the drill."

Even though everything he's saying makes perfect sense, it doesn't sound as though Brennan's fully convinced by his own argument. There's nothing to be done about it now, though, and everything will look better—or at least clearer—after some shut-eye. Maybe.

I fall asleep thinking that even though I took Grady's advice about speaking my mind with Brennan—on accident, mostly—it did not, as predicted by the rugged farmhand, bring the Donnellys any closer to acceptance.

The time change plagues me into the following morning, my screwy internal clock rousing me as soon as the sun peers over the horizon and leaps into my room. My eyeballs might as well be on fire, the lids weighed down like lead, but try as I might, sleep dances just outside my reach.

My stomach growls, reminding me there had been no dinner last night. Even if breakfast is still a little ways off, maybe I can scare up some more of that soda bread. Or I could make something for the Donnellys—something American to show them that fitting me into their family could be fun.

The idea takes root as I tug my unruly—and apparently

Scottish—hair back into a braid. All of the loose pieces stay put with the assistance of a half a sheet of bobby pins. Jeans and a clean sweater, plus water splashed on my face and a good toothbrushing, almost make me feel like a human being.

Since my watch claims it's only a few minutes past six, it's no surprise that the hallway that leads from my first-floor guest room into the kitchen is dark and quiet. In my daydreams mothers are up the day before Christmas Eve, putting last-minute touches on cookies and pies, but six is probably pushing it, even for daydreams.

Which is why the sight of Katie McBride at the kitchen's island, her feet dangling from a bar stool, takes me by surprise. She's clad in pajamas and thick wool socks that look homemade, hair mussed, one hand wrapped around a steaming mug of tea and the other holding a ratty paperback of *Wuthering Heights*.

The girl looks for all the world like she's never belonged anywhere but in this kitchen.

She looks up, her bright green eyes hardly hindered by the glasses she must have swapped for her contacts, and smiles. "Good mornin', Jessica. I've wet the tea if you're interested."

"Thanks." I'd still rather have coffee but the scent of the tea as it pours into the sturdy mug is different than what Mrs. Donnelly whipped up yesterday—all honey and cloves and cinnamon—and my mouth waters.

Taking the tea and shuffling back to my room is more

than a bit tempting but that would seem like running away. For all of her beauty, for all of her history with my boyfriend, Katie probably knows Brennan better than anyone else. I'm not above picking her brain under the guise of friendliness.

And yeah, maybe I want to see if *she* thinks it's over.

When I slide onto the stool at the end of the counter, she puts down her book without marking her place, takes a lazy sip of her tea, and cocks her head toward the paperback. "Have you ever read it?"

"*Wuthering Heights*? Sure. It's one of my favorites." I've always wondered what it says about me that the stories of tragic love speak to me more than the sweet kind. Another one of those questions best left unexamined.

Katie nods. "I read it every Christmas."

"Me, too," I allow, even though admitting we have anything in common makes me want to scoop my eyeballs out with a melon baller.

"And want to give Heathcliff a good smack as a holiday present," she laughs, the sound tinkling off the china in the cabinets. "But I have a feeling he's the kind of guy who never learns."

"I'm pretty sure Catherine knew what she was getting into, anyway." I take a sip of my own tea, which is lovely on my tongue as it was in my nose, and can't help but smile.

"I suppose you're right. Women know what kind of mess they've gotten themselves into with the man they choose. Or gotten themselves out of," she finishes in a softer tone, eyes faraway now, like they've taken a train ten years into the past. She looks so sad sitting here in the misty morning, like a leprechaun kicked out of the hive for giving away one too many pots of gold.

A droplet of sadness splashes into my curiosity. There's no good reason that I, Brennan's current girlfriend, should be interested in the regrets of his former, but who am I to argue with my gut?

I'm not willing to give up Brennan, but I am willing to let her talk. Weirdly enough.

The far-off expression dissolves with her next drink of tea, replaced with a conspiratorial grin and an impossibly charming accent. "So, Molly says Grady Callaghan's been bailing you out of trouble right and left since you got here. What do you think of Ireland? And the Donnellys?"

"Gosh, that is so true about Grady. What's his story, anyway?" I almost bite my tongue trying to stop the question before it escapes. I'm supposed to be finding out more about Brennan. My boyfriend. Not indulging my increasingly hard to ignore obsession with his childhood friend.

The glint in Katie's bright gaze says she didn't miss my flash of horror. "Grady's story is a sad one, I'm afraid, and he's pretty private about it. He's stuck in Fanore but he has his reasons. He and Brennan have always been competitive, but he's a good guy. A *really* good guy, actually."

"Ireland is lovely," I say to change the subject, cautious of my choices now. "I mean, even covered in snow and freezing cold."

"But you're from Missouri, yeah? It's one of the few places in the States that I haven't visited," she comments easily. "But I imagine you get plenty of winter."

My heart perks up at the mention of home. I hadn't expected to miss it quite as much as I do, especially since there's no Christmas-scented kitchen waiting for me there. "You've been to the States often?"

"Yes. My parents are both international teachers, so we've moved around a lot, and on our summer holidays we almost always spent time in the States."

"That's nice." Totally lame response, but I just don't care to hear about how much more well rounded and courageous she is than me.

"Have you traveled much?"

"Nope. This is my first time abroad."

"Really? Wow. I could make you a list of places you've just got to see, but it would be a hundred cities long." Excitement peels off her in wisps, trying to infect me.

I'm so jealous my hands curl into excited fists. Not because she's been there, but because it's hopeless to think I ever could. "I don't know if I'll make it much farther. I'm a bit of a nervous traveler."

"Really? I thought Brennan said you wanted to be a journalist." She sits slightly forward, watching me over the rim of her mug. "Won't you have to pay your dues covering international stories for a few years?"

It crosses my mind to be pleased that Brennan was *actually* talking about me in the car and that wasn't just something she said to appease me after her sudden appearance. But there's an edge to her words. A challenge, one that I'm more than willing to take. If things aren't going to work out for Brennan and me, fine. It won't be because of this girl, though.

"I do want to be a journalist but I'm afraid the boring kind that sits behind a desk on a network affiliate is more my speed." I smile, softening what could sound defensive. She can't know she gets to me with her perfect face and her happy laugh and the years of history in this house. "Brennan doesn't really get it, I don't think."

"Jessica, he's a guy. If their mickeys had ears everyone would be better off."

"I'm assuming a mickey is a penis," I choke out.

She nods and we dissolve into genuine laughter. It leaves me missing my sorority sisters, a raw ache that throbs a bit in my chest. Katie refills our tea, and even though there's a lull in the conversation it's not uncomfortable at all, at least not considering we're two girls who barely know each other.

I squash my instinct to like her, remembering why I'm here in Ireland. "So, tell me about you and Brennan."

She waves a hand, her eyes sad again like maybe they've been that way underneath all the time. "You don't want to hear about that. Ancient history."

I roll my eyes. "Come on. We're barely twenty. It can't have been more than three years ago."

"Not quite a year, actually."

Surprise nips at my neutral expression. I assumed they

had broken up before he left for the States for college. If she's telling the truth they were dating when he decided to leave. "Wow. So he decided to study abroad while you were still dating."

Her face shutters, closing me out, but it's feels as though I hit a sore spot. Katie obviously holds her relationship with Brennan close to her heart, as though she's determined to keep the truth of their romance a private memory shared by only two. When she responds, the familiarity between us has evaporated, her tone detached. "We gave it a go, although I'm not sure either of us really thought it would work out."

"Why's that?" I prod, even though the way she's biting all of the color out of her bottom lip betrays her discomfort.

"The typical long-distance stuff. We're young, it's a big world, you know. We were too in love to say good-bye without a good reason, though, and I know I always thought we'd find our way back to each other in the end." She shrugs, her chin jutting out. "No offense."

"It's not your fault. I guess it must have come as a shock when he broke up with you, then."

"Oh, he didn't break up with me. I broke up with him."

The development saps all of the hope from my blood. Leeches away the expectations I've harbored the past four months. It's the worst possible scenario—that he's not in love with me because he's still in love with Katie.

The land mine in question slides off the stool and wanders over to the counter, putting away the utensils and ingredients she used for her tea with a bounce in her step that says she knows she won this round. A vibration sets me on edge, as though someone plucked an invisible, taut guitar string that's stretched across the center of the room. How much more don't I know about Brennan?

"Why did he go all the way to the States for college in the first place?" The words stick in my throat, losing confidence as they peel off, thinner than when they formed.

"It was my idea, actually, but his parents definitely supported it. Brennan's never been off the island and is sure he wants to take over Grady's job and the farm. We thought he should experience more first."

The guy who majors in business, minors in German, and has never once said a single thing that made me think farming and Ireland had sunk so deep into his blood. The fact that he'd never talked about applying for a visa to stay in the States after graduation hadn't escaped my attention, but we've only been dating four months.

"Some people don't need to travel to find what belongs to them," I murmur, my heart in pieces because it knows what I can't say, what Katie McBride doesn't want to admit. I feel it in my bones, the connection between the two of them. It's not gone, and the strength of it fills me with an envy I didn't even know I possessed.

She laughs at what must be a sick, serious expression on my face. "Come on, Jessica MacFarlane. We're young. There is plenty of time to worry over the future."

The painful vibration increases, spiking my irritation. *Why* are people so intent on spouting that stupid mantra?

Instead of losing it in front of Saint Katie and giving the Donnellys one more reason to look at me as the intruder, I smile and hop off my stool as well, rinsing my mug in the sink.

"I'm going to go make myself presentable," she announces, smoothing her near-perfect bed hair. "I didn't expect to meet anyone else in the kitchen so early."

"Okay. I think I'll make breakfast. Try to ingratiate myself."

"Don't try too hard. The Irish hate that," she replies with a sour smile before sweeping out of the room.

Hmm. Whatever I make is going to have to be easy because too much of my brainpower is mulling over this morning's conversation with Katie. I'd be inclined to like her if she didn't have obvious plans to end up with my boyfriend.

Waffles. Everyone has the ingredients in their kitchen cabinets and the Donnellys are no different. I don't know if Irish people eat waffles, but it's batter and syrup. Who doesn't like that?

Chapter
6

The answer is the Donnellys, apparently. Brennan and his grandfather seem to feel different, at least managing to get forkfuls of breakfast past their lips. Mr. and Mrs. Donnelly pick at the pastries, which admittedly would have been better if they'd had syrup in the cupboards—or the *press*, as I've learned. I didn't think about that, but with fruit, whipping cream that no longer has a pie to call home, and fresh honey as choices they aren't terrible.

"These are delicious, Jessica!" Katie exclaims a little too forcefully. "I swear, sweet breakfasts were always one of my favorite things about the States."

"They'd be better with syrup." I'm trying not to be grouchy, but whatever.

"Yeah. Sadly that's never hopped its way over here." She gives me another maybe-fake encouraging smile and chews another bite.

"I'm going to bring some back the next time I come." Brennan leans over and kisses my cheek, sweet support warping around me. "To have on hand."

The insinuation that he's thinking I might be here to make waffles again some day doesn't have the desired effect. I'm not sure what's changed since I walked through the Donnellys front door. It's a combination of things, really—his parents not approving, all of my little "quirks" that make me unacceptable, meeting his literal hero of an ex-girlfriend.

And talking with Grady, a small voice whispers from the back of my mind.

No. Grady might be pushing my boundaries, making me think a little differently for the first time in a long time, but it's not like he can take Brennan's place in my future.

I cast a glance at my boyfriend, my doubts a towering stack of pebbles now. Maybe the place beside me in the future doesn't fit him, either.

Except it *should*. There's no reason for my worries.

I need time to think, to separate my frustration from clear thought, but with Christmas Eve tomorrow and my flight out not scheduled until the twenty-sixth, I'm stuck. In a situation of my own making.

The downward spiral of my emotions roars in my ears, louder than the reluctant chewing around the table, when Grady appears through the door to the kitchen.

The guy seems to have some kind of Jessie in Distress radar.

Ugh, Now I'm calling *myself* Jessie. No one has called me

that since my father died, over ten years ago now. More proof the handsome, irritating, fascinating farmhand is getting under my skin.

"Good morning!" he bellows at the family before squinting at our plates. "What in the *hell* are you eating?"

Mrs. Donnelly gives him an admonishing look that seems to confuse Grady further. "They're waffles. An American tradition, you know, and Jessica made them for us."

"Lovely things, waffles," Mr. Donnelly adds, then frowns as Grady gives his plate, which still holds the majority of his breakfast, a pointed stare.

"Waffles, right," Grady furrows his brow. "Don't the Belgians eat those?"

Brennan snorts but tries to cover it up with his napkin. Katie grins.

It's enough to make me giggle, as well, but I tamp it down, crossing my arms over my chest. "I think *lots* of people eat waffles. Though apparently not around here."

"Okay, well, now that's settled, the reason I'm here is that the McCormacks asked me to look after their horses while they're down in Dingle visiting their daughter and those wretched kids. Any takers on a morning ride so I don't spend all day running 'em?" He glances around the table, eyebrows shooting up when they land on Katie. "Well, if it isn't cute Katie McBride. What are you doing here?"

"I was doing some innocent shopping when I was kidnapped by a dodgy bunch of bed-and-breakfast owners." Katie sniffs, her smile infectious.

Grady returns it, as charmed by her as everyone else. "A typical Tuesday night in Ennistymon, then?"

"Pretty much. Saved me a bob or two for the taxi home, though."

"Oh, you two go on," Mrs. Donnelly huffs. "We couldn't let our Katie spend Christmas *alone*."

Grady bends at the waist and brushes a kiss on her ruddy cheek. "I know, Maeve. Lord above would fall down dead a second time if you left a single stray by the side of the road."

She swats him away but it's clear that she's pleased by his attention, and that her loves stretches to include every person around her table. With the possible exception of me, but if I'm being honest, they've handled my showing up unannounced and all of my slips and flubs with more grace than required—and her complaints about me after the first night were nothing more than a mother looking out for her son.

They're things *I* should be thinking about if I'm serious about Brennan. Finding the right match isn't all about motivation and potential earning, as Grady pointed out. We have to fit in other ways.

"Any takers for a ride or two? Katie, I know you'll embarrass me with your skills but the horses would love it." Grady turns coaxing dimples her direction. "It'll be grand."

She shakes her head. "Everything's grand with you, Grady, but I'm afraid I'm in the mood to do a bit more reading in front of the fire."

"Fine. Brennan? Granddad Donnelly?"

"Don't be a feckin' eejit, boy," the old man grunts.

Brennan shakes his head in refusal and his parents don't even respond, which looks expected.

"I'd like to go," I volunteer. It's the perfect opportunity to get some much-needed space, even if I won't technically be alone.

Plus, this way I avoid watching Katie and Brennan catch up on old times, only to remember how happy they were then, which sounds like a unique form of torture.

Maybe leaving them alone isn't a great idea.

"Are you sure you won't come, Brennan?" I coax.

"You ride?" Grady's question tilts way up at the end, interrupting whatever my boyfriend's reply was going to be—an excuse, by the look of things. Meanwhile the Donnellys' farmhand peers at me as though the concept of me on a horse is akin to me walking on the moon.

"I have, yes." It's true I'm not very outdoorsy, and it's also true I haven't been on the back of a horse since first grade, the last time I was at camp, but still. The old expression "it's like riding a horse" has to come from somewhere.

Or is the expression "like riding a bike?"

Too late now.

"Well, come on then. Got six horses to tote around before sundown."

"I've got to help clean up the kitchen first." Both Katie and Mrs. Donnelly protest, saying they can handle it, but I refuse. "No, I made the mess. Just give me fifteen minutes, Grady."

He nods, already looking put out, which is weird considering what I *thought* was a connection in the barn last night. The sudden change adds an extra snarl to the hopeless tangle of confusion in my belly.

"Meet you out front. The rest of you have a lovely day."

"Oh, hey, Grady." Katie stops him with a touch on his arm. She's gotten up and starts collecting plates and silverware.

"Yep?"

"Bunch of the old gang that's around for the holiday are getting together in Ballyvaughan tonight, around eight. You should come. Brennan's in, and so is Jessica. It'll be grand."

I jerk my head around to look at Brennan, who told me nothing of this little excursion, but he's ignoring my gaze in favor of another patty of black pudding. My stomach churns just looking at it disappear between his lips.

"Oh, yeah, it'll be grand. No doubt about that." Grady shakes his head, looking amused enough to make me suspicious, and disappears from view.

"Are you sure you won't come with me?" I ask again, wanting him to say yes but not willing to beg.

"I don't feel like being stinky and sore," Brennan says, reaching for me and sliding his hands around my bare waist as I try to shrug into a flannel shirt borrowed from Molly. "But you look sexy as hell in that farmer's getup."

"Don't get used to it," I tease, buttoning it up the rest of the way. Being naked—or even partially so—around Brennan is asking for trouble, and we agreed not to violate rules about sex under his mother's roof.

Being a devout Catholic she's definitely into the whole no-sex-before-marriage idea. Even though her son and I definitely *are* into it, this is her house. It's important to me to respect her beliefs. I'm so glad I remembered to squirrel that stupid pregnancy test away in my suitcase before anyone saw it.

Brennan pulls me in for another kiss. I don't refuse, even though I'm not feeling it. His tongue slides over my bottom lip, earning the groan he's looking for, and I forget for a moment that everything's shit, kissing him back.

"You are killing me, Jessica MacFarlane. I want you so bad."

"*Mmmm*," I murmur, wishing I wasn't breathing quite so heavily. "But it's only a couple more days. Just think how good it will be then."

He sighs and squeezes me once more before turning me loose, swatting my butt as I move toward the mirror. "I don't know how it can be better than it's been for the past six weeks. But fine."

"You're adorable when you pout; has anyone ever told you that?"

"Maybe." He sticks out his lower lip, eyes shining with desire. "Is it working?"

I laugh, Brennan laughs, and it feels so good to be at ease with each other. This is the first time we've been tested, and we'll make it through it.

"So what's with this get-together tonight?"

"Oh yeah, sorry I didn't have time to mention it. Katie invited us last night, but with all the drama with Pop it kind of slipped my mind."

"Sure, it sounds like fun. I'd like to meet your friends."

I watch him in the mirror and glimpse the tiniest grimace as it passes over his face. Desperation to somehow salvage this—us—sends my heart racing, blood squirming like worms in my veins, but the answer as to how doesn't come no matter how long I take to braid my hair.

Once a touch of makeup hides the dark circles under my eyes, I turn and spread my arms. "How do I look?"

"Damn well too good to be out riding horses with the like of Grady Callaghan," he grumps.

I stop, wondering if it's wrong to ask the question, then deciding I don't care. There's no way to figure out where I fit on the Donnelly game board without understanding all the pieces. "Do you not like him or something?"

"Grady? I like him fine. I like the idea of having my girlfriend out alone with him all day a little less."

The response turns his pouting decidedly *not* adorable, lifting the buried annoyances up onto my tongue. "Well, you could have come with me. But obviously you'd rather spend your time elsewhere today."

"What's that supposed to mean?"

"Oh, I don't know, that you'd rather curl up in front of the fire with your ex-girlfriend than hang out with your current one?"

He stands up, eyes flashing, teeth grinding together. "No one told you to go horseback riding with Grady today. In fact, no one told you to come here at all, and now you want me to rearrange my time with my family because you're not happy with the way your little manipulative surprise turned out?"

The words pelt me like shots from a paintball gun, exploding in ugly splotches as they slam into my torso, arms, neck. It stings and it smells, and I blink back the tears filling me eyes. "Well, if that's how you really feel about getting to spend some extra time with me, then I don't know what we're even doing here, Brennan."

His shoulders droop. "Look, it's not how I feel about spending time with you. I just . . . this is . . . I don't know. Not what I expected."

Not what I wanted seems to be more what he's thinking.

Brennan's eyes meet mine, and they echo the confusion tripping up my reactions at every turn. "But regardless, I don't like the idea of you being alone with another guy."

"Well, I'm not going to sit around here all day." I wait for him to change his mind about coming along, and when he doesn't, I take a deep breath through my nose then blow it out through my mouth, wiping tears with the back of my hand. "I'd better get going."

I pause, waiting for an apology that doesn't come, then head out into the cold.

Chapter

7

Ready then?" Grady growls when I step outside, squinting in the bright sunshine. He peers closer at my face and his frown deepens as he steps toward me. "Are you crying?"

"No." Not anymore.

I make it clear with my tone and crossed arms that questions aren't welcome even though the concern etched on his handsome face makes me want to fall into his arms and sob away my troubles. He respects my nonverbal cues, though it doesn't stop his expression of disgust.

The chill in the air does nothing to dampen the beauty of gray-blue skies stretching all the way to the horizon. Pristine white snow, nothing like the black slush that passes for the same thing in cities at home, and the gray rock and purple hues pushing through on the hillsides remind me that while the States can be beautiful in the winter, I'm not there.

I'm somewhere new and wonderful, and this is an adventure that shouldn't be wasted no matter how things turn out between my boyfriend and me.

I cast a glance at Grady, who's stretching his arms above his head and taking in the scenery with a rapt expression that would be more at home on someone who doesn't wake up to such a thing every single day.

Excitement dribbles past my sorrow. "I'm ready. How are we getting there?"

"The McCormacks are just a couple of plots over. We'll walk unless you'd rather not." His blue eyes, brighter than the sky today, dare me to object.

Thoughts of cold, wet feet and the likelihood of stepping in clumps of mud—or what I hope will be mud—dance through my head. The great outdoors and I have a relationship of respect. Which is to say I stay out of it as much as possible and it agrees not to go out of its way to kill me.

That said, there is no way I'm giving Grady the satisfaction of proving I'm not up to this little excursion before we even get out the door. "Sure, let's walk."

He raises his eyebrow but doesn't comment, taking off toward the sun without waiting. I take a few skips to catch up, then have to double-time it through the calf-deep snow to match his lengthy stride.

My breath plumes out past my lips harder and harder, clouds of wispy white dissipating before Grady can notice, but we've only gone about five hundred yards before he looks back to check on me. He slows his pace without comment, and I would breathe a sigh of relief if I had any extra air.

"Thanks for at least trying to prepare me for Katie," I start, feeling like chatting even though an hour ago I just wanted to be alone. And okay, wondering if Grady might be able to give me something—anything—that makes me feel better about Brennan having kept his past from me.

"Nothing can prepare a person for the loveliness that is Katie McBride," Grady replies, eyeing me. "And your boyfriend should have done that, not me."

Everything may not be wine and roses at the moment, but I'm not going to bad-mouth Brennan behind his back. "She *is* lovely. I even like her."

He snorts. "Of course you do. Everyone loves Katie. Literally everyone."

"She grew up here, too?"

"Yes. We all threw her in the mud when we were little, all chased after her when we got a little older. But she only had eyes for Brennan. Always."

"Is that why you get little lines around your mouth like you tasted something sour when you say his name?"

Grady stumbles a little, surprise raising his eyebrows. "What? No. I mean, I don't do that." It's the first time he's seemed out of sorts or less than confident. It's sort of endearing. "I don't have a problem with Brennan. I certainly never had any illusions of dating Katie."

"Oh yeah, why would you?" I toss back, sarcasm spicy on my tongue.

"Trust me, we've all had certain thoughts. But the two of them were inseparable."

"So what happened?" Our pace slows to a stroll.

Grady has professed a love of plans that rivals mine, and at the house he acted like he had so many chores on his plate for the day they couldn't possibly get accomplished in time for drinks tonight. Yet here we are, two uptight people with deadlines on the brain, taking our sweet-ass time.

It's enough of an accomplishment to make me step back and marvel, but the expression on Grady's face says I've breached an unseen boundary, circled wagons around life-long friends.

"She decided it was over, for Brennan's own good."

"You sound like you don't think it was. Over."

Grady gives me an exasperated look. "Why do you want to talk about how things may or may not be over between Brennan and Katie? Are you intent on making yourself miserable instead of enjoying your trip?"

"I don't. I just . . . I'm curious about your little town and Brennan's life before I knew him. That's all."

"Well, it's not whether it was over that I was disagreeing with," Grady explains, his voice softer now. Pliable. "It was her deciding without him."

There's a suggestion running deep under the words, hidden extras that promise Grady knows more than what

85

he's saying. Maybe more than he wishes he did, about what went wrong. The whiff of mystery flutters on the wind before dancing away.

We walk the rest of the way to the McCormacks' barn in companionable silence, with Grady stopping to point out nuances in the landscape every once in a while. The neighbors' llamas. The rainbow in the distance. The giant-placed boulders on the hillsides. It's all new to me, all fascinating, and for the first time Ireland grabs onto my heart.

The McCormacks' sturdy barn is as weathered as the Donnellys', more gray than brown and just as warm on the inside. The difference is that the stalls here are filled with half a dozen beautiful horses—three brown-and-white fillies, two male palominos, and a gorgeous black stallion.

Grady stops outside the last stall and turns around, crossing one ankle over the other, and leans back against the bowed wood. "Tell me, Jessie. How long has it been since you've ridden?"

I glance up, wondering if I'm hearing a double meaning that isn't there, and choke on my tongue at the twinkle in Grady's eyes. Instead of shying away I let a teasing smile onto my lips. "Too long, Mr. Callaghan. Too long."

Grady took the news that it's been years surprisingly well and coached me along the way as we saddled the horses— okay, he did most of the lifting and saddling—but now that

I'm standing alongside a palomino named Bach with one foot in the stirrup, nerves start dancing in my stomach.

"You're not going to puke, are you?"

"No." I reconsider, holding the reins tighter as the horse shies away from me, nervous because I am. "Probably not. Although you've already seen me do that once and the second time isn't nearly so embarrassing."

"Just as disgusting, though, I'd wager." He grins, dimples catching the light from the midday sun. He settles his hands on my waist and any other thought drops straight out of my head. It's so oddly natural. "You've got to be calm, because horses are jittery dicks when they freak out. On the count of three, yeah?"

I barely manage to nod before he gets to the assigned number and gives me a boost that leaves me sitting upright in the saddle. I take a deep breath that's too shaky and it has nothing to do with the horse.

"There, see? Grand." He swings up onto Garth, the second palomino, settling in with an ease that's both impressive and attractive. Which is weird because finding a man who could sit a horse has never been on my list of must-haves when it comes to a guy. "Hold the reins looser—there you go. Dig your heels in to go forward, the firmer the faster."

"Got it." Maybe. "Where are we going?"

"Out to the pasture, up a hillside or two. I wish the snow had held off because we could have seen some great ruins."

"That would have been nice."

I set off, letting Bach saunter a head or two behind Garth, trying not to let my horse feel how he intimidates me. Garth could splatter my brains with one well-placed hoof if he decides he fancies such a thing on this beautiful morning, but Grady's easy confidence settles my fears. By the time we hit the bottom of the first hill and start upward, I feel good in the saddle. Good enough to look around, breathe in the air, and answer Grady when he asks how Brennan and I met.

"At a frat party."

"You don't seem like the frat-party type."

The comment almost sounds like an insult wrapped in a compliment, as though he can't decide which he means. I decide to hear the compliment because the day is too perfect. "You don't have to drink to have fun at parties. News flash."

"I'll have you know that I don't drink all that much, either. For an Irishman."

I laugh in spite of myself. "Oh my goodness, Grady Callaghan—did you just make a joke?"

"It's been known to happen." He laughs, too, that honey sound that sticks to my skin.

"You know why I don't drink much—what's your excuse?"

He shrugs, that closed expression fighting for purchase on his face again. The pause goes on so long it seems like he might not answer, so when he does, there's no doubt the response isn't going match the lighthearted tone of my question.

"My pa drank. He drank so much he forgot the way home one night and never came back."

My heart climbs into my throat, beating fast in response to the anger rolling under his words like thunder. Katie had said Grady's story wasn't a happy one. "I'm sorry. That must have been hard on you growing up. A dad is someone you should be able to count on."

My dad had been that way. For a while.

"It was better without him, at least for me. My mam could have used him after she got sick, though."

Now my heart throbs, lanced open by the pain in his quick glance. It's all starting to make a little more sense, why a guy that's smart and young would hang around a town as small as Fanore. It's noble, which isn't a description most people earn in the world today.

"How is your mother now?"

His reaction is a jerk of the muscle in his jaw, as though he clamped down his teeth in an attempt to bite back the truth, and a tightening of his fingers around the reins. "She died last summer. Rare vascular disease."

The quiet truth sends my heart crashing into my stomach. Of course he's close with the Donnellys, since they've been a constant in his life since childhood. Working for them must have allowed him to make money while staying close enough to take care of his mom, but none of that explains why he's still here now.

"I'm sorry you had to go through all of that by yourself, Grady."

His half smile, content somehow, breaks my heart. "I wasn't alone. I was with my mam."

Tears prick my eyes and I smile, too, because it's so clear in this moment that beauty lurks in everything, even in loss. I'm inclined to analyze, to ferret out potential pitfalls or roadblocks in the future, but some things can't be planned. But if Grady can cast his horrible light in a sort of thankful glow, what else might be possible?

"You're lucky that you had a mom who loved you." The words breathe out in a whisper, pried loose from somewhere inside me that's rusted away over the years. There's hope underneath it. Raw, painful, hard to see. But there.

The glance he shoots my way is wide with surprise. "I'm sure your mam loved you, Jessie."

I shake my head, taking a few minutes to swallow the wet lump in my throat. The kindness in his words, the surety buffeting his tone, are hard to take. "In her way, maybe."

"What about your pa?" Grady nudges his horse through a gap in one of the piled stone walls and up a graceful hillside, checking to make sure I'm following.

Bach navigates without help from me, his nose a couple of feet from Garth's tail.

"He died when I was nine. Cancer."

"I'm sorry."

I shrug. "It was a long time ago. So, I can promise you it gets easier."

"Did it kill your mam? Him dying?"

He's pushing. Lifting up rocks with gentle fingers, hoping there isn't a snake coiled underneath, and even though it normally bugs me when people pry, I *want* to tell him everything.

"It killed her when he got sick—the dying took the better part of three years." I swallow, forcing myself to feel it again for the first time. The one or two times the story spilled out of me it's felt mechanical. A well-oiled tale of the destruction of a happy childhood. "Things were great. My dad made tons of money as an artist—he was a sculptor—but my parents weren't exactly responsible. They had so much money they didn't know what to do with it, so they spent it all on nothing. When Dad got sick there was no more money coming in, no savings. No insurance. No way to take care of him."

I look over to find Grady's horse standing still atop the ridge. Grady is staring at me with a mixture of understanding and empathy, and the combination bolsters my spirit in a way I've never experienced. As if he's stitching together the holes in my soul just by listening. It's been . . . forever, really, since anyone came at me with advice that isn't to just get over it and live, already.

A deep breath of clean air fills my lungs. There's nothing to see from up here but more hillsides, more sturdy and winding walls, more little farmhouses belching plumes of smoke from teetering chimneys. Ireland is like a promise that life doesn't have to be complicated. That a roof and family, some land and friends, are all a person needs to be happy.

"After he died we had nothing. Mom had never worked, never thought for a moment about what she wanted to do with her life. We didn't have anywhere to live. She sat me beside her on street corners begging for food, dragged me from shelter to shelter when it got too cold out, until a teacher in ninth grade finally called social services." I keep my eyes on the horizon, familiar shame coating me like black oil. "It helped, even though none of my foster parents were the best. They weren't awful, and I studied hard in high school, got a scholarship to college."

"Where is your mam now?"

"I don't know." I swallow hard, finding the courage to look at him again.

Grady does the oddest thing in that moment—he smiles. Dimples crease in his cheeks and he reaches out, palm up, asking for my hand. The reassurance in his expression sends my hand searching for his and our gloved palms tough, fingers interlocking, until he gives me a tight squeeze.

"To surviving in the world without parents. You're an inspiration, Jessie. Damn strong woman."

Nothing about bucking up, about letting it all go and moving forward. Just a confirmation of all I've been through, of how sort of amazing it is that I've gotten to where I am. It's hard to think about my own life in those terms—I've simply done what I have to do to survive.

For the first time pride swells within me instead of shame. It puffs out my chest and before long I'm smiling, too.

"We should head back down and grab two more horses. It's going to get cold fast once the sun starts going down."

"Sure."

And Bach follows Garth back down the hill, the day normal and happy in horse land. In Jessie land, everything is topsy-turvy. Upside down and backward, but turned in a way that makes me think I've only assumed it was right side up for the past decade.

The warmth of the barn washes over me, making me realize for the first time how chapped and cold my cheeks feel. Grady takes pity on me, unsaddling both horses, while I wander, my mind too full to be anything but blank. Excitement tumbles through me and right out of my mouth at the sight of an honest-to-goodness *sleigh* in the back corner of the room.

"Oh my laundry, can we hook up the horses and go for a ride?" I squeal, pointing when Grady looks up.

He gives me an incredulous look. "Do you know how long that takes?"

"No."

"Well, it's no simple trick, and it would only exercise two of the horses and we've got three left. Plus, the snow's not deep enough yet. Maybe after one more storm."

Disappointment sticks out my lower lip but I don't argue, since I have no idea how deep snow has to be to support a giant sled.

"Are you pouting?"

"What? No."

"You totally are." He smiles as he saddles the second of two brown fillies. "This is Peig. She's a little feisty, so you'll need to keep a tight hand on the reins. I don't suppose you brought any more carrots? They're her weakness."

"Nope, sorry."

We take the fillies out for a run, not going upward this time but toward the village. People bustle from the post-office-slash-grocery-store into the bar, boots laced up their calves and faces hidden by hoods and scarves, all of them taking a moment to wave and call a greeting to Grady and introduce themselves to me. All the while, I think how strange it is that these people see the old Jessica, while inside a new girl is kicking her way free.

Once the ladies are exercised and unsaddled, I help Grady brush them down before he leads the stallion, Uaine, out of his stall.

"What does his name mean?"

"Warrior." Grady grunts as he slings the saddle onto the giant's back, the horse nudging his fingers with soft lips. "Here you go, beggar."

Grady fishes a rice cake from his pack by the door, then sighs and gives the horse one more before giving me a sheepish look. "He's a gentle giant."

"You love him."

He scoffs. "He's all right."

I smile, dancing around, hopping from one foot to the

other and flailing like a moron. "This has been the best day."

Then my eyes meet Grady's and just like that, the world stops. We're made of magnets, opposite poles that suck us toward one another until I'm a foot away, my breath coming in futile gasps as my vision blacks around the edges. It's me and him, two people who should never have met, alone in a barn halfway around the world.

I have never, ever wanted to reach out and touch someone more, and the raw ache in Grady's face says he's battling the same desire, but in the end we both adhere to *the right thing to do*.

He clears his throat, shattering the moment. "I thought we'd ride him double back to the Thistle. I'll just drop you off."

"Sure."

We mount up, the solid comfort of Grady's hard chest at my back, the insides of his thighs pressed against the outside of mine, his crotch grazing my butt sending shockwaves in every direction. My stomach won't stop flopping and my hands sweat on the horse's mane. Grady doesn't seem to notice, guiding Uaine out of the barn and into the late afternoon, which has grown grayer and windier, far colder than this morning. Clouds gather on the horizon like thick, dirty cotton balls, promising more snow. Maybe enough for a sleigh ride.

"So, what's next for you?" I ask, hoping my voice doesn't

sound as strangled with lust as I feel. Also hoping to unravel more of what makes Grady tick.

"I've been thinking about it." His tone is conversational, shoulders relaxed as he leans forward slightly to check on me. "You did really well on the mounts today, by the way."

"That's what all the boys tell me," I tease without thinking. It's the kind of joke I'd normally reserve for my sorority sisters or maybe Brennan, and my face blooms with heat as he guffaws, vibrations sliding through him and into my back and turning into shivers down my spine.

"I bet they do, Jessie MacFarlane." His arms tighten on my shoulders as he asks the horse to veer right. "I haven't laughed as hard in months. Thank you."

"What have you been thinking about," I prod, unsure how to respond to the compliment. "School?"

"Eventually. I mean, I love working outside and not having set hours, and I doubt working all day in an office is going to be my gig. I'd like to travel first. Take pictures."

"Oh, right. Your black-of-night storm photography."

He snorts, acknowledging the jab. "I've never had any classes or anything but I enjoy it. The camera is a hand-me-down that used to belong to my dad, and maybe he passed along his eye for framing a nice shot, too. Don't let it be said the man was good for nothing."

"What do you shoot, landscapes or people?"

"A little bit of everything, but I'm not into family photos or wedding pictures."

"So pretty much you're not into the kind of photography that makes you money," I comment, pressing my back into his chest to let him know I'm teasing.

"It makes sense that you would notice that, since you're into the kind of journalism that earns you paychecks instead of accolades," he says fast, trading barb for barb.

Even though he's mostly kidding, the Jessie clawing her way out of the past, begging to have a future, considers the ramifications of a life spent behind a desk in a studio. Maybe it would be a waste of my life—this *one life*—to not have love for my work.

We ride the rest of the way home in companionable silence, my mind reeling with possibilities, taking on fear and uncertainty like a boat punched full of holes. But for some reason, this guy and this day have left me with a big bucket in my hands that's helping me bail water.

It's okay to not be okay.

The concept shines in my palm like a glossy marble, a piece of currency that's valuable because it's different. I cup it gently, my hand sweaty but determined not to let it go.

The first thing I see when the house comes into view is Katie and Brennan sitting together on the porch, their heads bowed together in quiet conversation. The second thing I notice is that the storm clouds on my boyfriend's face at the sight of Grady and me pressed together on a horse make the ones in the sky look positively friendly.

Chapter

8

Brennan leaps off the porch to greet me, as though either his pants are on fire or he's guilty of something. I look at Katie, sitting quietly, and know nothing happened. Nothing that could be considered cheating in the strictest sense of the word, anyway. Her belief in their story not being finished is too unshakable. I'm positive that, in Katie McBride's mind, I'm no competition at all.

A few hours ago I would have fought tooth and nail, made a plan to get rid of her once and for all, but the new Jessie isn't so sure what she wants anymore. Not really.

"Hey," I say, picking pieces of hay out of my hair.

"Hey, yourself." Brennan's voice is tight, the words squeezed too small, and his steely gaze follows Grady as he clomps back the direction we came. When he turns it back on me, accusations reach out and stab me. "Have a good day?"

I step back, pushing a pointed glance toward Katie, still watching us from the porch. "Did you?"

The fight bleeds out of him, pooling on the ground under our feet until we're knee-deep in a tepid pond of apathy. He gives me a weak smile, an attempt at a truce. "You smell like horse."

"Which is exactly why I'm going to go shower," I say, and manage a tired smile. "What time are we leaving for town?"

"You sure you want to go?"

"Are you sure you *want* me to go?" I snap, still bristling from his gall, acting like I've done something wrong while he's snuggled on the porch with his ex.

"Of course I do." His hands reach out, squeezing my biceps. His expression swings to apologetic, looking to smooth over any rough edges—his particular contribution to our relationship since the beginning. "We're going to head in right after dinner."

I take a deep breath, letting him soothe me. "Okay. I'll be ready."

Brennan shoos me away, pinching his nose closed with two fingers. For a guy who grew up on farmland he has a pretty weak tolerance for animal fumes.

I stand under the hot shower's spray, the stench of the day swirling down the drain but the feeling it leaves me with stamped much deeper. I stare at my reflection while I straighten my hair, wondering why I look the same—nothing's different about my flyaway chestnut hair, my long lashes, or the freckles dotting my cheeks.

I haven't changed yet. Haven't decided whether I really can, but the simple consideration lights my eyes. Pinks my cheeks. Brightens my smile.

Even my hair looks good when I'm finished, which is a rare and beautiful thing. At least Brennan's high school friends won't be talking about what a dog he's dating.

Dinner goes smoothly, for once, with Molly and everyone else excited about the Christmas festivities and Brennan and Katie hurrying through the corned beef and hash and potatoes so that we can get into town on time. We've all agreed not to stay out late—they said they want to pop in and say hello, catch up for a few pints and get out, which is more than okay with me.

Brennan gets behind the wheel this time but we all know I'll be the one piloting us home. I don't mind so much now that I've got at least some experience driving on the wrong side of the road, and it's not raining. And surely the need to stay out of my way has made its way through the livestock whisper down the lane.

Thick awkwardness followed us from dinner and into the toy car. Brennan and I might have come to a truce as far as not discussing the things that are pissing us off right now, but that leaves us with nothing but oppressive silence. Katie gives conversation a go or two but gives up when I look out the window and Brennan barely manages a grunt.

So, I don't know about my boyfriend, but for me, keeping my mouth shut seems like the best way to stop from screaming. Or crying.

The thing is, I don't even know why we're fighting. Because of Katie? Because of Grady?

Because I showed up here and uncovered the ugly truth—that Brennan never told me about his past, never let me in on his plans to return to Fanore to run the B&B, and when he looks into the future I'm not the girl he sees by his side?

I'm not convinced Brennan ever takes a peek into the future, which is a big reason I came here—to force him to do just that. It had never occurred to me that I wouldn't like what he saw there.

Ballyvaughan turns out to be the name of a town, and an adorable one at that, just over a half an hour drive from Fanore. There are actual side streets and more than one row of businesses—including bars and restaurants—to choose from, and as Brennan leads us into a traditional Irish pub called Greene's, I can't help but notice how handsome he is and my heart twists.

Katie looks beautiful, too, in a clingy but modest brown dress that skims her knees and highlights her eyes. Boots with a small heel complete her outfit in a way that says she's not trying too hard. I'm confident in the way my cranberry top and slinky black skirt offset my curves while my boots keep my legs from impersonating an ice statue until we get inside.

The pub is overly warm and like something out of a dream, all ragged booths and cherry-colored leather, dark wood, flickering lanterns casting deeper shadows in dark

101

corners. Bottles of liquor stack on the mirrored wall behind the bar, and the men with their backs to us can only be referred to as regulars. I want to take a picture but don't want to look like a tool, so I close my eyes, committing Greene's to a panoramic-style memory.

"Hey, it's Donnelly and McBride, just like old times!" a burly kid with dark brown curls bellows from the bar. He slams down a pint of Guinness and grabs Brennan in a giant hug, tugging him away from me.

"Put me down O'Brien, you big oaf." Brennan disentangles himself with a smile and the guy, O'Brien, goes after Katie.

A second boy, this one tall and skinny with a shaggy mop of blond hair, wanders over with a smile. An impossibly short girl with dull brown waves and eyes that are a faded blue behind her glasses follows.

"Emer! Finn! What's the *craic*?" Brennan hugs them, too, and then they greet Katie, meaning that all in all it's several minutes before anyone remembers or realizes there's a stranger in their midst.

"This is Jessie," Grady's now familiar half-amused, half-irritated voice interjects from behind me. "Brennan's girlfriend, despite his lack of manners."

I feel the barest presence of Grady's hand on the small of my back before Brennan scowls and pulls me to his side. The farmhand looks smashing, cleaned up in a way that's different to me. I can't help but notice the way his jeans fit his butt perfectly, fraying a bit at the hems where they hit the floor around his worn boots. His ripped upper body fills out a blue-and-gray flannel shirt that matches his eyes, leaving my heart to stumble.

"I was getting to that." Brennan frowns harder. "You know O'Brien doesn't give anyone time to breathe."

Grady gives me a smile but I shake my head. I don't know what's happening here or what I want to happen, or what's possible in this brand-new world, but I do know that I'm not a cheater. Figuring out my future with Brennan has to be my top priority, and Grady, no matter how intriguing, can't fix that.

"I'm Jessica," I tell O'Brien, leaving off my last name on purpose.

Brennan doesn't offer it, either. "Jessica, this is Danny O'Brien, Finn Gallaher, and Emer Flannigan."

"Nice to meet you all."

"You're an American," Finn observes while Danny attacks Grady in a fashion similar to the greeting he bestowed on Brennan.

"Guilty."

"Well, how about a pint?"

"She doesn't really—"

"Sure," I reply, cutting Brennan off, then shrugging at his questioning look. It's not going to kill me to hold and sip it, and by the time the end of the night rolls around, there's probably not much chance any of them will remember how much I did or didn't drink.

Danny turns back to the bar to order three more, and

Brennan leans down to murmur in my ear. "No one drinks until everyone has their glass, then we all toast. Make sure to look everyone in the eye."

I nod, committing the practice to memory, then take the lukewarm black beer from Danny. Once everyone has a glass we raise them and Finn begins a boisterous toast. "Here's to a long life and a merry one."

"A quick death and an easy one," Emer chimes in, raising her glass.

"A pretty girl and an honest one," Brennan murmurs, not looking in my direction in a way that feels purposeful.

"A cold pint and another one!" Danny finishes, pushing his glass into Katie's so hard the caramel-colored foam sloshes onto their hands.

I toast each glass in turn, meeting everyone's eye with a smile, then take two giant gulps of the surprisingly pleasant beer. Twenty minutes later I still can't shake the appreciative, intense expression in Grady's eyes when they met mine over the rims of our glasses of Guinness.

Or how hard it was to breathe when his gaze slid all the way down to my toes.

I drained the first beer and asked for another in an attempt to erase what turns out to be a rather stubborn visual, leaving my limbs tingling and my cheeks flushed and numb. The feeling is nice, kind of like any serious problem floats too far away from the thinking part of my brain to reach.

"It's so good to see you guys together again," Danny

gushes, then blushes when he notices me listening. "I mean, it's great to see all of you. Grady, what are you up to, man, I haven't seen you in forever!"

The friendly Irish boy does his best to change the subject, and I know he didn't mean me any insult, but there have been *several* comments about how good it is to see Katie and Brennan, plus at least three adorable stories that involve the two of them and high school. They're doing their best to ask me questions, but once we dispatched with the boring story of how we met and how I'm enjoying Ireland, everyone lost interest.

I don't blame them. This is a night for catching up with old friends, not making small talk with ones you'll probably never see again. Katie and Brennan keep inching closer to one another without even realizing it, and when I come back from my second bathroom break—the spot next to Brennan has disappeared.

My chest tightens and I turn toward the bar, ordering another pint.

"Are you sure you want to do that?" Grady sidles up next to me, one eyebrow arched toward his hairline and his arm too close to mine.

I shift away from the heat of him. The spark of his skin. "Why, aren't you hoping I'll get wasted enough to take my top off and dance on the bar?"

"I hadn't entertained the possibility, to be honest." He bites his lips, cutting a glance toward Brennan, who hasn't noticed my absence. "But unless that's how you're planning on capping your night, you might want to slow down. You're not used to drinking, and Guinness has more alcohol than most beer."

"Thanks for the advice."

The bartender hands over my beer and I slap a few euros on the counter, leaving Grady alone. This whole day is a strange, uncomfortable mash-up of lovely and shitty, but at the moment the buzz keeps my emotions from swamping my lack of good sense.

I shoulder my way into the circle of friends, trying not to feel glad when Grady pushes in beside me, our hips brushing. It's sweet that Grady feels the same . . . friendship blooming between us and that he's tuned into my comfort here. Or lack thereof. But Brennan is my boyfriend. Brennan is the one I want to do those things. I slide my hand into his and feel a gush of relief when he squeezes back.

Time wears on, and we keep drinking. The hour or two we were going to stay turns into three, until my eyelids are heavy and my feet ache from standing, and as the pleasant drunk feeling starts to tip toward dizzy and sick. I finish the rest of the beer in my hand and set it on the table, stumbling a little on my way to the bathroom and back. I've lost count of the number of times I've gone, and nausea turns in my gut.

Why did I drink so many beers? Who am I?

Stupid new Jessie.

"Well, I think I'm going to get going," Grady says,

putting what I think is just his second empty pint on the counter.

"Aw, of course Callaghan is the first one to leave," Danny complains, punching him on the arm.

"Well, you know, we can't all be coddled like you are, O'Brien. Some of us have work to do in the morning, Christmas Eve or no."

"Sure, sure." Emer stands on her toes to give him a hug, one that lingers a few seconds longer than it has to.

A stab of jealousy startles me. There's no way Grady doesn't have his own sordid dating history because there's no girl alive with two eyeballs and a pulse who could pass the guy without looking twice.

"See you later, man," he says, and gives Finn a handshake, then turns to Brennan. "Are you going to be okay getting home?"

"Yeah, Katie's driving." He gives me a pointed look, an annoyingly obvious reminder that I was supposed to be the DD, but it bounces off my alcohol-armored skin.

"Do you want me to drive you, Jessie? You're looking locked enough to fall over." Grady hesitates by the door, keys in his hand.

"Does that mean pretty?" I slur, tipping sideways so that he has to grab my elbow to hold me up.

Brennan frowns. "It means wasted. And you are."

"Well, maybe a little. A *wee* bit," I snort. I'm tired, too. So, so tired. "Are you going to stay?"

"Yeah. I mean, this is my only night to catch up with everyone."

Never mind that we all agreed not to stay out late. Never mind that I'm his girlfriend and I need to go to bed. Never mind, apparently, that he doesn't like me alone with one Grady Callaghan.

"Fine. I'll go with Grady."

"Fine."

Only because you have to, I think, letting Grady take my hand and pull me out into the cold.

"You've made a fine mess of things, haven't you?" Grady puts an arm around my waist, helping me walk to his rusted green truck a few blocks away.

I'd push him off, but putting one foot in front of the other proves quite a bit harder than it was a few hours ago. The cobbled, uneven streets slick with crusted snow combine with the blurry world to keep me leaning on Grady. "I'm sure I don't know what you're talking about, but it's none of your business if I did."

He sighs, opening the passenger door and boosting me inside. The world spins outside the truck and my stomach lurches, coating my tongue with a nasty taste. Closing my eyes helps, but only a tad.

"You're not going to throw up in my truck, are you?"

"I'm really not sure."

He sighs again and starts the engine, letting it idle

108

while the air blasting from the vents transforms from bitter cold to lukewarm, then shifts into gear. We bump through the night in silence for a while, which is good, since if I open my mouth there's no telling what might come flying out.

"Rough night?" he asks, softer this time. Peering under those rocks again.

I'm too tired to play the angry snake. "You could say that."

"It's none of my business, but why don't you talk to Brennan instead of fighting with him?"

"It's not going to do any good." I slouch in the seat, sticking my booted feet on the dash.

"Oh, and getting plastered is doing the trick?"

A smile tugs at my lips, then a laugh burbles up from my center. It's ridiculous, he's right, and I never, ever make a decision in the moment. This one had turned out poorly, but guess what? I'm still alive.

"You are a real piece of work, Jessie MacFarlane." Grady grunts, but a quick glance reveals he's grinning, too. "I'm glad you came to Ireland."

"You are?" I sit up straighter, crossing my legs. The world spins again and I press my eyes closed, groaning.

"Yes. But I might change my mind if you vomit."

"Whatever."

The roads twist and turn, lazy through the countryside, and the stone walls catch my eye, piquing my curiosity not for the first time. "What's the deal with the walls? I mean, at first I thought they were property divisions or livestock pens but they seem more haphazard than that."

"Trust you to use big words when you're pissed," he grumbles, squeezing the wheel tight around a curve. "But you're right. People use them that way now, but their origins are more practical. There have always been a lot of rocks in the area, and in order to farm, they had to be picked up. So people stacked them."

"Huh. That's kind of boring," I hiccup, then giggle. "It explains why they look like they've grown straight up out of the ground, though."

"They're not like that in other places in the country. County Clare is special."

"Of course it is." I hiccup again, and this time Grady laughs. The honey sound of it falls over me, landing right between my thighs and burning.

"The other story is that during the potato famine the people who were out of work stacked walls for the rectories and churches in exchange for food." He smiles. "We Irish don't take kindly to handouts."

"Thank you," I blurt out, still too warm from his presence. His voice, his laughter.

"For what?"

"Driving me home. Listening to my bullshit. Making me feel like I'm not a loser. Take your pick."

We've reached the Donnellys' and Grady pulls up, choosing a parking spot and sliding the truck into park. He unbuckles and turns to face me, fire burning in his bright eyes, promising me something I don't want to accept.

"You really are gone in the head, aren't you?" Grady peers at me.

"What?"

"Those things? They aren't hard to do for you. You're making my Christmas rather spectacular, even if yours is turning out shitty."

My breath catches, heart thudding when his gaze refuses to let go of mine. "If you weren't here, I think I'd have thrown myself off one of your famous cliffs by now."

Grady reaches over and clicks my seat belt open, then grabs my hands and pulls us toward each other until we're in the middle of the bench seat. His fingertips are rough, calloused, as they trail down my cheeks. My body sways, listing to the right, then the left, and it's impossible to tell if it's still the booze or if Grady's gentle touch is knocking me off balance.

"There's nothing wrong with you, Jessie, and there's nothing wrong with wanting security in the future. But you've got to give yourself a break. There are guys in the world besides Brennan Donnelly. If he's not the one, you'll find someone else."

"Someone like . . ." I'm drunk enough not to care that this is inappropriate. That I'm leading him, urging him to give a name to the tension strung between us like twinkle lights, and acknowledge the desire crackling in the air.

He tips his head to one side, fingers tracing the outline of my lips. "You're a smart girl. I have to believe you'll know it when you see it."

Our faces hover inches apart, our eyes locked. His breath mingles with mine, both coming too fast. The heat spewing from the vents makes the car too warm. My eyes drop to his mouth, licking my lips at the thought of what it might feel like on mine. Knowing there will be fireworks but also comfort, and proof that there are, in fact, options for me.

His hand slides to the back of my neck, pulling me forward slowly, maybe to give me the chance to stop him.

Stop him, Jessie. You have a boyfriend. This is wrong. Even the voice in my head is slurring. My stomach roils.

I don't want to stop him.

Chapter

9

The knock on my door might as well be a jackhammer in my skull.

Light spews into my bedroom at the Donnelly B&B, stronger and brighter than it has been the past couple of days. It assaults my aching eyeballs as I try and fail to get enough moisture into my mouth to answer the knock. Finally, I manage to croak out a "come in."

Brennan enters, showered and dressed, looking handsome and put together and generally making me feel more disgusting than I already do. His tight smile doesn't do anything to improve my mood as he sits down on the edge of the bed and I struggle to sit.

"Rough night, huh chicken?" He jerks his chin toward my body.

I look down to find last night's clothes askew and stuck to my sweaty skin. It smells like booze in here, as though it's coming out of my pores, and the greasy feeling in my stomach worsens. My memory is a puzzle with missing pieces, and every muscle in my body tenses when I recall being in the car with Grady. Talking about how there are other fish in the sea, my blood on fire as he leaned closer and closer.

There's nothing after that. I don't remember coming in the house or finding my way into bed or getting myself the glass of water and ibuprofen sitting on the bedside table.

"Yeah, a little," I start, cautious. My head pounds and I reach for the drugs. "I'm sorry I lost it on you. I don't know what got into me."

He shrugs. "It happens. Especially when you suck down Guinness like it's a watering hole in the desert."

"I'll have to remember that."

"I guess Grady got you home safely." The way he says it, as though implying that something happened, sinks my stomach into my toes.

Because I don't know. Something *might* have happened.

"I hate to point this out again, but you could have driven me home," I snap to cover up my discomfort. Also because I feel like shit. "You chose Katie. Again."

"I didn't choose *Katie*. I chose to stay out with my friends whom I haven't seen in months." He takes a deep breath and closes his eyes as though counting to ten. "This isn't why I came in here."

"Oh?" Wariness makes me bite my lower lip. "Why did you, then?"

"I've been feeling bad about not telling you about Katie. About her being here."

"It's okay. It's right to invite her for Christmas if she doesn't have anywhere else to go."

"No, not that." His fingers trail up and down my arm, but for some reason the touch annoys me when it's meant to soothe. "I mean springing the fact of her. We haven't talked too much about our pasts, because we've been having such a good time in the present, right? But if I'd known you were coming I would have told you about her."

"Grady said your parents love her. Like, they-pretty-much-named-your-kids love her." I bite my lip harder and wish there was a polite way to put some space between us. I feel disgusting. Also, I might have kissed another man a few hours ago.

The slick, oily feeling in my intestines climbs up toward my throat.

He grimaces at the mention of Grady but his silence is all the answer I need. Between the lingering effects of last night and the discomfort swirling off him, almost gagging me it's so thick, I'm about to run for the toilet.

"They love her. I loved her, too. Katie and I . . ." He pauses, as though trying to decide what to say. Whether to be honest, maybe, or to sugarcoat it. But Brennan doesn't own a single pair of kid gloves. "It wasn't like a silly high school romance. It was real and everyone knew it."

"So, what happened?"

"I left for the States. She decided we should move on." He swivels his head so he can look into my eyes, gives me a sweet smile. "I met you."

"Yeah, but what *happened*?" I wonder if he knows, if Katie even told him. An image of Grady not wanting to talk about it yesterday pops into my mind. He might know the truth.

"It's ancient history. It doesn't matter why she made that choice, it only matters that you know I've moved on. Things have been a little awkward since you got here, with the surprise and then running into Katie and everything getting tossed off-kilter. But nothing has changed, right?"

It's crazy to me that he can sit here and say that as though he actually believes it. I got drunk last night. Me. I feel like two people right now, the old one fading while the new one is struggling to define herself. To figure out what it means, all of the possibilities.

I don't know what it says about Brennan that he can't see it. Can't tell. Maybe he's never seen me at all.

My hair is sticking under his shoulder when I nod in agreement. Because it's not fair to expect him to read my mind. We need to have a different talk, a more relevant one, but now isn't the time. It's Christmas Eve, and I've already disturbed too much of the Donnellys' holiday.

"Right." My best smile seems to work.

"Good." He presses a short kiss to my lips. "Mam and Katie are in the kitchen whipping up some last-minute dessert. They said to see if you want to help."

I nod again, grateful for the chance to get out of the room. To spend Christmas Eve in the kitchen with the other women. "Sure. I'm just going to throw up and I'll be right there."

❧

I spend five minutes tying up my hair and smoothing on a bit of makeup, brush my teeth a second time, then don a bright red sweater and a pair of deep-gray corduroy pants and black flats. I feel ready for the holiday and the spirit of the day wriggles its way into my veins, spilling comfort and happiness through my blood.

The warmth of the kitchen wraps around me as securely as the strings of the apron Mrs. Donnelly hands over when I join her at the counter. She's got the space covered in open cans of apples, along with the traditional cake ingredients and a few of the same spices that went into my pumpkin pie—minus the nutmeg.

"What are we making?"

"Apple cake," Katie answers, sliding a recipe across the counter toward me. "We usually wing the amounts, but I figured you might like to have it written down. It's one of Brennan's favorites."

My mouth waters just reading the mixture of ingredients, and my excitement flickers at the finishing touch. "Ooh, we get to make a custard sauce?"

Mrs. Donnelly winks at me. "That's the best part."

The three of us fall into an easy rhythm of questions and

answers, with a fair smattering of laughter mixed in with our cake. We finish up and they both disappear with excuses of needing to shower and dress for the evening, but the happiness at living my dream holiday—minus the boyfriend troubles—has sunk deep under my skin.

Brennan's nowhere to be found, so I put on a coat and boots and go for a walk in the new dusting of snow. The fresh air is exactly what I need. It clears my head and settles my belly, and by the time the farmhouse comes into view again I'm so excited for tonight. For gifts and dinner and warmth from the fire, and everything else that's making me feel better about everything. Life.

Especially the future, no matter what it holds.

Then Grady pops up, arms full of firewood, before I can take refuge in the warm, Christmassy house. An evil glint in his bright eyes startles a grin out of me, then a grimace.

"How are you feeling?"

"Fine." I try to step around him and up the porch but he blocks me. "I'm cold."

"No, you're not." He peers at me, confused now. "What's wrong?"

"If you're going to recount the sordid details of how I cheated on my boyfriend last night, I'd really rather not hear them." Tears fill my eyes as I look up to find exasperation on his face. "What?"

"Nothing happened. You literally passed out in the middle of a sentence and I carried you to bed, gave you some water and pills, then left." His arms tighten on the stack of wood. "But it's nice to know you think so highly of me. See you."

He steps around me and I pinch the bridge of my nose, headache roaring back. "Grady, wait."

It's too late. He's striding away with long steps, and there isn't anything I can say, anyway. Whatever happened last night, whatever's *been* happening, can't be a thing. I have a boyfriend, and Grady's just a farmhand in Fanore, Ireland.

Plus, he hates me now. That should make things easier.

I brush away the odd sense of loss and step into the foyer, shrugging out of my coat and kicking my boots off on the rug, breathing in the reminder that it's Christmas Eve.

The inside of the Donnelly home smells amazing. Exactly like Christmas should, with spices and sugar and cooking turkey twisting together, forming braided scents in the air. The sweetness of it dispels my lingering feeling of *ick* over Grady and sparks the tiniest flicker of hope that maybe things from here on out will go off without a hitch.

This will be the first real Christmas I've had in a real home with a real family since I was six years old, and even though that should mean the holiday holds bad memories for me, it doesn't. A night like this, a tree like this, presents like these and a family like the Donnellys' have been the focus of a million daydreams.

They're about to come true, and even if life is slightly less perfect than I'd prefer, this is a thousand times better than the past decade. I swallow hard, gratitude coursing through me, tears blurring my vision.

"Molly, is that you?" Mrs. Donnelly calls from the sitting room. "It's time to light the candle and you're still the youngest!"

"It's Jessica," I say, popping into the room with my best smile, unwinding my scarf in the process. Mrs. Donnelly's at the front window beside a taper candle, a box of matches in her hand. A fire crackles in the stone fireplace and Grand-dad Donnelly snores in the recliner, mouth hanging open.

Brennan's mother is still wearing an apron but has swapped out house clothes for a pretty, deep-emerald dress that sets off her attractive face. The room seems to glow even without the candle, from the soft lamps in the corner to the muted television playing a black-and-white film, and the bright-green holly wreaths scattered in between. The smell of cinnamon and cloves add nuance to the picturesque room, and Mrs. Donnelly offering me a real smile pushes it into perfection.

"Oh, hello dear. It's time you were back—you'll want to run and change for dinner after we light the candle." She presses her lips together, but the sparkle in her eye gives away her happiness in the moment. "Family! Get your arses in here so we can light this candle before dinner goes to shite!"

Thuds and shuffling footsteps signal her success this time around, and her shoulders relax. Her good mood infects me further and I settle into the scene. "Why do you light the candle on Christmas Eve?"

"It's an old tradition. The candle is a beacon of safety, a symbol that Mary and Joseph are welcome in this home as we celebrate the birth of their child."

"That's nice." It is nice, a beautiful symbol that's a reminder of what the holiday means at it's heart and not what it's become because of the retail industry. "And having the youngest girl in the house light it is tradition, too?"

She nods. "During Penal Times a lit candle in the window also signaled safe passage for priests who were being persecuted by the Protestants."

I sense the conversation wandering onto more unstable grounds but we're saved by the entrance of the rest of the family, Molly and Brennan shoving one another lightly as they come through the door.

"Settle down, now," their mother admonishes, handing the box of matches over to her daughter. She must think about what it will be like to hand over the candle-lighting duties to Brennan's or Molly's daughter one day, to watch her family keep expanding and love trickling down through generations.

It's something I always think about over the holidays—what it will be like to be surrounded by my own family some day, if I'm lucky enough to have one. In this perfect, glowing moment it's possible to believe in the dream, and that these people might even be a part of it.

Molly lights the candle with a dramatic flair. Mrs. Donnelly asks everyone to bow their heads for a prayer and we all comply, though I can't help but sneak glances at everyone while their eyes are closed. I follow suit with a warm face when Molly peeks, too, catching me.

"Our heavenly father, we thank you, as ever, for bringing our family together on such a wonderful occasion. We're grateful for Brennan making it home from school yet again. That Katie made a timely appearance and saved my husband's life, because he's a glutton who can't keep his hands out of the icebox. Above all else we thank you for the gift of your son, born this holy night, and strive to do our best work in his name. Amen."

"Amen," I mumble along with the rest, noting that they're obviously not thankful for my arrival. Only Katie's.

I shake off the omission, deciding that being too sensitive is only going to make things harder, and take Brennan's hand as we file into the dining room. The table is set with beautiful, delicate china decorated around the edges with an intricate pattern of holly. The plant seems to have significance in the Irish culture and adds so much to every space. I help Mrs. Donnelly, Katie, and Molly bring the turkey and potatoes and steaming platters of green beans and leafy salad and a million other goodies in from the kitchen.

The rest of dinner is as lovely as the run-up, with quiet laughter and gentle teasing between siblings and parents and children. I think about having a glass of the honeyed wine they pass around when they open the second bottle, but my stomach absolutely refuses to entertain the idea. Grady laughs with the rest of them but I don't miss the glances he shoots my way, ones that say he *doesn't* hate me, and each one heats up my blood to an unbearable degree.

After we've cleared the table and washed the dishes in the kitchen, Molly hands me two clean place settings and nudges me toward the dining room.

"What are these for?" Maybe they set the table for ghosts.

"Oh, it's another of Mam's old traditions," Brennan explains, coming up behind me and slipping strong arms around my waist. "Calls it the Laden Table. Another welcome for travelers like Mary on Joseph, out on a night like tonight."

"That's nice." I repeat the sentiment from earlier, since neither of them heard me then. It's a lame reply but my mind has wandered, still swimming in hormones and hangover.

He kisses my shoulder, then moves up my neck. I pull away, uncomfortable, giving him a swat and a reproachful look. Molly twists her lips like we're grossing her out, putting the finishing touches on the table.

"I'm going to get ready for church," she announces, flouncing toward the door before pausing to giggle. "I'm kind of tired, bro, so maybe you can wait until Sunday Mass to do your confession. I want to get home before dawn."

"Ha-ha," he says, and sighs in her direction, then pulls me into his arms as she disappears.

I let myself relax at his closeness, at the familiar smell of him. All of my dreams, harbored and nurtured by the last four months, glimmer. "You guys go to church tonight?"

He startles, as though I just asked him to sacrifice Nanny Goat for Christmas dinner. "You don't?"

"No. I usually volunteer at a homeless shelter or something."

It's not that I have a problem attending Mass. My best friend in high school was Jewish and Christina attends a non-denominational service in Fort Worth that I tag along for on occasion. Things have turned around for the better today, and sitting with them through another tradition will top it all off—in a good way, this time.

"I'd love to go." I give him a smile and a kiss and scoot down to my room to change clothes.

But a million thoughts of Grady, the way he looked at me across the table, how maybe he doesn't hate me, after all, fill my mind along the way. Maybe I'd better see about that confession thing, too.

Chapter

10

I get less sleep than a little kid listening for the *clip-clop* of reindeer hooves on the roof, but the thoughts going through my head until dawn aren't so innocent. My boyfriend is seriously one of the hottest guys on campus. He comes from a fabulous, stable family. He's freaking Irish for Saint Patrick's sake, accent and all. We've got four months invested in this thing and they've been steady and safe.

And I'm lying here thinking about Grady Callaghan.

It's not even his face (more interesting than handsome) or his body (definitely earned by a lifetime of hard labor) that's sparking my increasing and undeniable attraction. It's because I know more about Grady Callaghan—deep, true things—than I know about my own boyfriend, and we've been dating four months. And Grady knows those kinds of things about me, too.

It's making me think that there's a way to keep my future

safe without planning every last detail. Or trying to, anyway.

It's crazy to think that I came here with the idea that it would make Brennan see me in a different light—a serious one—so that the plan for my life can stay on track. I'm leaving in a few days with a new plan. To maybe *not* have a plan other than finding what and who I love and being able to take care of myself.

An odd sense of freedom, accompanies the thought. I can do anything. Go anywhere. Be a field reporter, travel with nothing but my iPhone and my wallet, or work at a network. I can be single, get engaged if I find the right guy, and it doesn't matter. Not knowing doesn't have to mean following my parents into poverty. I can do things right, make sure I have a safety net, and maybe take a few chances, too.

Like Grady, that stubborn voice whispers from the back of my mind.

I shove it away and get up, deciding that a warm glass of milk will put me to sleep. My penchant for the old-lady cure to insomnia fuels endless jokes in the sorority house.

The Donnelly B&B is so quiet I can almost hear it breathing through the vents. My feet don't make any sound on my way down the hall to the kitchen, but when the light from the fridge illuminates Grady on a stool at the bar, a decidedly not quiet curse word pops like fireworks.

"That's not at all ladylike."

I snort, putting a hand to my chest to slow my heart. "Because that's my main goal in life."

I remove the gallon of milk from the top shelf and a coffee mug from the press, popping it into the microwave before confronting him.

"What are you doing here?"

"There's some weather blowing in and Maeve likes to start Christmas morning early."

A glance out the kitchen window reveals the first, lacy flakes fluttering from the sky. The microwave releases my hot milk and I slide onto the stool next to Grady, content to watch the snow and let the beverage warm my belly.

"I can't believe you drink warm milk when you can't sleep. I thought only old people did that."

The comment distracts me from the beauty outside, but one look at Grady Callaghan reminds me there's plenty to be found inside, too. He cuts off my retort by tipping his own mug in my direction to reveal its identical contents.

He winks. "I like to add cinnamon."

There's nothing to do but shake my head and try to remember why I'm in Ireland in the first place. "I thought you were all mad at me for questioning your honor or whatever."

"Maybe I was cheesed off at you for questioning your own honor."

The suggestion halts my attempt to keep him at arm's length. Or keep dancing around whatever's stirring up the air between us.

"I normally wouldn't," I reply, finding my voice. "But I'm not sure I trust myself around you, Grady Callaghan."

That seems to please him, and he spends an inordinate amount of time smiling into the bottom of his mug after draining it. When he finally looks up to meet my gaze his blue eyes are a veil, hiding his feelings from sight.

"Well, we got ourselves a little pickle, then. But you're the girl with the plan, Jessie MacFarlane. I'm going to let you lead the way."

We're sitting so close the heat from his body thwarts the chill sneaking in under the thresholds and around the old wooden windows. He smells like cinnamon and pine trees, like crisp wind and a hint of the barn.

It tugs me even closer and he leans in, one hand scooting forward on the counter until our fingers are touching. I stare at them, expecting to see sparks. Expecting one of us to pull back.

Eventually I tug against the magnetic field that keeps shoving us together, putting space between us. I have a boyfriend.

The fact that I've never wanted to be single so badly propels me off the stool and down the hall, my throat clogged with the words I didn't get to say. It's weird, but back in bed, a hand pressed to my fluttery chest, I can't make myself believe I just missed my last chance.

Morning comes way too soon, if my puffy, tired eyes are any indication. There's no telling where all of these revelations will take me, but they're definitely taking me about five thousand miles away. And who knows, this new, relaxed me might find Brennan more attractive than ever.

I do what I can with water and makeup, and the end result isn't too bad. The spirit of Christmas finds me, helping me banish the useless thoughts of Grady to the corners of my mind. They're hidden behind the expectation of giving gifts, of sitting in a room that smells of fresh evergreen and tea, of gathering around a table later this afternoon and celebrating the one holiday that's escaped me for years.

The family—plus Katie and Grady, though they might technically count—gathers around the tree. Granddad Donnelly reclines in a big cushy chair while Molly, Brennan, and Grady sit cross-legged in front of the fireplace, golden flames dancing behind them. Katie and Mrs. Donnelly move to make space for me on the couch, and Mr. Donnelly settles in a wing-back chair.

"Happy Christmas," they chorus almost as one voice, the happy sound pinging off the frosted windows and warm bricks.

"I made you some tea," Katie says with a smile, shining in a pair of black button-up pajamas and pants that skim the floor. There's something about her this morning that's fragile, as though she's got cracks around the edges, but she looks away before I can guess what it is.

"Thanks," I say, tucking my knees underneath me and wrapping my chilly hands around the mug.

Brennan hops up and comes to plant a kiss on my forehead. "Happy Christmas, chicken."

"Back at you, gorgeous." It's easier than I imagine, pretending nothing has changed.

"All right, Molly, get to passing out gifts." Mrs. Donnelly instructs.

She groans at what I'm assuming is her job as the youngest, but Brennan pitches in after a minute, the two of them dragging brightly tied packages from under the tree and distributing them around the room. I'm touched by the pile that stacks up in front of me. It's not as big as the others but is on par with Katie's. My surety wavers again. They obviously bought me a few things before Mr. Donnelly collapsed the other night.

I sense eyes on me and look over to find Grady watching me, his gaze a confusion of emotions that speed up my heart. Moisture leeches from my mouth, and it isn't until Katie clears her throat that I realize Grady and I have been staring at each other way too long.

Her eyebrows are raised and I look away, hoping to avoid her questions. "Brennan, did you pass out the ones I brought, too?"

"Yep, in the TCU paper. All done."

"Okay, for Jessica's sake. We all open our present from the same person at the same time so we can show them off," Molly explains. "Let's do Granddad's first; they're always the best."

"And the same," her brother adds with a smile.

"You kids are ungrateful wretches and you know it. I bet Jessica's going to like my gift."

"I'm sure I will."

"I think you and I might be friends, after all, but you're going to have to stop being so nice. It could make a person sick." He gives me a toothless grin. "Like black pudding."

That makes me snort. "I'll keep that in mind."

We dig through our piles, coming up with what has to be a jar wrapped in newsprint, and tear off the paper. Inside is a jar of home-harvested Irish honey that I am sure is delicious.

"Thank you!" I tell him, hugging it to my chest. The others echo my sentiment but set the jars aside quickly, as though they're going to join a dozen more just like them in a cabinet.

"Don't go wasting it on any waffles," he replies in a gruff tone that's offset by the smile stretching his cheeks.

"Granddad, knock it off," Brennan huffs, giving me an apologetic smile.

I shake my head, tears stuck in my throat, to let him know that it doesn't bother me. Good-natured ribbing from Grandfather Donnelly only makes me feel more a part of the family.

We open gifts from Molly next, which are copies of her favorite book by her favorite author—at least this past year—and pairs of hand-knit wool socks from Katie, like the ones she had on the other morning.

She nudges my shoulder, whispering, "I had to give you a pair of mine, since I didn't know you'd be here, but I washed them."

"I would have accepted even if you hadn't," I whisper back. "I don't have anything for you."

She waves me off, turning to admire her handiwork on Mrs. Donnelly's feet. Katie doesn't seem herself, not making eye contact and fluttering from one conversation to another as though she can't or won't let her mind or her voice sit still. A shiver wracks her body and she hugs her arms over her chest.

"Do you want a sweater?" I ask, concerned by the abject misery on her pretty face. "I have extras."

"I would love that. I can't shake this chill for some reason."

She puts out a hand to stop me when I start to get up. "I'll get it. In your room?"

"Yeah, I left it in my suitcase. Should be near the top."

Katie slips into the hall, trailing her odd melancholy behind her as Molly announces it's time to open Grady's gift. She grabs at her newsprint-wrapped gift with all the glee of a five-year-old in the same situation while Grady ducks his head and blushes as though he'd like to protest but there's not much point to asking people not to open your gifts on Christmas morning.

Everyone tears into his or her present, but I'm smiling so big at mine I can't look around right away to see what everyone else received. It's a black-and-white framed picture of Nanny Goat with an ice pack wrapped around her foreleg with an ACE bandage . . . that's quickly disappearing into her mouth. Subject matter aside, the photograph is expertly framed, backlit by the sun setting across the water and dappling the gray boulders under the goat's feet.

"This is amazing," I say with a laugh, looking up to find his eyes. In them I see embarrassment and expectation and hope for something I'm too afraid to name. "Thank you."

"You're welcome."

I look around at everyone else's gifts then and find that they're all beautiful photographs. Brennan received one of his parents laughing by the kitchen sink; Molly, a gorgeous candid photo of herself. The Donnellys' received different photos of their children, and Grandfather a still life of a pint of Guinness.

Everyone's in the middle of opening their TCU T-shirts and golf shirts and Mrs. Donnelly has exclaimed over tea when Katie clears her throat from the doorway.

I look up—we all do—and horror explodes inside me. It splatters on my organs like goo, making it hard to breathe as she stares right at me, tears spilling onto her cheeks.

She's got my unopened pregnancy test clutched in her hand.

"It's not what you think," I start, leaping to my feet and taking the little pink box from her while the family gapes, and turn a pleading gaze on Grady. "Tell them."

"It's true," he says in a rush, holding up his hands in mock surrender. "It was a joke. I bought it for her while I was out getting groceries because I caught her throwing up that pudding."

Mrs. Donnelly's face regains a bit of color and Granddad

can't stop snickering. Mr. Donnelly appears bemused by the entire thing, and I stare at my boyfriend, hoping this isn't going to look like something it kind of is—a private joke between me and the farmhand he doesn't seem to love.

But Brennan's eyes are on Katie.

I follow his gaze, and find her on the floor, her arms wrapped around her knees and tears streaming down her face. Sobs wrack her bony chest and, like everyone else in the room, I'm completely taken aback.

For her part, Katie seems to have forgotten the rest of us are in the room. She raises her head and stares at Grady, the accusation she'd reserved for me changing targets. "How could you make a joke like that?"

All of us are staring at Katie, completely transfixed. What's super weird is that she's only talking to Grady, as though he's the only person in the world who might understand what's set her off.

"Katie, *a grhá*, what are you talking about? Are you okay?" The concern brimming in Brennan's eyes, the way they're focused on her as though he'd throw himself under a crashing boulder if it was causing her tears, breaks my heart for so many reasons.

He's at her side in a heartbeat, but she pulls away when he tries to put an arm around her. "Stop."

"Why? What's wrong?"

She keeps crying, her green eyes almost glowing as they stray, unfocused, out the front window. "Did you never wonder if something triggered our breakup? It was all so easy for you to understand, that one day I would wake up and change all of our plans."

"*Easy* for me? Have you lost your brain? It *killed* me, but you said it was what you needed. Not what you wanted, what you *needed*. How could I argue?"

Brennan's words totally suck for me, but anything I'm feeling pales in comparison with the pain etching lines on her stunning face. It's so pale her freckles look copper in the early morning light. We all watch, rapt as though they're players on a stage, afraid to move and interrupt a moment that must have been a long time coming.

"You should have argued. You should have asked." She turns her fiery gaze on him.

He sits back as though physically burned but his voice grows more desperate. As though he's holding the water, waiting for her to tell him where to toss it. "What would you have said, *a ghrá*? I'm asking now. What changed your mind? What happened?"

Katie's emerald eyes drop back to the picture. "I lost her."

"Lost who? You're not making sense."

"The baby. Our baby. I lost her."

If I could put the ingredients together that create the word stunned, it would include everything in this room right now. The tension in the air. The way all the color drains from Brennan's face. The slight gasp that emits from Molly, the quick movement of Mrs. Donnelly's hand to cover her mouth. The twist of my heart.

The horror on Grady's face at the realization that his spontaneous joke became the catalyst of this eruption of emotions, the loss of a secret that maybe has been waiting to escape for months.

His expression convinces me that he's known all along that Katie had been pregnant, but maybe he *didn't* know she'd never told Brennan. The gruff distaste for the guy he'd grown up with could be easily explained by thinking he'd abandoned his girlfriend in her moment of need.

The silence, the lack of reaction from Brennan, goes on a moment too long, and Katie stumbles to her feet. Brennan makes a grab for her hand but misses. The sound of her sobs echo from the foyer, where she pauses—maybe to put on her boots—before the front door slams.

Brennan looks lost. Like a statue that someone put down in the wrong place.

"If you don't get off your arse and go after her, man, I am going to smash your face," Grady growls.

The threat spurs my boyfriend into action and he leaps from the couch. He turns in the doorway, gaze ending its search when it lands on my face. He's asking silent permission—I've seen the request a million times when he wants to stay late at a party or go to a game with his friends, but this time it's more than that.

He's asking for permission to go after Katie, but I know, in reality, I'm granting him permission to leave *me*.

It's harder than I think it will be, maybe harder than it should be given the situation, to give him that nod. But I do. And then he's gone.

"Did you know about this?" Mr. Donnelly asks his wife in a soft voice that's full of more reproach than he's used since I've met him. Even over Nanny Goat.

"No, of course not. And there's no way she confided to her parents. Poor dear."

"Her parents are missionaries," Molly explains softly, for my benefit. "Super strict."

I'm honestly surprised that the Donnellys aren't more upset to find out their son's been violating God's laws, but they love Katie like a daughter. They might be disappointed later but right now they're worried about her.

"You knew," I say to Grady, more a statement than a question.

He nods, still pale. "I knew about the baby. That she lost it. I caught her tossing drinks in the trash a couple of times and she refused to ride in a really big horse show, so I put it together." He cuts a glance at the Donnellys. "I thought she told Brennan, though."

"That poor girl," Mrs. Donnelly reiterates, wiping tears from her eyes.

We sit in silence, nothing left to say. After a few minutes, Molly starts stuffing discarded wrapping into a giant trash bag, the bright paper and stringy, happy bows out of place now that the family has been rocked. No one feels much like celebrating, Jesus's birthday or not.

Everyone slowly drifts from the room, Mrs. Donnelly and her daughter to the kitchen to see about breakfast, Mr. Donnelly to check on the animals, Grady in tow. I don't have anything to do because this isn't my house. Isn't my family.

"Aw, c'mon lass. No one looks good with a face as long as a horse's."

I've almost forgotten Granddad Donnelly is here, too, but there he is leaning on his cane and looking at me with the kind of exasperation I reserve for my roommate when she barfs peppermint schnapps into the sink.

"I'm worried, is all."

"*Humph.* Worried about yourself." He shakes his head at me. "Sometimes roads in life don't lead the place you think when you set out. Don't be too daft to realize when you've gotten to where you belong, anyway."

He clomps off, back into the front room. A moment later the sounds of wrapping paper being torn finds my ears. I can't help but smile at the thought of him in there tearing into his presents alone, even if he did just call me a horse face and spout nonsense.

Anyone can see Brennan and Katie aren't done. So obviously this road has led me to a very pretty dead end.

Chapter

11

It's hours before Brennan comes back. We didn't even eat dinner together; Mrs. Donnelly left it all out in the kitchen for people to come through and fix plates, but Mr. Donnelly and Grady haven't returned, either, not that I've seen. Maybe they're avoiding the excess of estrogen.

I'm sitting on the porch, bundled up in coats and hats and blankets, reading *Wuthering Height*s in the last rays of Christmas Day sunshine. It glints off the melting snow, little drops forming the soundtrack of my day as they fall off the gutters and splash into puddles. The wind has started to pick up, another storm brewing on the horizon, when Brennan traipses up and sits next to me on the padded porch swing.

He's soaked through and vibrating with tension, his fingers twisting together, knee jiggling, My boyfriend is normally as put together as I am, but right now everything about him is askew—hair out of place, dirt smudged on his pants and face—and my heart goes out to him.

I cover his big hand with mine and he grabs onto it for dear life.

"I was going to be a father." The softness in his voice, the wonder, can't overtake the raw edge of loss. There's nothing to say so I don't speak, just squeeze his hand tighter. "How could she not tell me?"

It's a real question. He turns his head toward me, searching for answers I don't have. Can't fathom. "I don't know. It's a pretty personal thing and it sounds like you had already decided to go to school in the States. She didn't want to ruin that for you."

"That's what she said, too, but it doesn't make me feel better. It makes me feel damn well worse, to know that she didn't think I could handle it." His fingers tighten on mine. "I would have done the right thing."

"Exactly. Katie knows that, too. She wanted you to live your life."

"She can't decide that for me!" He pulls away, running his hands through his hair so hard it stands up everywhere. "I never wanted to leave Fanore, to leave her. I only went abroad for school to get everyone to shut up."

I swallow hard, because only the most terrible sort of person would make this about her. But it stings, to hear that he'd be better off, happier, if he'd never met me at all.

Brennan seems to realize the way his statement might

affect me and turns, horror hanging on his already ravaged face. "I'm sorry . . ."

He trails off, because we both know there's nothing else to add to the sentiment. He's sorry that he hurt my feelings, that the truth spilled out with no filter. Sorry that things have turned out this way.

He's just sorry. But it doesn't change anything.

"I'm sorry, too."

An understanding stretches between us, an acknowledgment that this thing we had was real but it's over, that maybe it was never going anywhere, anyway.

"You know why I really came here?" I ask, still holding his hand.

"Why?"

"I was worried we weren't moving fast enough. I wanted to make you see that I'd make the perfect wife after graduation."

The glance he gives me is full of his trademark amusement tinged with exasperation. "Oh, chicken. You had to know I wasn't even on that wavelength."

I nod. "I think I did. It was desperation, flying all the way out here to surprise you. Because that's how I get when things start to derail. When I can't predict the outcome." I bark a short laugh. "I certainly couldn't have planned for any of this."

"Well, I might not have been ready to go ring shopping over the summer, but I never expected any of this to go down, either, I can promise you that." He turns and our eyes meet, then he pulls me into a hug.

"It's over then, I guess?" I mumble against his shirt. It smells like sweat and some other girl's tears.

He pulls away, tucking a strand of hair behind my ear. "I'm not going back to school. It's hard to say how things will end up with Katie and me at the moment, but she's a mess. Never dealt with the whole thing because nobody knew the truth, and her parents are going to take it rough. She needs me."

My heart twists. Someday, I'll find a guy who feels this way about me. Who understands what I need and is willing to give it to me no matter what I've done to hurt him.

The thought makes me smile. "You're a good guy, Brennan. She's lucky to have you, and I'll eat my hat if you two don't end up together. So will half the people in this town, from what I hear. Maybe more."

He smiles back, but it's sad around the edges. Distracted. "You're going to find someone way better than me, I promise."

It's odd that Grady's face flashes in my mind at that moment. I take it inside with me and lay it beside me in bed, letting my tears fall. Grieving for the loss—not of Brennan, but of all my plans. I don't have any backups in the works, but for the first time I think maybe that's okay. I'm smart. I'm getting a college degree.

Everything will be fine.

It takes me a few minutes to change my plane ticket to the earliest flight out the next day. It's leaving from Knock, not

Shannon, which is farther away, so I'm up and out the door before anyone else is awake. I leave a note for the Donnellys, thanking them for their hospitality. Last night I'd told Brennan I was leaving early, and he hadn't argued except to tell me to be careful because a storm was blowing in.

All the more reason to get out of here now.

The rental car is right where I left it, and the dogs run off when the engine turns over, breaking the stillness of the snowy morning. I have to wait while the car warms up and melts the snow crusted on the windshield. A brief thought of staying crosses my mind, reinforced by the memory of navigating these roads in the rain the other night, but the weather could get worse. The snow started not that long ago—if I wait it out, I might not be able to leave at all.

Decision made, I back out of the spot and step on the gas, navigating my way down the winding lane toward the main road with care. The livestock stay clear of my car but my tires slip off the lip of the road and into thick drifts more than once. My hands sweat on the wheel and I pray that the main road shows up sooner rather than later.

When I reach the road, the snow isn't any shallower. It was stupid to think that in a town this small someone would be out plowing roads the day after Christmas. *Main* is an arbitrary word around here.

The GPS on my phone can't find a signal, so I pull over and snatch a map out of the glove box. To get to the airport in Knock I'm supposed to go back through Ballyvaghan, so I take a left on the road out of Fanore.

I'm taking a curve as slow as humanly possible when the tires slide again. The brakes lock up when I step on them, and my heart jams into my throat.

"Shit, shit, *shit*." I chant, twisting the wheel right, then left to no avail. On one side of the road is a rocky hillside that goes pretty much straight up, and on the other, one of those now-depressing stone walls is the only thing separating me from the shoreline.

The thick snow on the side of the road stops the front of my rental car from smacking into anything hard enough to crunch it, and for a moment I sit there, limbs trembling with adrenaline, swallowing my heart back into my chest.

My worst nightmare comes true when I put the car in reverse, step on the gas, and . . . nothing happens. The tires spin over and over but they're off the road and deep in a snowdrift, so I finally give up and wrap my hands around the useless steering wheel while the heater blows stuffy air in my face.

Tears sting my eyes but I blink them back, rolling my eyes at my own drama. I put my shoulders back and my mind to the task at hand. The car will run out of gas eventually, and once the heat goes off it's going to get real cold, real fast. My suitcase is in the trunk, which means I've got more layers of clothes. A few packages of crackers and at least one bottle of water are lurking in my carry-on bag in the backseat, so I won't starve. The snow outside will melt in an empty bottle, too, if it comes to that.

My heart rate slows as confidence builds up from my

center. I've got this. The plan to spend an Irish Christmas winning over my boyfriend might be a bust, but this place sure as hell isn't going to kill me on the way out.

I get out of the car and dig through my suitcase, dragging out a second sweater and a warmer pair of gloves, then wrap my red pashmina around my neck and face. I crouch down to inspect the back set of tires. Given that this tiny little toy of a car is likely rear-wheel drive, they've got to be my problem.

I'm thinking that maybe I could dig out some snow, or maybe use the car's floor mats underneath them to gain some traction, but even those long shots are decimated when it becomes clear that the rear axle is high centered on something—snow, a rock—and the tires aren't even touching the ground.

"Well, fuck a duck." I tromp back to the driver's side—then around to the *actual* driver's side—and kicking snow off my boots before climbing back inside the car.

My fingers ache from the chill, and I hold them in front of the vents for a few minutes, then down my bottle of water. I fill it with snow so it will be melted when I'm ready for more, then I take a deep breath.

It'll probably take me more than two hours to traipse back to the Donnellys—or even to a closer residence where I can use a phone—but there's nothing else to be done.

"Well, let's go, Jessie. Onward and upward." All I know is that I'm getting to the damn airport.

I'm about to shove open the door when a strange,

tinkling sound meets my ears. It sounds like sleigh bells, a jingle that I've only heard in movies and daydreams, and if I was anywhere but Ireland I would dismiss it as crazy fancy.

But I *am* in Ireland and when I step out of the car, Grady Callaghan leaps off the sleigh, giving Garth a pat on the rump and performing an awkward, sweeping bow.

"What are you doing here?" I ask, my jaw falling open. It's like a Christmas card.

He brushes snow off his coat and I can't help noticing his coveralls. And thinking they're kind of sexy. "Got yourself in a bit of a pickle, right? And what is my latest résumé entry?"

"Showing up when I'm embarrassing myself?" I laugh, unable to stop myself.

"Yes, but we've got to quit meeting like this," he jokes, bending to inspect the rear tires. "Turn that thing off. You're not going anywhere."

"No."

"Jessie, the thing is stuck in the shuck. We'll have to pull it off, and I don't have any straps in the sleigh," he explains, more patience in his tone than I probably deserve.

"I mean, I know the *car* isn't going anywhere but I need to get to the airport."

"Yeah, I know. We can drive the sleigh back and get my truck."

I narrow my gaze at him and put my hands on my hips, realizing he never really answered the question of what he's doing out here. In a *sleigh*. "Where were you going?"

"What do you mean?"

His obvious stalling makes me roll my eyes. "You were just out for a lovely morning ride in your neighbor's sleigh?"

"Oh, that." He tugs on the hem of his stocking cap and bites his lower lip, looking off toward the ocean before snapping his blue, blue eyes back to my face. They linger, hesitant, and what might be a blush touches his cheeks before he shrugs. "Coming after you."

It's not the answer I expect but it's the one I wanted. "You were coming after *me?* In a sleigh?"

"You were so excited about getting a sleigh ride the other day and now it's finally snowed enough, so I didn't want you to miss out." His cheeks redden further. "And I'm coming after you *in a sleigh* because I couldn't let you leave Ireland without telling you something very important."

I smile, hot all over and with a sudden and uncommon urge to tease. "What, pray tell, is important enough to chase someone down in a snowstorm?"

He shifts his weight from foot to foot, then seems to make a decision. "All right, then."

Then Grady Callaghan steps forward, cups my jaw with both of his big, gloved hands, and draws my lips to his.

My fingers and toes are cold but my chest boils, blood swirling fast through my veins. My surprise fades as quickly as snowflakes on warm skin, and I find myself kissing him back as though there was never another option. The lips that were tentative, tasting, maybe even asking, turn hungry against mine, devouring like it's his very last meal. My own lips part, tongue eager to allow him in, to drink in the fresh, heady wine that is Grady—a boy who intrigues me but was all wrong.

It doesn't matter. All that matters is the way his mouth feels against mine, how his arms hold me tight so our bodies mold together through layers and layers, and the surprising strength of the need spilling through me.

He pulls away, his hands falling to my shoulders. Desire and curiosity fight for prominence in his bright gaze, neither winning out until I give him what feels like a dazed smile. "Oh, good. You're not going to pop me, then."

"Not for the kiss, anyway." My mind swirls, trying to figure out what this means, whether I'm a terrible person for enjoying Grady so much when I've just broken up with Brennan, and what we're supposed to do now.

"Stop."

"Stop what?" I ask, biting my lower lip.

"Worrying about a million things neither of us have any control over. I kissed you because I hate the thought of you walking out of my life. Without at least asking whether you might want to keep in touch with me after you get home."

My heart thuds at the prospect. At how this little kiss, this chance encounter, feels like something so much more enormous. At the possibility that with Grady's help, I could learn to sit back and see what happens instead of freaking out about all the things that could go wrong.

Because he's showing me that sometimes things go right even when you don't ask them to.

"I don't want to not see you again, either." I give him a playful look. "Not that you need to hear that."

"I'll always need to hear that, Jessie MacFarlane." He draws me against his chest, hugging me tight and bending to bury his nose in my hair. "But I am freezing my arse off, so how about we get in the sleigh."

"I thought you'd never ask," I squeal, running over and letting him boost me up into the red velvet interior. It smells like a bouquet of musk and man and winter—and yeah, a little bit like a barn. The woolen blanket on the seat scratches my hands but once Grady is under it with me, his thigh pressed against mine, I can't come up with a single complaint. "No hot chocolate?"

"Good Lord, who do you think you're dealing with here?" He reaches into the back and pulls a thermos from under the seat, tossing it in my lap before he flicks the reins.

"You brought hot chocolate."

He looks over, cheeks still red, but maybe it's from the wind. "If there's one thing you need to know about me, it's that I take my sleigh rides very seriously."

"I'm glad to hear it."

"Okay. Let's get you to the airport." Grady urges the horses into a trot and the snowy morning rushes past my cheeks, fingers warm around the thermos.

I don't expect the relief over his not pushing the issue or

trying to get me to stay. It's refreshing, that Grady under-stands so much without my having to tell him—that my whole life is rearranging, and dealing with unexpected feel-ings or a new relationship, no matter how lovely, is going to take time for me to sort out.

It kind of makes me want to jump him, but he's kind of busy. Driving a sleigh.

"Oh, and the airport is in Knock," I tell him, snuggling into his side.

Grady looks down, blue eyes shining with happiness. "That's a bit beyont a tiny jaunt, you know?"

"I know. You still up for me?" I hold my breath because maybe I'm not just asking about the ride to the airport. I might be changing, might be considering a different path, but I'm not stupid enough to deny I have issues that are going to take a while to dispel—and Grady knows every single one of them. There's no point in pretending I'm per-fectly fine.

Acting as though I had it all together didn't get me anywhere with Brennan and this thing with Grady, if it happens, is going to be different.

He gives me a smile, dimples popping, as though he's read every thought in my neurotic head. "Oh, I'm thinking that being *up* for you isn't ever going to be an issue."

Grady snaps the reins again and the horses break into a gallop, leaving me to burn with hot lust at the images accompanying his sexy-as-hell reply. We fly toward the McCormacks', living a different present than I could possibly have foreseen when agreeing to take this trip almost four thousand miles from home.

And just like that, Grandfather Donnelly's words make sense. Since my trip to Ireland ended with Brennan and me going our separate ways instead of better than ever, it might seem as though my plan missed its mark.

But glancing sideways at Grady next to me in the sleigh, a snow-covered Ireland surrounding us, and an unstoppable grin making my cheeks ache, it's not so hard to believe that maybe I've ended up in, if not the right place, the one I was meant for all along.

Epilogue

The road to Fanore is still narrow, still treacherous, and still impossibly dark, but at least this time it's not raining.

It's snowing.

The streets wind and twist even more than they do in my memory, which is saying a lot, but when I make the turn off toward the Thistle Farmhouse B&B, at least I know to slow down. And watch for goats. I let out a breath once Mini-car Extraordinaire slides past the spot where Nanny Goat and I had our altercation last year, then jump when a warm, calloused hand covers mine.

"Oh, look; it's where we first met."

I shake my head, still not daring to take my eyes off the road. "Where you treated me like an annoying American for the first time. So sweet."

"Well, you *are* an annoying American," Grady points

out as we slide into the parking lot unharmed. "But now you're *my* annoying American."

Caramel lights melt through the B&B's windows like butter, slipping onto the porch and reaching into the parking lot, but not quite reaching our car. Snowflakes tumble downward, dotting the windshield and melting on the hood as I switch off the ignition, undo my seat belt, and turn toward the passenger seat.

Grady sits there, in the flesh for the first time in over six months. He'd been to visit me once while he'd been in the States applying for a couple of photography internships, but the visit had been too short and involved too many other people.

I'd jumped at the chance to visit Fanore for Christmas again, this time with an actual invitation.

Grady's rough hands brush my jaw, bringing my thoughts back to the present. Then his lips are on mine and we're struggling to get close enough around the stick shift and console and too many clothes, but I can't ever get close enough to Grady.

His tongue sweeps over my bottom lip, opening me up for his pleasure and I tip my head, giving him all the access he wants. My hands drift down, toying with the inch of bare skin between his collar and chin, earning a groan that sends heated tingles all the way to my toes. We're both breathing hard when we pull apart, his forehead pressed against mine while we fight for normal heart rates and proper oxygen.

"You are going to kill me, Jessie."

"I hope not. We've barely gotten started and you'll have to last the whole summer."

A silly smile deepens his dimples. "You and me in Greece. All summer. You in a totally inappropriate skimpy swimsuit."

Grady and I both got internships with an up-and-coming news-reporting website—me doing social media reporting and him covering the photography end. It was pure luck they assigned us to the same location.

"I can't believe we both got internships at the same communications company." I poke him playfully and he catches my hand, running fingers over my palm. Electricity zaps every nerve ending. "It must be the luck of the Irish."

He rolls his eyes, leaning in to capture my lips with his again. We get lost in tongues and hands and skin for a little while longer, and when we stop to breathe I notice it's cold. "We should go inside. You know the family is waiting with a midnight snack."

I can picture it now—not a daydream this time, because it lives in my memory—Molly skipping around, trying to get Katie's attention or sparring with her brother. Mrs. Donnelly setting the table, wetting the tea, checking her desserts. Mr. Donnelly yelling at his kids to settle down and his father, old Granddad, presiding over the mess of wonderful that he helped create.

The holly wreath on the front door beckons us inside. It was so nice of them to invite us both for the holiday. Two little orphans, for all intents and purposes, who managed to find each other in the most unlikely of circumstances.

"Shall we?" Grady asks, getting out of the car and offering his arm as though he's a gentleman.

I know better, and what's more, I prefer it that way. An idea goes off like a lightbulb over my head before we make it three steps and I sneak him a conspiratorial grin that makes him groan, this time for a different reason.

"I know that look, little Jessie. What devious plan is on your mind?"

"I was just thinking we should go check on Nanny."

"She's fine, I fed her before I came to pick you up," he insists, taking another step toward the house.

"Yeah, but I mean, maybe you and I should go check on her. Just to be sure. In the barn. Alone. Where it's warm and no one ever goes except you . . ."

The lightbulb goes off for him and the wicked grin he gives me in return makes me think I could love this man with everything I'm worth until the end of my days.

"Ah, yes. Nanny Goat. She *was* looking a bit off, now that I really think about it." He grabs my hand, tugging me along. "I'll need your help, of course."

I trot along beside him, happiness shooting out from my smile and my chest and out the ends of my fingers. There's no way my body can contain it all, and if happiness were made of real energy, the whole town of Fanore would experience a power surge.

Grady tugs the barn door shut behind us and grabs me

in his arms, twirling me around until my feet lift off the ground and, once again, the complete turnaround my life has taken in a year makes me want to stop and stare. Touch it to make sure it's real.

"I just realized I've never showed you how soft the clean hay in the loft can be," he muses, setting me on my feet. "We should try it."

I lean in and kiss him with everything I've got, tasting and teasing and trying to understand every last bit of Grady Callaghan, even though we've got all the time in the world to do just that.

I pull away, his shirt fisted in my hands, and give him my most serious nod. "We should try everything."

Sleigh Bells
and
Second Chances

Chapter
1

The bounce of the wheels on the runway jars me wide awake, the lingering effects of blessed Tylenol PM trailing hazy clouds in my mind. Reality trickles back in with the awareness of bad breath and gritty eyelids, and from there it doesn't take long for the sense of dread to return to my gut.

London. Christmas, alone in a hotel room. A job that's going to be ten times harder because of the *particular* band I'm assigned to babysit over the next two-plus weeks.

The flight to Gatwick isn't any longer or shorter than it's ever been. I spent every summer from the time I was seven until I was eighteen in England with my father and my older brother but I haven't been back since.

I sigh, flicking my phone out of airplane mode and wading through the onslaught of text messages while the plane taxis to the gate. Two from my mom, the first lamenting my absence over the holiday and the second a not-so-subtle request to please reconsider contacting my so-called father while I'm in town; a couple from my roommate, Jessica, promising to call me when she arrives in Ireland next week; and the rest from my boss at BGG Entertainment, with reminders where and when to report for duty.

We're sitting on the runway like we're in some kind of purgatory—not really in England, but nowhere else, either. My conversation with Jessica plays in my mind and reminds me of the reality waiting on the other side of the Jetway.

"I know you're not looking forward to missing your favorite holiday with your mom, but I'm going to be in Ireland. We could get together for New Year's!"

My roommate's pretty face twists into her most earnest expression, the happiness sparkling in her dark eyes a permanent fixture since she came home from Fanore last Christmas. Trust the most uptight girl in the world to somehow fall in love with an Irish hunk in three days flat.

"I don't know. I'm probably going to have to work." *It's mean, maybe, to rain on her parade, but even the promise of a familiar face abroad isn't enough to untie the complicated knots in my stomach over the prospect of this trip.*

Familiar faces abroad tied more than half of them in the first place.

"You're going to have to work on New Year's? I thought you said it was a Christmas Eve concert and then a New Year's Day appearance on some telethon or something."

"You've got it backward. Christmas Day and New Year's Eve."

Jessica makes a face. "This isn't like you. You always see the bright side of everything. Even that Calc final you probably just bombed."

"Hey!" I toss a pile of socks her direction. Anything to derail packing. "I'm going to work in the music industry. I don't need to know how to do math."

"Hopefully they won't want you to, like, make sure artists get paid."

"That's what accounting departments are for," I inform her, smiling a little. "And I know. It's London, not the dark side of the moon. I'll find something to entertain me."

"Um, like hanging out with one of the coolest bands in the world?"

"Yeah, sure."

Jessica blows her bangs out of her eyes and stuffs one last handful of sexy lingerie into her suitcase before attempting to zip it closed.

"Are you going away for three weeks or the rest of your life? Jeez!"

"I know, it's ridiculous. Usually I'm much more organized— have my outfits planned for every day and how often I'll change— but for some reason I'm too excited to focus."

"I'm pretty sure Grady would be happy if you didn't bring any clothes at all."

Her cheeks bloom red even though they've gotten together—in

the biblical sense of the word—several times since they met a year ago. Jess laughs, the sound so full and happy that it expands into every corner of our room. "I'm sure you're right, but I doubt the Donnellys would appreciate it."

"It's so weird that you're spending Christmas with your new boyfriend and your ex-boyfriend's family. Especially considering your massive fail last year."

"It wasn't a fail, Chris. I met Grady."

"And he has somehow managed to pull almost all of the sticks out of your ass. I've got to hand it to him, although I don't want any details about the ass stuff."

She laughs again, so much more easygoing than the Jess I moved in with a year and a half ago. I don't like her more or better this way but it does make living with her less of a hassle. And she's happier, so that's good.

"How did your finals go?" I ask, in an effort to keep the conversation focused on her. I'm not ready to talk about the myriad reasons going on a tour of a slaughterhouse for Christmas would be preferable to going to London.

"Good, I think. And I turned in my application for another summer internship. I can't let you be the only one with awesome prospects."

"I never thought you would," I murmur.

Some people might find Jessica's competitive streak annoying but it works for us. We push each other.

"Okay, seriously. I'm going to need you to spill what's really bothering you about this trip because it can't all be because of

your dad. I know you haven't seen him in years but it's a couple of weeks. Maybe your stepmother isn't evil, you know? Stereotypes are a bitch."

I roll my eyes at my roommate, who has moved to smoothing the hospital corners on her bed. "Disney says they're evil, Jess. They wouldn't lie *to us."*

"Right, because sweet mermaids exist and it's not weird to want to have sex with a giant hairy beast?" She raises her eyebrows, inviting an argument.

"Props for the nice mermaids clarification."

"Everyone knows mermaids exist, and they're evil as hell. Anyway, I love you, Christina Lake, but you're no sweet and innocent princess."

Other passengers struggle to life, bringing me back to the present as they stretch stiff legs, gathering their bags from the overhead bins and shuffling toward the exit. I join the parade off the aircraft as it spills into the bustling morning at Gatwick. The lulling whirr and circle of the carousel does nothing to quell my nerves, and I dig some gum from my purse, wishing I could go straight into work and get the hard part of this trip over with.

You're over him, my mind insists. *It was four years ago. You cried, you moped, you've been dating and moving on—seeing him won't change anything. No problem.*

I let the mental pep talk straighten my shoulders and push lingering uncertainty from my mind as I drag my giant suitcase and slightly smaller duffel off the carousel and struggle toward customs. The line is short, since it's pushing toward noon and the Christmas travel season won't truly start for another several days.

"Are you traveling for business or pleasure?" The bored customs agent studies my passport, not looking up, as she waits for the answer. The gray hairs at her roots and temples say she's asked the same question so many times she can recite it—and probably guess the answer—in her sleep.

"Business."

"What's your business in London?" She picks up the stamp, her meaty hand hovering above the little blue booklet.

"I'm a music industry intern and I'm here for the New Year's Day concert at the O2."

"You're here early," she remarks, pressing her stamp to the half-full page in my passport.

"They've got publicity running up to the event," I explain, then realize I should probably be doing my job even now. "It's for charity, the concert."

"That's nice. What charity?"

"Um . . ." How can I not know that? My bosses didn't say and I hadn't thought to ask. "I'm not sure yet."

She gives me a look like I might be the biggest idiot she's encountered so far today, maybe this week, and slides my passport back under the glass. "Have a nice holiday."

"Thanks," I mutter, stowing it in my purse and tugging my suitcase into the food court.

The rumble coming from my stomach distracts me from feeling badly about failing as a publicity intern and I grab some fries and a cheeseburger from the nearest fast-food joint. I'm planning to chow my impromptu lunch in a taxi before my phone rings. The caller ID displays my mother's number. I manage to flop into a hard plastic chair and manhandle my suitcases while not spilling my food before pressing Accept.

"Hello?"

"You made it!"

I roll my eyes at her fake surprise. "Yes, mother, I made it. As I'm sure you know because you've been using the Internet to track my plane."

"You know me too well. How was the flight?"

"It was fine. I slept most of the way."

"Have you called your father yet?"

I suck in a deep breath and hold it while I count to ten. My father, so called, hasn't spoken to me in almost four years, and even though he divorced my mom ten years prior to *that*, she hasn't stopped prodding me with lectures about offering the olive branch.

Which would be maybe easier if I knew why I'd been cast aside to begin with. An answer that would be gotten more easily if we actually talked, I'm sure.

"No."

"Christina . . ."

"I'm still thinking about it, Mom. I'll probably call him, maybe see if he wants to have coffee, but don't expect me to spend a happy Christmas around the tree with his happy new family."

"Fair enough, sweetheart. But don't blame them for your father's actions. We know how he is."

I barely stop from snorting. My father's first novel sold for a giant advance almost fifteen years ago, and not only did he become a pompous fame whore, the constant attention made life harder for all of us. He'd managed to settle down, but not before leaving my mom.

And he can still be a jackass.

"I know you're probably anxious to get to your hotel and unpack," she continues. "You don't have to work until tomorrow?"

"Right. First thing in the morning."

"Well, try to have fun and do some exploring. As many summers as you traveled England, you've never really spent time in London."

I roll my eyes again but can't help but smile. Exploring a new city is one of the things about this trip that might not suck. "I will."

"And Christina . . . don't let that boy pull the wool over your eyes again. There aren't enough tissues in the world."

My heart seizes but I grit my teeth. Tell it to be still. "Don't worry about that. Cary White is the furthest thing from my mind."

It's true, as it has been for years, but things would be a whole lot easier if he was a little bit further from my job, too.

Jessica texts me before the cab makes it halfway to the hotel BGG booked for me at the last minute.

Have you met the band yet? Are they as hot in person?

The text makes me smile despite my mood. My room-mate at the sorority house knows most everything about me, but *nobody* outside my immediate family knows about my history with Pursuant's lead singer. It's not that I'm embarrassed. It's just that Cary is a part of my past, and when I pledged the sorority and met Jessica, TCU was my present and future. It had to be, in order for me to survive.

Once Pursuant hit the big time, I kind of figured no one would believe me, anyway.

Not going into work until tomorrow.

Oh, well, I expect to be invited to the New Year's concert if I can convince Grady to come to London.

I think I can manage that, my fingers type out as the taxi pulls up at a quaint English inn. Talk soon.

XOXO

"Here you are, lady. The Pilot Inn." My middle-aged Indian driver twists in the front seat after putting the car into Park, nodding out the window to my right.

My eyes scan the green shrubbery, stiff with ice and the remnants of a recent snow that's long melted from the streets and sidewalks, then scale the yellowed stone walls. The little inn is picturesque, but if the amenities are stuck in the days of Elizabeth Bennet along with the exterior, I'm going to have a chat with my boss at BGG tomorrow.

I mean, if they fire half of their intern staff for getting

baked at a show and bring me in from halfway around the world *over Christmas*, they can at least put me up somewhere nice.

"Thanks." I shove some pounds into his hand and scramble out while he heads for the trunk, where he narrowly avoids a stroke while liberating my suitcase from his car. I hand over five extra pounds for the inevitable chiropractor visit and give him a salute before taking on the burden myself and wheeling it inside.

The interior is so modern and sophisticated that I pause and gape in the doorway like a tourist. Which I technically am, I suppose. There's a coffee and breakfast area, a nice glassed-in restaurant with windows that overlook the downtown skyline, and outdoor seating that, in Texas, would be packed with rowdy students every afternoon for happy hour.

"Wow," I murmur under my breath. I guess finding fault with my bosses' British counterparts will have to wait, because this place is so adorable there's no *way* I'm leaving to stay with my dad in his stuffy old mansion.

The woman behind the front desk is probably a few years older than I am—not yet thirty—with mousy brown hair and bright red lips. "Good morning. Checking in?"

"Yes. Christina Lake."

She clicks away on her keyboard for a few moments before looking up with an apologetic smile. "I'm sorry, but official check-in time isn't until four this afternoon and I'm afraid your room isn't ready."

"Okay . . . well, I suppose I could have some tea."

"We'll be happy to hold your baggage if you'd like to go for a stroll. The river walk is lovely and the weather is mild. It's supposed to get much colder over the next days." The receptionist borders on chirping, which is like nails on a chalkboard to my traveled-all-night ears.

A nice, warm cup of tea tempts me, but the thought of getting to spend an hour or two alone sounds even better. I manage a smile, tamping down on my tired impatience. "Thank you. I think I will do that."

"Let me get you a takeaway cup of tea. Green or black?"

"Black. I think some serious caffeine is in order."

I leave my bags with the concierge and take the to-go cup of tea from the perky receptionist before wrapping a scarf back around my neck, jamming a stocking cap on my head, and stepping outside. It's not that cold, not for December, maybe forty degrees or so. A brisk walk might be just what the doctor ordered to clear my head, and like my mother said, London and I are not well acquainted. We might as well say hello.

I don't even make it to the Thames, which is only a couple blocks away, before my phone rings. The number is local but not one I have stored—meaning it's not my father's—so I pick it up without hesitation. "Hello?"

"I'm going to need you to come in today instead of tomorrow," a pert female voice informs me without an introduction.

It's not polite, but it's also not hard to guess the caller is my new boss, so I don't snap back at her. My sluggish brain struggles to recall her name. Daisy or Hydrangea . . . some kind of flower. "Okay. I can leave in ten minutes."

"A car will be there in five."

She hangs up before I can respond. Part of me, the childish part, wants to continue my walk to the river and at least take a few fresh, deep breaths just to be a brat. The rest of me, which has spent my whole four years of college gearing up for a career in music and the past twelve months as a BGG intern lobbying for one of only a few jobs that will be offered after graduation, squeezes my phone like its my new boss's neck before turning back toward the inn.

By the time I get there, I'm raring to go. The sooner I can get started, the sooner I can put the awkwardness of seeing Cary behind me and get on with my job.

I'll be here a little over two weeks. My own particular past in this infernal country is going to make them challenging, but if I can get through them and do a kick-ass job in the process, one of those jobs—and the future I've wanted for longer than I can remember—is as good as mine.

Eyes on the prize, Christina. Eyes on the prize.

Chapter
2

Sleep would have been nice, given the travel and the nerves over seeing Cary White again, but my boss—Clover? Rose?—obviously has other ideas. By the time the BGG-hired car maneuvers through the nightmarish London traffic my stomach is no longer an organ at all, really, just a writhing mass of vines and snakes and castor oil that's never going to function normally again.

It takes the grouchy driver half an hour to get us to the BGG offices, housed in a modern glass building that stretches high into the heavy, gray winter sky. The girl at the front desk looks me up and down, asks my name three times, and calls upstairs while popping her gum. I do my best not to snatch the temporary badge she gives me or put a hole in the sign-in sheet—or her forehead—with the pen but only because it would look bad on my résumé.

The elevator ride to the twenty-first floor soothes my

nerves somewhat and I step out to face another ditzy-looking secretary with a mouth full of gum. There's no way to guess whether my restraint would have held a second time, because a pretty girl with slippery black hair and the greenest eyes I've ever seen steps around the corner, rescuing me from my own personal Sophie's Choice.

"You must be Christina. I'm Violet."

Violet. Sheesh.

She flashes the secretary a look after a particularly loud pop of gum. "We can go to my office. Would you like some tea?"

"Yeah, please. Milk no sugar."

The secretary frowns at the request but gets up and heads into a small kitchenette. I follow Violet down a carpeted hallway and over a threshold into a sparse but tasteful office. One large window makes up the back wall, spilling light over the desk, and a few framed records hang on the cream-colored walls.

"Have a seat," Violet says, sitting behind her desk and tapping the keyboard on a large Mac desktop to wake it up, effectively making me feel about as important as a fly trapped under a cup.

"I'm excited to be here." I try a smile, knowing this woman is going to be the only buffer between the band and me for the duration. "And anxious to get started."

The grouchy secretary pops in and sets two steaming cups of tea on the desk but there's no way even tea will settle the anxiety I've got working. Now that I'm here, on the job, the only thing I want is to see Cary again, face-to-face. Get it over with so I can prove I'm over him.

"I don't know what your intern coordinator is like back in the States, but I don't really go for sucking up." She raises a flashing, hard gaze to me, appraising. "Show up where you're supposed to be when you're supposed to be there, and keep your nose clean—no dalliances with boys or drugs— and no excuses. Got it?"

"Got it." I swallow disappointment. It's not as though Violet's the first boss I've had that assumes intern equals incompetent child or whipping boy, but it would have been nice to have found her pleasant.

"Aside from Christmas Eve and Christmas Day, when I'll be in Cornwall visiting my parents, I'll be supervising your work on Pursuant's public relations and reporting to your regular bosses."

I try not to flinch at the mention of Cornwall, but the arch of her plucked and shaped eyebrows tells me that plan failed. "What?"

"Nothing. My father has a summer cottage in Cornwall, that's all."

"Riveting." She purses her lips. "Who's your father?"

"Gerard Lake."

She tries to act as though she's not startled but fails, her mouth pulling into a frown before she gives me a look that says she's sizing me up all over again. Violet doesn't comment on my parentage. "Pursuant's lead singer used to summer there with his family, as well."

173

I swallow, avoiding her gaze and trying to will away the sweat forming on my upper lip and under my arms. The relief over her not wanting to talk about my father is short-lived. There's no question that now would be the time to tell her Cary White and I are acquainted, but with the way she's behaving and what she just said about steering clear of boys, I'm afraid she'll fire me on the spot. Better to let it come up naturally and hope by then she'll be impressed enough with my abilities to let me stay.

That there's no one to take my place should play in my favor, too.

She pulls a sheet of paper off the printer, ignorant of my internal turmoil. "Here's their itinerary from today through New Year's Day. The first event is tomorrow morning, a radio interview. Then they have a photo shoot on Wednesday, some magazine interviews, and then a couple days of sound checks at the venue."

"At the O2?"

"The telethon and concert is New Year's Eve at the O2, but they're playing a private show Christmas Day for some big-time donors at an intimate little abandoned theater."

"Gotcha. So what are they—"

"Everything you need to know is outlined in that material. I'm very thorough and very good at my job." She shoves the rest of the pages across the desk and stands.

I take the paper, scanning the dozen or so appearances I'll be expected to attend with the band. It's nothing I haven't done with local acts in Dallas or bigger ones in New

York City last summer. Simple. Glorified babysitting, really, especially since Pursuant has been doing promotion for years. Old pros.

"Well, come on." She taps the toe of her nude designer heel on the polished wooden floor in the hallway, dark eyebrows raised my direction.

"Where are we going?"

"To meet the band, of course."

A bolt of fear slices through me, clean and sharp enough to draw a gasp of air past my lips, but it's short lived. I ignore the curious look she shoots me, tip my chin up, and walk out of the office on shaking legs. There's no reason to get so worked up over this. I have a job to do and I'm going to do it.

I follow Violet back into the main office and then into the hall toward the elevator. We take the lift down to the seventh floor, where the oppressive, thick silence can only mean one thing—recording studios. There are lights outside of all the doors—some lit green, others are dark, a few are red—and Violet leads me to the last one on the right. We loiter in stiff silence and wait for the red light to blink off while I try to come up with the best way to deflect her irritation if Cary blurts out our whole history like a moron.

The light changes to green. Her hand turns the knob and swings open the thick, padded door. We step over a second threshold into the control room of the studio, thick glass separating a couple of producers wearing headphones at the sound boards from the band.

And there they are. The members of Pursuant, all familiar faces, but my eyes are drawn to one in particular, the sight of him like a punch in the gut. Cary looks exactly like he did the last day I saw him, but I already know that. I've seen that face in supermarket checkout lines, on cheesy morning shows, gathering awards like raindrops on his palms. I've grown numb to it. Immune to the effect those blue eyes had on me at one point in time.

This is different. So unexpectedly forceful that I have to bite my lip to keep from crying out.

In person, I see the things I remember instead of what a photographer wants me to see. The way his eyes crinkle around the edges. How he tucks a longer strand of hair back when he's listening to feedback, the way he bites down on his bottom lip as he's making notes on his sheet music.

The way, the moment he looks up and sees me watching him, his dark blueberry eyes sparkle like someone lit them on the Fourth of July.

His pure joy leaps to me, swirling in my chest like a happiness tornado, and for the briefest of moments everything feels right with the world. I clamp down on the geyser the same moment the light in his face falls away, making way for shadows.

He leans into the microphone. "What is *she* doing here, Vi?"

Cary's voice shakes as he asks the question but his tone leaves no doubt that he's not pleased over either the surprise or my presence, or maybe the combination. My nerves quell, soothed by offense and irritation. So, Cary thought he could go the rest of his life without having to see me again and he's not excited to find out he's been wrong.

Welcome to the club, jackass.

"Do it again. And try to suck less this time, you bunch of posers," one of the producers, a balding man with thin shoulders that can't begin to fill out his thin black sweater, snaps at the guys through a microphone that's turned up super loud.

None of them seem to take offense, just count off the start again. The sweet strains of chords and melodies filter through the high-quality speakers, and as Cary's voice rasps over the words, my heart jerks. I'm eighteen again, my toes curled into the cold sand as a fire crackles nearby and he sings with a guitar on his lap, just for me.

Violet whirls on me, cutting me off from the past. The snap of her green eyes promises I'm about to be anything but grateful. "Something you forgot to mention?"

Her question hits me like a smack to the cheek. It burns, my face fiery at being caught so soon in my omission. The glittering anger in her stormy features seems to point to her looking for a reason to fire me. "Um, I sort of know them. We met in Cornwall. A few months before they signed their first deal."

Violet narrows her green eyes, fastening on my face as though it can somehow let her read my mind. It feels a little bit as though it does. "And?"

I shrug. "And nothing major. Cary and I had a little summer fling but it ended before the holiday was over and I haven't talked to him since."

It's harder to say those words to a stranger than it should be, even though they're as brief and clinical as I can manage. It's true, but it's not the whole truth. The confession tastes like acid, like secrets that would rather dissolve than be revealed.

She presses her lips into a thin line. "I've dealt with more than my fair share of groupies in this line of work and I don't have time for any such nonsense from you, not while you're supposed to be running the show."

I open my mouth, hot tears pricking my eyes at the embarrassment. "I swear to you, that's not why I'm here. Cary White is about the last person I'd choose to see if it were up to me, but this is my job and I'm committed to it. I'm a professional, I want a career in music, and nothing that happened when I was a dumb kid is going to get in the way of that."

She studies me. "So we're still clear on the no monkey business?"

"Crystal."

I let out a quiet breath of relief as she turns back to watch Pursuant run through the song, apparently unwilling to sack me just yet. Probably because if she does, there's no way she's going home for the holiday.

The band hit the refrain and the words of this song pluck at my carefully forged, but not battle-tested, armor.

I never told you about the mistake I made
But you could never have forgiven me, anyway
I walked away, I couldn't stay
Now you're my secret mistake

My mouth goes dry, and I turn to Violet, keeping my voice low. "Is this a new song?"

"Yeah, it's their first single off the new album. They're going to share it for the first time at the interview tomorrow."

I swallow hard. "Did Cary write it?"

"He writes most of their songs, yes." She glares at the glass, refusing to look at me. "Did you do *any* prep for this assignment?"

I know that he writes their songs. All but a couple on three-plus albums, and all about walking away, about regret, about great loves that were smashed and abandoned because of secrets and mistakes and stupid pride.

As hard as I've tried to tell myself that it doesn't mean anything other than my ex-love has a knack for good writing, it feels like they're about me. About us. I've been tortured by lyrics and radio DJs in love with this band. In the beginning it made me cry; now it pisses me off.

The song ends again, and this time Cary doesn't wait for his feedback or an okay from the producer. As he bends down, disappearing from view to put away his guitar, I watch

179

the other members of Pursuant as they stow their own instruments and head toward the door that leads toward me. Alfie, the bass player, with his wild blond curls and long face, enters first. David Moore, Pursuant's second guitarist and never my favorite, rubs a hand through his thick, mouse-brown hair and refuses to meet my eye. Simon stuffs his drumsticks in his back pocket and gives me a small nod. He's not as handsome as the others but he's definitely part of the best-body conversation. Last is Cedric, the keyboardist and their quiet conscience.

He'd been a good friend, once upon a time, and gives me a soft smile as the band steps into the control room. "Well, if it isn't my favorite American."

"Since you hate all other Americans, it's a dubious honor." I step into his arms when he opens them, giving him a quick squeeze. "It's good to see you, Ced."

"Likewise, little Bug."

All of the guys had called me Bug once upon a time. Whether it was because I was attached to Cary's hip—and he mine—the summer we knew each other or because my presence broke up their happy band full of singles I'd never known, but aside from David, they'd all liked me well enough. I thought.

"Hey, Chris," Simon says, looking nervous as he checks over his shoulder for Cary.

I give them a general hello, my stomach flipping as my ex steps over the threshold. Into the same room as me, breathing the same air, like we did four years ago. As though it's

180

never changed, and the six of us have been hanging out this whole time with no worries.

"Cary, I wasn't aware of your previous . . . acquaintance with Christina before she arrived, but she's assigned as your publicity intern through the New Year. I gather it's been awhile, maybe it's awkward, blah-blah-blah, but she's assured me that she's able to conduct herself in a professional manner. I know you will, too."

The other guys look like they might burst into laughter at the barely concealed smackdown. In another time, another place, another Christina might have been inclined to snicker at the little-boy chagrin on his handsome features, too.

"I'll manage," is all he says, cutting a curious glance in my direction.

Cedric slings an arm around my shoulders. "Always was good at talking us up. She'll be fine."

"Time will tell. I'll be around in a supervisory capacity until a couple of days before Christmas, and I'll be back before New Year's Eve. Any questions?"

They shake their heads. I want to avoid looking at Cary, as though he's the sun, but Violet's watching me, looking for any sign that my promises were bullshit, so I only let my gaze settle on him as long as it does anyone else.

Disbelief at how hard it is to see him and not ask what the hell happened, to not melt into a puddle at the beauty of him, is like roaring static in my mind. It's all hitting me with too much force. It's too unexpected, to have spent three years thinking this was all behind me only to have it blow up in my face. I feel like no time has passed. Like he broke my heart yesterday and I'm still standing here holding the pieces.

"Now that we're all done whining, can we get back to this song, then?" One of the producers stares at Violet and me, looking less than amused about the interruption. "It sounds like shit."

"Yes, de-shit away." Violet waves a hand, her eyes glued to her phone. "Christina, come with me and I'll get you all of the access cards you'll need for your stay."

We leave without any further drama. Cary doesn't look at me, I don't look at him, and in general neither of us handles this life development in a mature manner whatsoever.

Kind of like how we parted ways the first time. I mean, someone tells you they love you, makes you feel it with every breath they take, every look they send your way, and leaves without a word?

Maybe I'd been naive to assume seeing him again would be easy. But just because I'm floundering a little doesn't mean I'm going back under those waves.

"Well, that was about the most awkward room I've ever encountered in my entire life," my new boss comments as we step into the hall. "And I got divorced after I caught my husband in bed with not one but two other men."

"I'm . . . not sure how to respond to that."

"That makes two of us."

Chapter

3

Christina!"

I stop with one hand on the door that leads out into the cold afternoon and close my eyes. Violet had been quick, handing over an access card and reminding me that all the phone numbers for the band, for her and her boss at BGG UK, plus the contact information for every interview that's set up over the coming weeks are in the packet she gave me before dismissing me like I'm a less-than-adequate servant.

I thought I was home free, but the familiar, heart-twisting sound of my name on Cary's tongue stops me in my tracks. My car idles at the curb, less than ten feet away. Too far to help me avoid this confrontation. Embarrassment floods my cheeks at the thought of how I behaved in that studio a bit ago, not two minutes after promising Violet that professionalism wouldn't be an issue, and I know we have to do this.

Rip off the Band-Aid.

The hesitancy on his face when I turn around does nothing to ease the tightness in my chest. "Yes?"

"Oh. Um." He stuffs his hands into the pockets of his skinny jeans and I refuse to let my eyes wander south the way they're trying to. "I wanted to say something."

"Okay." My heart pounds so hard it's hard to breathe, never mind talk, but nothing matters more than not letting him see how being within three feet of him makes me actually want to die. Makes me want to throw myself into his arms. Makes me want to jump him so I don't die.

"I'm sorry for how I acted upstairs. It just . . . it took me by surprise, seeing you again." He steps closer, and the familiar scent of cinnamon washes over me. He dumps it into his tea like sugar and there was always a dusting of it everywhere—on his fingers, his counters, sometimes clinging to his eyebrows or hair, depending on how exuberant he'd been that morning. "A warning would have been nice."

"It's been four years. I guess I thought you wouldn't care."

He winces at even the most glancing blow. "Blimey."

"Look, this isn't my idea of a good time, either, but they didn't give me a choice and I wouldn't have said no, anyway. It's a great opportunity and I'm supposed to be a professional."

"Supposed to be?" He gives me a half smile that I return without thinking.

"Yes." I stop smiling at him and frown instead. "It's been awhile. I grew up."

Cary pauses, biting his full lower lip and looking out the window again. His eyebrows go up at the sight of the car. "Where are you staying? With your dad?"

The question underneath the question, as though he knows somehow that my father and I have had a falling out since the last time we spoke, shakes my insides with a tremor that makes it hard to stand. There was a time in my life when I would have trusted him. No one whose arms would've felt better around me, whose scent and laughter and understanding could've kept the world safely out.

But that ship has sailed. *Long* sailed, and even though he forced me, I did wave good-bye.

"I don't see how where I'm staying is relevant to my doing my job." I clamp down on the emotions struggling to smother me and cross my arms over my chest. Chide my lady parts for turning to sizzles and fizzes at his nearness. "Was there something else?"

Cary's shoulders slump. He bites his lip again, but when his eyes find my face and hang on, he starts to change. His spine straightens. The sparkle returns to his gaze and he steps closer, reaching out to touch me.

I pull away.

Cary frowns, confusion knotting his brow. "Do you want to get some tea?"

"What?"

"Tea. Or coffee, you bloody American. You and me. We could catch up—it's been forever."

The words fall over me, hit my shoulders like boulders

before they crash into my chest and smash my heart. Tears prick my eyes, and the show of weakness serves me well, spiking hot anger. "No, Cary, I do not want to have *coffee* with you. I don't want to *catch up*, and it's been *forever* because you left. Remember?"

I fling the accusation his direction but it seems to bounce off his chest, off his skin, and slide to the floor in puddles that look like exploded sobs. The tips of Cary's ears turn red, a sure sign he's embarrassed, but what I see in his face looks more like pride than anything else.

When he doesn't say anything else, I spin around and push open the door, and don't look back even when I hear him say what sounds like "that's my girl."

I huff into the backseat and tell the driver I'd like to head back to the hotel. Despite my best efforts, I can't stop myself from looking out the window as we pull away from the curb. Cary's there, standing just outside the door watching me go, the most interesting expression of hope and devastation tangling on his face.

Then a shriek pierces the morning, and Cary's surrounded by two or three girls shoving notepads in his face asking for autographs.

The attention forces him back in the building and a frown finds my lips. His girl, indeed. He's going to have to forget that idea, because even if he told me the whole truth and got down on his knees to beg forgiveness, there's no way I could ever be strong enough to let him close again. It's

186

been too long of a road, with too many paths that head straight uphill, to turn back now.

After four years, I've finally crested the summit. I'm afraid that even coffee would send me tumbling all the way back down to where I started—and into a million tiny little pieces.

The ride back to the hotel takes longer than the drive into town this morning, and all of my anxiety has given over to exhaustion by the time we pull up in front of the Pilot Inn. My eyelids are heavy and nothing—literally *nothing*— sounds better than crawling into comfortable clothes and collapsing until tomorrow morning.

My feet drag into the lobby and over to the bellhop, where I hand over my luggage tag.

"Um, I'm sorry, Miss, but your bags have been claimed."

Fatigue makes my confusion hard to overcome. "What? By who?"

"Your father. He said you'd want to be going straight-away once you returned." He nods toward the coffee shop seating, a slight sheen of sweat popping out on his forehead at my consternation.

Instead of asking more questions, I follow his gaze.

And there he is. Gerard Anthony Lake III.

It's been over four years and he looks older. My father's cheeks sag, there are unfamiliar wrinkles on his forehead and around his eyes, and a new paunch hangs over his belt. But it's him.

To his credit, he doesn't open his arms for a hug or act like I'm supposed to be happy to see him. He does smile. It's a little thin but genuine, and it hurts more than a little.

"Hey, Chrissie."

It doesn't seem as though it should be possible, to be so angry with someone and want them to hug you and make everything okay at the same time. The only thing I know to do, the only thing that's worked to keep me in one piece, is to hide behind walls that separate my squishy parts from the world. From him.

"What are you doing here?"

"Your mother called. She let me know you'd be in country over the holidays and thought I might be willing to open my home."

I am going to kill my mother. She's the best person I know, so it's going to be a real sacrifice, but she just cannot go around sticking her nose in my business like this. She divorced the man over ten years ago. If anyone should understand the desire to never see him again, it should be her.

He was a choice I made, she whispers in my mind. *A bad choice, but he's your father. You don't get another.*

Shut up, Mom.

"Well, it's awfully magnanimous, but as you can see, the label is putting me up in a hotel."

"It's Christmas. You want to stay in a hotel?"

"Why not? It's just another day."

"It is *not* just another day; it's your favorite holiday and Imogen's ready to cook all of your favorites." His smile turns rueful. "Or, she's ready to ask the cook to prepare all of your favorites."

Imogen is the stepmother I've never met—the mother of two stepsisters, both younger than I am, who I have also never met. Apparently they're all more worthy of my father's time than I.

"How sweet." I move past him and make a grab for my suitcase before I do something stupid like let how tired I am encourage me to give in just to get some sleep. "But I wouldn't want to intrude on your *family* holiday."

That barb finds its intended mark and he has the good sense to look ashamed of finding a brand-new family to replace the one he tossed into the trash. I get hold of my suit-case and make for the front desk as my father huffs at my side, working hard to keep pace. He's breathing heavily as I pause just out of the receptionist's earshot.

Apologies shudder in his pale blue gaze, an icy, cold thing that I inherited. "I don't want to force you, Chrissie. I know I can't, but I was hoping to convince you that holidays are for family. We're still family."

I bite back all of the rude, hurtful retorts even though every single one of them would be true. I've earned my anger—he abandoned me when I needed him the most—but right now I'm too tired to argue.

"I'm really beat, Dad. I haven't gotten any sleep since I landed and it's been kind of a rough morning." I pause, gathering the courage to look him in the face. "Let me think about it, okay?"

His smile fades, less sure than it had been a few seconds ago. It makes me feel better, for some reason, that he has his doubts as to whether this is a good idea.

It's strange, not addressing the rift between us. I think of Cary wanting to catch up, of me denying him the chance to address the gulf separating the two of us, and am forced to look the idea straight in the face that I might be more like my father than I want to admit.

"Okay. Okay, Chrissie." He wrings his plaid cap in his hands before smoothing it out and pulling it down on his forehead. "I know we have a lot to talk about. Just . . . think about it."

I give him a tight-lipped nod and watch as he strolls out of the hotel and into a town car idling at the curb. Coffee with Cary, Christmas with my dad and his new family . . . just what does London think it's up to? I'm here to get Pursuant through two weeks of publicity and a couple of shows, not to chuck all the progress I've worked my ass off for over the past four years.

With that thought in my head I get the key to my room and head upstairs, my determination to keep focused renewed.

Chapter
4

When someone knocks on my bedroom door at midnight, I sit straight up in bed. My heart gallops, banging against my ribs, and it takes a couple of minutes to remember who I am, where I am, and to let the wrinkled bedsheets loose from my clutches.

The knock comes again, assuring me it's not part of a dream, and I tiptoe over to peer through the peephole on shaking legs.

My heart slams to a stop at the sight of Cary on the other side of the door. He's a bit disheveled, longish hair tucked behind his ears and circles around his eyes, the tip of his nose rosy from the cold.

"I can see the shadow of your feet, Bug. Can I come in? It's bloody freezing."

"What do you want?"

"Please?" he asks, voice sweet and somehow sexy, instead of answering.

I glance down at my choice of pajamas, a pair of shorts and a cami, but decide not to change, since at least I'm wearing a bra. Whatever.

The door swings open, letting in the chilly air from the hallway and raising goose bumps along my arms and legs as Cary brushes past me. The smell of him—cinnamon and sweat, a saltiness particular to him, all of it familiar—washes over me, so potent my knees almost go out from under me. Had I thought that he would somehow cease to have any effect on me just because he broke my heart?

My ex–summer fling leans against the desk, dusky blue eyes fixed on me. They lower all the way to my toes, then lift in a slow sweep. By the time they land on my face every inch of me is boiling from the inside out, so hot I can hardly recall what it is I'm supposed to be wary of—why I would ever think of not letting him back in.

We stare at each other like people trying to decide if an oasis in the desert could possibly be real, or if it's going to turn out like all the disappointing others. My skin tingles, breath struggling to get in and out of me and somehow, I'm closer to him. A couple of feet away.

I cross my arms over my chest, too aware of my body, of how it's reaching for Cary, for the connection that's somehow still crackling between us, without permission.

His dark eyes look wet as they search my face. "My god, Chris. Is it you? Are you real?"

He reaches out a hand, fingers grazing my waist before latching on, and the electricity of his skin against mine looses a lightning storm in this room.

Oh, fuck it all.

I'm in his arms. My hands are in his hair, our lips and chests and stomachs and thighs are pressed tight together. His mouth is desperate, tasting and licking until mine opens for him. A moan rips me apart, dragged loose from a long-ignored piece of my soul, and my throat burns. Tears wet my cheeks but I don't let him stop when he tries to because nothing would be worse than losing his touch in this moment. Worse than letting the world outside that door, the world of the past four years, into this bubble.

I curl my fingers tighter in his hair, earning a growl as my lips travel to his ear, licking the spot he likes, then down to nip at his neck. Cary White trembles under my touch and sensual power floods my blood, my body aching with the need to have all of him against me, around me, inside me again.

His hands skim the bare skin of my stomach as he whips my tank top over my head, then reaches around to make quick work of my bra. I free him of his jacket and sweater, then his undershirt, until our bare skin sparks as it touches. My senses are heightened, every brush of the fine hair on his chest against my breasts thrumming a shudder that starts there and ends in my toes.

Cary takes control, spinning me around so that my back is against the desk. He sets me up on it as my fingers make quick work of his pants, then dip below the band of his boxer briefs. My touch quickens his movements as he rids me of my clothes, dropping them on the floor before wrestling a condom from his jeans and slipping it on. Cary's forehead presses against mine, his arms around my waist as he draws me to him, our eyes locked together.

There's a question in his, and permission in mine, and I grab onto his lips with mine again because if he speaks, if I speak, all of this will disappear like shadows in the sunlight. I don't want to examine anything; it feels too good to let it go, even if the way, way inside of me knows we're making things harder than ever.

My legs tighten around his back and then Cary is inside me, filling me up, and we move together with a compatibility born from experience and familiarity and something more, something that enveloped us from the moment we met at eighteen years old. It had been as though my whole life had been a path leading to that moment, no question it would eventually lead me to him, and as our bodies give and take in the here and now, I cry at the sheer rightness of it.

And maybe because, no matter how over him I am, how I've moved on and proved that my future can still be amazing, it feels as though I never got off that same path.

That it will keep leading us right back here.

Sparks sizzle through me as his mouth leaves mine and trails to my ear, down my neck. The flick of his tongue against my nipples makes me shudder and his steady, firm movements drive all rational thought from my head. Blackness clouds the edges of the room until all that remains is Cary, and me, and the pleasure washing over me, boiling out of me in gasps and tears as I cling to him.

He holds me tight, whispering my name in a desperate, hoarse tone that tears at my heart as he shudders against me for what feels like forever. Neither of us moves, or speaks, and the past is here around us, as surely as the bed and the sheets, and the smell of him.

We're in the back of Cary's hand-me-down Land Rover, and I was so crazy in love it had not crossed my mind to be ashamed of the cliché. He'd brought blankets and tea, we'd watched the sunset, and taken our time stripping off each other's clothes in the dim twilight. We had stripped each other's souls bare during the weeks we'd been dating, falling in love, and it hadn't occurred to me to pause before crossing this threshold, too.

We watched each other afterward, sweat drying between our bodies and wonder swirling in my blood.

"Are you okay?" he asked, one finger trailing down my cheek. Concern and wonder sparkle side by side in his blue eyes.

"I'm fine, worry wart. Do you think I would have done that if I didn't want to?"

"No." He smiles then, our happiness spilling out and mingling in the tiny slivers of space between us. "I just know how hard things are with your dad, with him moving on, and I . . . I never want to hurt you, Chris."

His strange melancholy confuses me and I lean up to kiss it away, enjoying the salty taste of his lips and how it mirrors the nip of the sea on the breeze. "Then don't."

I couldn't have known then what was coming for me in a few weeks. That he would disappear without a trace, without looking back, to leave me questioning everything that had seemed unbreakable to my silly, naive eyes.

I open my eyes in my hotel room. Older, but apparently not wiser, I wriggle off the desk and away from him, pausing to grab clean clothes from my suitcase before scurrying into the bathroom.

The mistake we just made—*I* just made—has become a hundred percent clear by the time I'm facing him again in yoga pants and a long sleeved T-shirt. I swallow, trying not to look at him. "You need to go."

His eyebrows disappear behind his shaggy bangs. "You're tossing me? No. We need to talk."

"I think we've said all there is to say." I nod toward the desk, my flesh warming. "We fell into old habits. I'm not blaming you but this can't happen again. I'll lose my job, Cary, and you and I both know that there's nothing but lingering hormones between us. I'm not getting fired for sex."

No matter how good it is, I think to myself.

"I see." A smile struggles to escape him, but he manages to restrain it. Barely. "You've got this whole thing figured out, then? I'm just a shag?"

No. I haven't figured out why you left me like that to begin with, but I have figured out that I can't survive it again. Sex is sex, but letting you back into my heart? Impossible.

"Don't make this any harder on me. You left me a blubbering idiot four years ago and we haven't spoken since. I know this whole thing is weird, but maybe you coming here tonight has kind of cleared the air."

Oddly, I do feel more relaxed. It could be the massive orgasm, but I think it's more than that. This is Cary and me, and if we've gotten to a point where we can hook up for nothing but old times' sake, then it could be that I'm over him after all.

The smile breaks through then, dimpled and flashing and devastatingly adorable. Cary leans down and brushes a lingering kiss to my cheek, lowering his head to whisper in my ear. "I never, ever want to make your life harder, Bug. I'd think you'd have figured that out by now."

His words take me aback, as though there's more to them, something unsaid but intended, and I search his face for clues.

Cary just shrugs. "I'll see you in the morning, then."

"Good night."

I close the door behind him and curl up on my bed, staring at the desk and wondering if any of that really happened. If it was a dream, it's one I've been having for years, even if my experiences have proved over and over again that they just don't come true.

Things are looking a bit better in the light of day. I got plenty of sleep after Cary left, and since my first duty as

Pursuant's publicist is a radio interview at eleven, I managed to sleep in a little, too.

The interview is scheduled downtown in a little over two hours. Violet made it clear that I'm responsible for my own transportation, which means it's time to get going.

The subway into the city passes too slowly, and I don't even want to think about taking it home during rush hour. The band has another recording session after the interview but I'm not sure whether I'm supposed to stay for that. I'm feeling less nervous about seeing Cary than I was yesterday, so whatever we want to call last night, apparently it worked.

The guys are already in the green room at the radio station when I arrive, even though I'm eight minutes early. Not the requisite ten, but close enough for horseshoes. Maybe not hand grenades.

"You guys are like, an embarrassment to rock stars. Why are you so early?"

It's ten thirty, almost midday for some people, but if memory serves—and it always does, when Cary's concerned—none of them are naturally early risers.

"Good morning to you, too, gorgeous," Cary says, his dark blue eyes lingering on my legs. The attention makes me both pleased and mad at my choice of a dress this morning.

"Yeah, yeah. Good morning."

David makes a face, staring down into his coffee. "We're a band, not rock stars."

"The media would argue with you on that."

"Fuck the media."

I roll my eyes. Apparently David hasn't gotten any better natured since I last saw him. At any rate, he's only proving my point. "Okay, well, the interview is supposed to start at eleven, so I'm sure they'll grab you in the next ten or fifteen minutes to get you miked and prepped. Did you all go over the questions?"

Simon snorts. "Like the wankers ever stick to the script. They're forever promising no personal stuff but that's never how it goes."

"That's what people want, dipshit." Cedric rolls his eyes. "Like, five people care about our next album and the rest just want to know who we're shagging."

My cheeks feel a tad hot at the knowledge of exactly who one of them was shagging just last night. Cary's eyes wander over to me again, making matters worse.

The pancakes I had for breakfast climb halfway back up my esophagus at the mere thought of having to listen to Cary talk about his latest fling. He's avoided any serious entanglements, if the tabloids are to be believed, but his bed hasn't exactly been cold since Pursuant made it big.

I don't know why it would be.

Simon, Cedric, and Alfie watch me with varying degrees of concern. Thunderclouds darken David's angular features and Cary stares at his notes, pretending to reread the prep for this morning's interview. The tips of his ears are red again and no matter how many times I tell myself I don't care why he's acting like my coming here is some kind of early Christmas gift, it doesn't work.

"Are you going to hurl?" Simon's eyes are wide.

"You *do* look like you've got the collywobbles," Cedric observes, scooting father away from me. "The loo's just down the hall."

"I'm fine." I swallow, pushing all unwanted mental images out of my head.

One of the station's producers shows up then, saving me from death by massive embarrassment but not, sadly, curing the aforementioned collywobbles.

"If you guys are ready, we'll go on back to the studio and get you prepped." She's older, maybe in her forties, and it seems as though they couldn't have found anyone who could care less that one of the hottest bands ever to come out of Britain is sitting in her green room.

It's sort of refreshing.

The next twenty minutes follow a protocol I've witnessed at least a hundred times, and my mind kind of checks out. I'm here to babysit, to try to make sure none of them say anything stupid or offensive that doesn't get edited out before the interview airs, then get them back to the recoding studio for another session.

My phone buzzes with a text message, and a frown tugs on my lips at the sight of my dad's number.

Dinner tonight?

So, he's not going to give up, not even for a day. I put the phone to sleep, focusing on my job instead.

My folding chair sits about ten feet away from the morning show DJ and the band, who all sport thick headphones, mikes, and relaxed expressions. It's hard to guess how many of these they might have done at this point, but it can't be a small number.

"Good morning, London! This is Rick Raider, and I'm coming to you live with all six members of Pursuant! How are you blokes doing?"

They murmur various greetings and responses. I don't have to remind them that smiles can be heard, each of them forcing grins as they speak to sound radio-ready.

"Now that you're here, how about we chat about your new album—it's dropping in less than a month, folks." He pauses for a breath. "Cary, I'm assuming you authored most of the songs."

"That's right. Simon cowrote two of them with me, though, and Cedric's debuting his first. Pursuant is a group effort, as always." My ex maintains the same story no matter who's listening, but everyone knows the band would fall apart if he left. He's the Justin Timberlake to their *NSYNC. "We're excited about the first single, which we're going to play for your listeners right now, if you're ready."

"Of course, of course. Now, what's this one called?"

" 'My Forever Mistake.' "

"You heard him, listeners—that's Cary White of Pursuant, and this is their new single!"

The first strains of the song pluck at my heart—it's the same one they were putting down at the studio yesterday. The one that, like so many of their titles, seems to be about me.

It plays in the background while the DJ makes small talk

with the guys, and the chorus plays too low for me to catch the heartbreaking words. Then it's over, the band is back on the air, and Rick Raider asks the last question I want to hear.

"Cary, it seems like many of your tunes center around the theme of regret, of missing out, of losing someone. Tell me, who inspires your lyrics?"

Cary's eyes find mine as he purses his lips, considering his answer. I fall in, swimming in the deep blue looking for my own answers, too far down to be seen or heard.

"That's personal, I'm afraid, but we're all inspired by someone. By some*thing*. I lost someone so right for me that it's hard to believe I can find anything like it again. It's an emotion I'm still untangling through my writing but maybe I'll figure it out, eventually, and you people will finally get to stop listening to me whine."

Our gazes are locked. His words stumble through my mind like drunken sorority girls trying to find their way home after someone's twenty-first birthday. Cary thinks we were right for each other. I've known—*known* in my soul— the same thing since the day we met.

Yet he walked away. He never called, just sat around mooning and writing songs. Why?

As much as I want to know the answer to that, the thought of asking terrifies me.

"The rest of us would be extremely grateful for that, mate," David says, the acid in his tone distracting both Cary and me, and erasing any hope David had of convincing anyone he was kidding.

The publicist in me tenses, sensing potential disaster. This interview could go off the rails quick if they can't get David's brooding personality under control.

"I mean, we don't mind as long as Cary's songs are still resonating with listeners," Alfie says, doing his best to smooth things over before they get awkward.

My shoulders relax slightly and I shoot Alfie a grateful look and a small nod. He smiles back and gives me a thumbs-up. They've got plenty of experiences covering for David's mouth, too, I suppose.

"So, is this someone the reason you don't have a steady girlfriend, Cary? Or are you keeping more secrets from us?"

There it is—the inquiry we all knew was coming.

Simon rolls his eyes but Cedric grabs the opportunity to save his bandmate. And maybe me, judging by the glance Ced shoots my way as he starts to answer. "I don't know about Cary, but I'm single."

"Yes, we heard about your recent split with that little Disney actress from America. Looking for a nice English girl now, are we?"

Just like that, the conversation veers away from Cary and his songs, with his love life fading in the process. A rush of gratitude toward Cedric burns in my chest even though a tiny part of me wanted to hear the answer. If he's seeing someone right now or maybe his appearance last night could have been about more than clearing the air.

"You can see Pursuant on New Year's Eve at the O2. Are you guys looking forward to that?"

"We've never played a venue as big as the O2 and we are seriously stoked to be invited," Simon answers, his eyes sparkling with genuine glee.

The O2 is a huge deal. I'm in a little bit of denial that I'm going to be *working* on a show there so I can't imagine how the band is feeling. They've well and truly made it, and the part of me that's been rooting for them since the very beginning blooms with pride.

"Right, and you'll be donating the proceeds to C.U.R.E. Epilepsy, yes? Is this a disease that's affected some of you, or did your label choose?"

The guys look at each other, no one seeming to know how to answer, and my mind goes blank. They're raising money for epilepsy?

My heart sticks in my throat and throbs. I have to get out of the room, so I stumble out of my chair and slip out as quietly as possible.

The hallway is cooler than the studio, the green room cooler than that, and the space to breathe calms me down. I sink down onto a bench and put my head in my hands, squeezing my eyes shut.

"I'm very sorry, but there was nothing we could do." The doctor in a lab coat, harried as though there was somewhere he needed to be, puts out a hand to steady my mother. "He suffered a massive seizure that could have led to the crash. Does he have a history of epilepsy?"

My mom chokes on sobs while she shakes her head. My

disbelief that Tim had a seizure is somehow larger than my utter astonishment at the idea he could be dead.

Mom sat there for a long time with a blank expression, signing forms when they brought them, nodding to a social worker that stopped to talk, and I sat at her side. I called my father to deliver the news.

I wanted to call Cary. Needed his solid, reassuring presence but he'd already left me.

Was already gone. Just like Tim.

A warm hand on my shoulder startles me from the tormented reverie. "You okay?"

I look up into Cary's soft eyes, edged with worry, and don't think twice about stepping into his arms when he offers them. It's still so raw, Tim's death. Still so hard to believe.

Cary's chest is hard against my cheek. Solid. I let him hold me for a count of ten before reluctantly stepping back. If anyone happened to see us, there would be rumors everywhere before we left the building, and I can only imagine what Violet would have to say about that.

I wipe my nose, batting Cary's hand away when he tries to swipe at a tear. "I'm okay. Did you . . ." I suck in a breath. "Was it your idea?"

The tips of his ears color. "I know how much you loved him. This is something I've been wanting to do for a while. Still can't believe it's what brought us back together."

"We are *not* back together, Cary. We're *working* together."

I soften at the chagrin on his features. "But thank you. It's very sweet for you to remember him this way."

"Interview's over," he informs me, changing the subject.

The memory of my brother's death still has funny raw edges, hard to see and painful to the touch. I blink them away and focus on the task at hand. "Any issues?"

"No. We talked about the New Year's Eve event and Raider invited us back once the album drops. Cedric and Alfie were more than peppy enough to make up for David's . . . David-ness."

"Good to know." Relief slumps my shoulders, but all in all, I'd call my first day on the job in London a success. I check my watch. "You have two hours before you have to be back at the studio."

"How about lunch?" Cary asks, more than a little hesitant. "I'm starving."

"I have some errands to run," I say, a little too quickly. Our interactions have to stay professional from here on out, and if last night proved anything, we can't be trusted alone together.

"What about dinner?"

"I'm um . . . having dinner with my dad." Great. Now I'm going to have to *actually* have dinner with my dad, since lying is one of the things I absolutely never do.

Cary's eyebrows go up. "Really?"

I shrug, thinking again that maybe hearing my father out will make me less like him. "Yes. It can't hurt to listen, right?"

"Those are my thoughts exactly, as you well know. I'm proud of you."

I've been focused on the future these past four years, on a career I love and making my mom proud, on proving to myself that my first love doesn't have to be my last, that my bombed-out relationship with my father has been on the back burner. Maybe there's no way to really grow up without at least acknowledging it's still on the stove.

But I'd still like to know how Cary even knows about it. "Thanks."

"Will you say you'll think about it? Spending a little time with me?" He holds up his hands in mock surrender. "In public, I promise. I . . . I've missed you, Christina. Not your body, not the sex—although I've missed that, too—just talking to you. Listening to you. Leaning on you, and holding you up. It's like I've been living four years without an arm."

His words are arrows, each one piecing the skin and burrowing deep before I can even think about yanking them out. As usual, Cary's way with words allows him to look right into my soul and verbalize how I'm feeling. It's irritating and endearing and the reason I encouraged him to start writing songs in the first place.

"I'll think about it. I promise." Our eyes connect, and he gives me a satisfied nod. "And I'll make sure you don't need anything once we get to the studio, but I don't think I have to stay the whole time."

"Oh, what, are you too good to listen to us practice

now?" Cary gives me a fake pout, sending sizzles all the way down to my toes. "As I recall, you used to be a fixture in Alfie's parents' garage."

"Well, things have changed." I find the courage to meet his hypnotic gaze, and the will to not press a hand to my chest.

He's staring back. "Not everything."

Chapter
5

I do leave the recording session before the band is finished—
it's just touch-ups and rerecordings of certain bars and
measures at this point—because I can't stand listening to
the same song one more time and because they had plenty of
supervision.

Also because David Moore, asshole guitarist extraordinaire, keeps staring daggers at me through the glass partition. Cary had been in good spirits and I'd caught David
noticing how his lead singer looks at me, how he reached out
to touch me without thinking about it.

How I couldn't make myself move away without effort.

David had not only noticed but also had trouble control-
ling the anger and redness creeping up from his neck and
ending at his hairline.

He's never liked me. Never. Why has always been a
mystery. I'd been too wrapped up in Cary that summer to

give a whit what anyone else had thought. Not even my dad, who had the gall to remind me on more than one occasion how hard I'd sneered at a life spent in the limelight.

I drop my messenger bag in the desk chair in my hotel room and close my eyes, summoning the courage to call my father. I might have chickened out, come up with some excuse for bailing on what I'd told Cary my plans are for the night, but the look on his face when he told me he was proud of me pushes me forward.

Not only because it feels good to know he thinks this is the right decision but because I've ignored for years the hole left behind by my father's abandonment. If nothing else, it will be a relief to finally be able to ask what put it there. It's the only way to keep moving forward.

My dad's voice is surprised when he picks up. "Chrissie? Is that you?"

I close my eyes. I'm already on overload as far as reconsidering how I feel about people who have tossed me out like yesterday's garbage, but I *am* the one that called. "Yeah."

I can almost hear him frown over my use of the slang as opposed to the proper *yes*. It's his pet peeve, which is exactly why I used it in the first place. To his credit—or maybe because he has an agenda—he doesn't mention it.

"What's up?"

"Oh. I was thinking . . . I'm free for dinner tonight if you still want to get together."

"I'm wrapping up a few hundred more words, then I'd planned to take the night off, so that sounds great."

Exhaustion creeps through my limbs. "Where's Imogen and the girls?"

"They went to her mum's for the evening, I'm afraid. They'll be back late." He pauses. "Do you want Indian?"

That he remembered my favorite food makes me smile in spite of everything. "I had it for lunch."

"All right. Italian, then. I'll send a car."

The sound of his laptop keys clicking lets me know his attention is about to totally fail as far as I'm concerned, and history tells me there's no point in arguing. "I'll be ready."

We sign off and I run to the loo. By the time I've done my business, washed my hands, and smoothed my stocking cap–tousled hair back into place there's a car waiting out front. A congenial older man named Alfred introduces himself before admitting me to the backseat and piloting us through town with a crisp expertise that explains how he arrived at the hotel so quickly.

We cross the Thames and head toward Hyde Park, the streets and buildings becoming more and more familiar as we creep toward my father's hoity-toity neighborhood. My brother and I never spent more than two nights there before leaving for Cornwall, and we never stopped making fun of him for buying such an opulent home when he has no interest in things like decorating.

He makes so much money from his books that he literally has no idea how to get rid of it.

My dad's waiting out front in a trench coat and hat,

holding up a hand to tell Alfred not to get out, before opening my door. "Care to walk? It's only a couple of blocks."

I nod, he helps me out, and we pass the chilly stroll in near silence. He points out some storefronts and signposts he thinks might interest me, and I note that the night has grown colder than anticipated. It's stiff, but not altogether unpleasant.

Even so, the warmth of the restaurant comes as a relief. The candlelight flickering on the wine-colored walls and the whispered conversations of people dressed in fancy clothes make me wish I'd changed, but my father doesn't act like it bothers him. He's wearing a pair of cords and a thick, cable-knit sweater, so at least we're both casual.

Except my father is handsome enough, and distinguished enough, to make anything he wears seem like he pulled it off a designer rack. I'm no schlub, but there's something about a successful, good-looking white man in his forties that intimidates the shit out of people.

The silence between us is awkward and forceful, holding a cold hand over my mouth until it's hard to breathe or focus on the menu in front of me. I ask for a glass of red Zinfandel, hoping the booze will at least take the edge off my nerves, and then request a plate of spaghetti and meatballs when the waiter comes back to take our order. I don't even know if it's on the menu but he doesn't tell me I can't have it.

My dad sips his scotch. I watch him, trying not to be too obvious about it, and trying not to think about how shitty things are between us. Even when I was a sullen teenager tired of spending my summers abroad, away from my friends, we'd always had an ease with each other. Laughed together because of our similar sense of humor, which tends toward the cheesy.

Tears fill my eyes out of nowhere, brought on by the sheer magnitude of what we've lost—after Cary left and Tim died, my dad's desertion was the knockout punch that cut the number of people in my life that mattered down to one.

I blink several times, staring into my wineglass, which is almost empty. *He* made this decision. *He* put this rift in between us and I'll be damned if I sit here and sob about it now.

"I wanted us to have dinner, Chrissie, because I know I owe you an explanation."

"You don't owe me anything," I reply, on autopilot. My voice sounds like it belongs to a robot.

"You're my daughter. I helped bring you into this world. I loved you before you took your very first breath. I owe you anything and everything you need." He pauses, waiting for me to disagree, pushing on when I don't. "I want you to know that I'm under no illusion that any explanation will excuse my missing the past four years of your life."

The waiter pops around to bring us refills on our drinks. My father knocks back half of his scotch on the rocks before wiping his mouth and continuing. "It's a rough moment when children realize their parents are human after all, but it happens to all of us. For me, it was the day my mother stopped getting out of bed. Just stopped. A week later my

213

father gathered her up in his arms, put her in the backseat of the car, and drove her to the hospital. She was never the same." He shakes his head. "Your brother's death caused a similar break for me. I'm not proud of how I reacted, but losing Tim destroyed me. I didn't just cut you out, Chrissie, I cut everyone out. Imogen and I didn't speak for weeks, and the only reason we made it through is because she's the one who forced her way in to roll me out of bed. Hauled me to a therapist and helped me start to put together the pieces of a new life."

A new life. Not repair his old one. The admission tastes bitter on my tongue, and the tears threaten to reappear. "You could have said something. Anything. Written a letter. It destroyed my life, too, and then I lost you."

"I know."

"And if you've been better, been dealing with it, why haven't you contacted me? I'm only here now because of a freak work assignment, not because you wanted me." Anger pushes a tear down my cheeks no matter how hard I bite my lip.

"I'm ashamed of how I treated you. I don't deserve to be a part of your life, and it's not fair of me to ask for your forgiveness." He reaches a tentative hand across the table toward mine, our fingers brushing as his own eyes shine with unspilled regret. "But then your mother called. You stepped into that inn and my God, Chris, I've already missed too much. I want you to spend Christmas at the house. Get to know your stepsisters and Imogen. I don't deserve it, and you're under no obligation to let me back into your life, but I'm here to say that I miss you. I love you. I always will, no matter what you decide."

It's all too overwhelming. My father is the second man in as many days to ask for undeserved admittance back into my life. The memories of the good times we've shared, and the bad, are complex and confuse my emotions but at the end of the day, he's my dad.

Things aren't going to go back to the way they were overnight, because trusting that he's not going to disappear if life gets unbearable again will take time. I can already feel my heart pulling back, putting space in between me and this man who destroyed the childhood idea that parents never leave you.

"Are you better now?" I ask, my voice timid to my own ears.

"I've been in therapy for four years, and I'm on a limited amount of medication. I've been level for a long time, and my life with Imogen and the girls keeps me grounded."

"It hurts that they've been your daughters all this time. Makes me feel like I was some broken thing you tossed into the trash before buying something new." There's so much anger. No matter how hard I swallow, how strongly my mind lectures my heart that what happened had nothing to do with me, it just keeps welling up and over.

"Winnie and Eliza can't replace you, just like Imogen didn't replace your mother. I love them as separate beings. Not a new family, but an expanded one. I want you in my life, Chrissie, and so do the girls." Dad looks around, maybe praying that the waiter will rescue him from my endless accusations.

Sorrow for him thickens my blood, but my anger doesn't go away. I don't want to think of my dad sick. Medicated and devastated.

But it can't just erase how being abandoned changed me at my core, forever.

"I'm not proud, but we're being one hundred percent honest tonight, so here's the whole truth—it was easier not to see you. Your face reminds me of Tim's face. My memories of you include your brother. But I've learned the hard way that pain isn't something that goes away, or eases, because we pretend it's not there."

"You should have let me make the choice. After you knew you messed up and you missed having a relationship with me. You should have come to me and I could have decided."

"You're right." His fingers close around mine. "You're so right, bud. You're a better person than I'll ever think about being, and I should have trusted you to do the right thing. But better late than never, right?"

That seems to be the theme since my plane landed at Gatwick. Change has never scared me the way it does some people. The way it does Jessie, or it did before last Christmas.

What does scare me is letting not one, but two men back into my life who have destroyed my heart in the past. I'm an adult now, or near enough, and it's time to decide what

216

my life is going to look like going forward. I'm not sure right now, but I know I need some time.

I swallow the last of my wine and take a deep breath to steady the beat of my heart. "I'll think about it, okay? Coming to stay with you for the holiday."

A smile breaks over his face, and even the most cynical person in the world—which isn't me—couldn't deny that he's truly happy at the tiny step forward.

We're silent while the waiter sets down steaming plates of spaghetti and meatballs for me, lasagna for my dad, and a piping-hot basket of bread in between us. My mouth waters and my stomach grumbles at the scents of garlic and tomatoes, basil and oregano, making me think it's all kind of amazing, how life goes on.

How maybe, no matter the mantra I've repeated every night when I couldn't sleep, it never is too late.

I'm on the verge of asking Alfred if he wouldn't mind using a wheelbarrow to ferry me from the car to the inn by the time we put away dinner, another glass of wine, and share dessert. We've done a fair bit of catching up as far as everyday things like school and friends, and I've told him the amusing anecdotes about Jessie's Christmas in Ireland last year—to some very amusing quips about the problems with Irishmen that I'll have to remember to repeat—but we were both too tired to continue delving into deeper issues, I think.

We'll have to talk about Tim sometime. About that last summer I spent here and how it ended, about how I'm scared to get close to anyone now, in case they're going to leave me in one way or another.

Even so, my heart feels lighter. Possibilities inch closer to my fingertips, almost within reach.

"So, you're leaving in the morning?" It feels so good to talk to Jessica that I flop back on the bed, reveling in the lightness.

"First thing. I don't know how I'm going to be able to sleep. How are things there? What's the band like?" I make a noncommittal noise, and can feel her exasperation oozing through the phone. "Chris, for heaven's sake, we've been friends for almost four years. I know you're all out of sorts and it *has* to be something more than just spending Christmas abroad. Out with it."

She's right. Living together has made us as close as real sisters, not just ones who wear the same letters, and keeping this from her any longer feels like wasted energy. "Fine. I sort of had a fling once with Cary White."

The answering, stunned silence is priceless, and almost worth the cost of talking about this with her. Or anyone, really. Even so, the sensation of my layers peeling back, long-kept secrets on display, coats my skin with itching discomfort.

"Cary White. You *sort of know* the lead singer of Pursuant and you never thought to mention it . . . wait a second. *He's* the Brit you had a summer fling with before you came to

TCU? The reason you were celibate most of freshman year? *How?*"

I wish—not for the first time since I was eighteen—that I could erase those ten weeks of my life from my memory. They're too strong. Too vivid, and in a strange twist of physics, only seem to grow clearer instead of fading gently into the past where they freaking belong.

"It was the last summer I spent with my dad in Cornwall before he married what's her name."

"Imogen, I believe," Jessica supplies drily.

"What kind of name is that, anyway?"

"A British one. Now get on with the tale."

"Anyway, Cornwall is pretty and it's peaceful but it's not like there's a ton to do." If it's not London or Liverpool, Americans have no clue where anything is in the UK. Hell, I still don't think Jess knows that Ireland isn't even *part* of the UK. "Cary's family rented the house on the shore two down from ours and, I don't know, take it from there."

"It sounds like a fairy tale or something. Cornwall."

"It was an amazing summer," I admit. "He was my first . . . pretty much everything. We partied with his friends in the band, we spent tons of time alone, just the two of us, and we never fought about anything."

"But."

I shrug, refusing to give in to the lump forming in my throat. "Then the summer ended, like they tend to do. I left for TCU, Cary left for Oxford, end of story."

"How can that be the end of the story? No promises to write, to visit, to keep in touch? I mean . . . did you guys fall in love?"

"What does that have to do with anything?" I shake my head. "We never made any promises. It was a summer romance, Jess. This is how those things turn out more often than not."

I don't tell her that Cary left without a word. That I thought we had another week together but I woke up one morning to find him gone. Just gone without a word other than a simple two-line note held down by a rock in our favorite spot on the boardwalk.

"You're the one, Chris. Don't ever doubt it."

The lump starts to throb, clogging my throat and forcing tears into my eyes. "I haven't talked to him since."

"And now you're going to be with him pretty much every day. Prep their schedules, make sure the venues are set up, sit in on rehearsals and interviews . . ." Jessica blows out a breath. "This is fucking intense, man."

"Tell me about it." I blink, staring down at my hands until my eyes are clear and I can swallow without needing a fire extinguisher, then catch the suspicious teasing in her tone. "What?"

"I'm just saying. Christmas in London with your old Brit flame . . . who just happens to be an international rock star now. This is going to be interesting."

"I don't know if they're *stars*, actually. Is Pursuant a household name? I think that's the test."

"You are such a pain in the ass when you want to be. Just admit it's not as easy as you thought it would be, seeing him again."

I consider rummaging through my heart and my head in an attempt to decipher how I truly do feel about Cary White again after all these years. "We had sex the other night. I think that got rid of any lingering feelings."

"Oh my God. Because sex often gets *rid* of feelings. What's the matter with you?"

"Nothing's the matter with me! It's out of my system, everything is professional, and I'm here to do a job."

"Hmm."

We hang up a few minutes later, me conveniently forgetting to mention that Cary's asked to spend some time together outside of my official duties . . . and that I haven't exactly decided to tell him no.

Chapter
6

"We've been at this for hours. How about lunch?" Cedric ducks under his guitar strap and lowers the instrument to the floor, not waiting for the go-ahead from the producers. They're almost done with this album and have spent all morning rerecording small snippets of songs that don't mesh just right.

According to the bald commandant to my left, anyway.

"I'm starving," Alfie agrees, eyes lingering on his sheet music.

"Lord, me too." Simon clutches his belly. "I think the mike might have picked up my stomach growling."

"You'd better hope it didn't," the producer mutters. The guy apparently has a nonexistent sense of humor, which somehow causes everything he says to make me want to giggle.

"You would have had a hundred girls throwing cookies

at you at the next show," Alfie jokes. "Which would be about the best thing anyone's thrown at us, to be honest."

"That's true," Cedric replies with a serious expression. "Bras taste like shite."

"Guys, focus. Lunch." Cary raises his eyebrows at me through the glass. "You in, Chris?"

I could say no, but there's not much point. We're spending the next two weeks together whether I beg off or not, and I'm hungry, too. Cary and I are going to have to figure out how to be together without making everyone else in the room throw themselves out the nearest window just to avoid the awkward.

"Sure. Where to?"

He names an Indian restaurant a few blocks over, and even though I turned it down when my dad suggested it, it sounds good today. The place is a hole-in-the-wall, chosen because they're less likely to be recognized and hassled. Pursuant isn't the kind of band that inspires screaming, crying, teenage girl fans to plaster their bedrooms with posters but they *are* widely known. There are plenty of girls who want to sleep with them, plenty of all kinds of people who'd like autographs or just to shake their hands and say hello.

It's less intrusive than it might be, but most people don't have a real sense of when it's okay to interrupt a person eating dinner and when it's not. I do insist on walking over on my own, begging off as they cram into the back of one of BGG's town cars like sardines.

The Indian restaurant is almost empty when I get there

even though it's smack-dab in the middle of what should be a lunch rush. The quiet atmosphere reinforces my guess as to why Cary suggested the place, but I hope the lack of foot traffic doesn't mean the food's shitty.

I definitely haven't had good Indian food since I moved to Texas. Now I'm going to eat it every day.

Cary's seated at a table for two toward the back of the restaurant, looking strangely out of place in the ripped red-vinyl booth. I realize how long it's been since I've seen him alone. Even in pictures, Pursuant is always together. Everyone knows Cary is their beating heart, but he'd never claim to be that essential.

My mind wants to turn my body right around and take me back to the hotel where it's safe, but my determination to keep things professional and friendly drags me right up to him.

To Cary, who saw me naked and sweaty and panting two days ago.

"Hey." I sling my messenger across the back of the chair. He jumps up to help me with my coat and his warm fingers brush the nape of my neck as he slides it free. Tingles drip straight down my spine and I have to swallow in order to form more words. "Where is everyone?"

"Oh, they won't be coming." He tosses my coat in the booth and waits for me to sit.

I do, because my knees are all wobbly and my brain is working on understanding what's going on. "Why?"

Cary plops on the opposite side of the table and picks up his menu as though he has no idea what he's going to order. He's going to ask for beef roast and *porotta*. I'm going to ask for chicken curry and *neer dosa* and we'll probably end up sharing.

"I wanted to talk to you alone, but in public, like we agreed."

"So you tricked me? Really nice." My mind's all caught up now, but it's numb in the face of the truth—I'm about to spend at least an hour alone with him.

The waiter ambles up, in no hurry as he asks us what we want to drink and if we're ready to order. Cary requests exactly what I guessed but I go for the *kaali daal* instead, which is supposed to be great in the winter.

The real reason I go off script is to remind my companion—and myself—that we don't *have* a script anymore. Because there is no *we*.

"I'm sorry about that."

"Yeah, you look real sorry," I mutter, my eyes trained on packets of sugar as I rip them open and dump them into my steaming tea. The air smells like cinnamon, a result of my inadvertent lunch date doctoring his own beverage. When I look up, Cary's watching me, something curious in his almost purple gaze. "What?"

"If you had asked me four years ago, I would have sworn up and down that you couldn't be prettier. But you're more beautiful now than you were that summer."

My whole body goes hot at his words. I manage to maintain some sort of composure, barely, and cock my head to one side. "You look about the same."

Which is to say, heartbreakingly gorgeous, but he doesn't need to hear that.

"I suppose that will have to do. You liked me this way, once."

There's no good response to that so I press my lips together, making room for sips of tea but no words over the next several minutes. There's a huge hunk of wood hand carved into a monkey or elephant or something reclining on the table between us. It almost blocks my view of this Cary, of the present, and all at once it's clear to me that living the next weeks this way is going to end in a nervous breakdown for at least one of us. Nurturing the awkwardness between us won't let me look forward, and being forced to look back isn't healthy for anyone.

You have a job to do. Suck it up.

"There's really nothing to talk about." My words, or maybe my tone, make him tense up like a puppy that's used to being kicked. "We dated four years ago and now it's over. Maybe it's harder because we didn't say good-bye or get any closure, but I'm over it. We've grown up, we've moved on, all of that. Maybe we can figure out a way to work together without tiptoeing around the past."

"You're over it. What about the other night?"

The way he says it, like there's no way he believes that's possible, starts a low simmer of rage in my blood. I've missed

226

Cary, been sad about losing Cary, wanted to know what happened with Cary but now—facing him, watching him look so incredulous at the idea that I could have moved on—makes me realize for the first time that I'm *angry* with Cary.

"What did you expect? That four years later I'd still be crying myself to sleep every night?" *Shit.* I wish that hadn't slipped out, even if I had spent the first three months crying myself to sleep. "And the other night was two people who used to have great sex succumbing to temptation or familiarity or whatever. That's it."

"I don't want you to cry, ever." He gives himself a shake, maybe realizing for the first time how hard this whole thing is for me, too. "I'm sorry for the way things ended between us, but I don't feel the same way. About the sex."

"Why didn't you just tell me good-bye?"

And there it is—a huge pile of regret and sorrow and anger that I hadn't even realized still tormented me after all of this time writhing right in the middle of the table for everyone to see.

We both stare at it, and I wonder what he's thinking. How it got so big, turned into such a defining *thing*.

How a relationship that spanned two months could create a mess that four years apart couldn't clean up.

"I was an idiot, Chris. You scared me. The prospect of saying good-bye, of having everything change into something not so simple, scared me. I told myself it would be better for you, especially after we signed our first contract a couple of weeks later. You never wanted this kind of life."

There's no denying that I'd made no secret of my desire to stay anonymous for the rest of my life, especially after seeing what fame did to my father, but even so, his excuses boil my anger over. "And you didn't think I deserved a say in that decision? Or even a chance to hear you say the reason it wasn't going to work out is because you're chickenshit?"

"I know. I'm sorry. All I can say is that I was young and dumb, and I've regretted it every single minute of every day since I wrote you that note and left Cornwall."

The apology, thick with emotion and honesty, clogs my throat. My eyes burn, until Cary's penitent, eager expression blurs across the table. It's not enough, saying he's sorry, but it's a better salve than I expected. I close my eyes and when they open, my world has started to tip back to even again.

"I guess we can agree that we were both eighteen, and both stupid to think a summer romance—no matter how lovely—would last."

"*Hmm*" is all he says as he pulls an embroidered handkerchief from his pocket and passes it across the table.

"You carry handkerchiefs now? I really *don't* know you anymore." Teasing him makes me feel more like myself, gives me something solid to cling to. He apologized, I accepted. We're two adults looking back on an old romance and I'm on the other side of it, just as I thought.

Right.

"It was my nana's. She embroidered them like it was going out of style and when she died a couple of years ago, my

228

mum found drawers of them. At first I thought it was kind of douchey. And also gross, because who wants to put a linen full of snot back in your pocket, right? But now . . . I can see it working in my favor."

"Because you need *extra* tricks to impress the ladies." I start to roll my eyes, but stop. "I'm sorry about your nana. I know you loved her."

"And I'm sorry about your brother, love."

I swallow hard. Of course he knows about Tim—he said as much yesterday when he told me about the concert.

He *doesn't* know that I spent the entire visitation and half the funeral staring at the door, waiting for him to show up. For the one person who loved me as much as my brother to put his arms around me, help me gather the pieces of my heart from where they'd exploded.

But Cary hadn't come. He'd known—*must* have known what losing Tim would do to me—and yet he hadn't come.

Water under the bridge, Christina. You don't have to forgive him for everything. You just have to work with him, and Cary's trying. Try harder.

"Thanks. It's getting a little bit easier now, remembering that he's not here."

The first few years had been torture. Going home from college and expecting to see him with his feet up on the kitchen table, an entire plate of pizza rolls oozing on the table in front of him. Expecting text messages making fun of Mom on pretty much a daily basis, and ones on special occasions to make me roll my eyes about my father and his antics.

"I know how crazy you were about him. He had to grow on me, since he almost stopped us from meeting, but you know we were fast friends after that."

"What?"

"You know, because you weren't going to come to Cornwall that last summer since he was staying home."

The comment makes me frown, my brain clicking backward over less obsessed-over moments from that summer. "How did you know that?"

"You told me," he replies quickly, something flickering in his gaze as he drops it to his tea. "Didn't you?"

"Did I?"

I actually don't remember talking about not wanting to be in Cornwall at all once Cary and I met.

Our food arrives then, smelling like heaven and loosing curls of steam toward the cheap, hanging paper lights. Cary's the first to push his dishes toward the center of the table and ask for extra plates, and despite my intention to eat my own food as some kind of statement, I do the same. It's familiar and intimate, our forks clashing as they scrape at the same food, our eyes meeting over the scents of spices and the past, and despite everything a shiver of heat and recognition stutters through me.

And it's not as though we're looking back. This moment, this Indian food, doesn't have a rosy tinge of romance because of our past, but perhaps because of what still is, and even though the (metaphorical) elephant has been shooed away and even though Cary's observation about my brother has the stink of not-quite-truth to it, I'm alive in this present.

We eat our food and toss each other morsels of small talk, smiling and laughing and generally doing a great impression of two people who had fully planned on never seeing each other again for their rest of their lives being damned glad it didn't turn out that way.

Cary insists on paying the bill even though BGG gave me a stupidly big expense account, then raises his eyebrows at me. "So, was dinner with your dad productive?"

"Yes. What makes you think it wouldn't be?"

"I just thought . . . you haven't been back to England since that summer. I assumed you and your father had a falling-out after he married Imogen. You weren't too excited about the idea of her all those years ago and that was when they were just dating."

My eyebrows knit together. "You remember all of that?"

"Oh, love. I remember everything."

Chapter

7

M_y phone rings, the display pulling up a local number and saving me from melting into a puddle of Christina at his statement. There's something going on with Cary—it's as though he's starting to look at our unexpected reconnection as a chance to . . . I don't know. Not go back, but somehow change the past?

It dumps real, potent terror into every cell racing through my veins.

"Hello?"

"Is this Christina Lake?" A gruff, pissy male voice grunts.

"Speaking."

"This is Ollie over at the Grouse. We need to push back Pursuant's sound check to three. Water leak."

"Okay, I'll let them—" A *click* sounds in my ear. "Know."

"Who was that?" Cary asks, spooning beef roast into his mouth.

"I'm assuming one of the managers at your venue for your Christmas Day venue, but the guy has negative manners. Where did you find him?"

"That's Ollie. I think he's pissed off because his name is Oliver."

We're both grinning now, over nothing really.

"They had some kind of water leak and they've pushed your sound check back to three."

"Let me text the other guys. Simon will be glad. Apparently he had like, three girls over last night and he's super tired."

"Three?"

"What can I say? The guy's making up for eighteen years of getting blown off."

"Um, that would mean he started getting blown off at birth."

"He did! His mum wouldn't even let him on the titty."

A laugh bursts out of me, surprising me more than it does him. "That is so wrong."

He's a fan of bawdy humor. How is that the thing, among all of the things, that slipped my mind?

We finish our food with a running commentary on the few other patrons in the restaurant, none of whom seem to recognize my old friend, which is good.

Also bad, since it means nothing is going to distract him from getting what he wants from me.

"So, how are you planning to pass the two extra hours in your schedule, Chris? A nap, maybe? I could go for one myself." The mischievous glint in his dark-blue eyes brings to life the boy I could never say no to.

"Don't even think about it, Romeo. I've gotten that out of my system, and besides, I don't fancy getting fired and losing out on my future plans for the likes of you." I give him a stern look. "You said if I agreed to spend time with you to catch up it would be in *public*."

He snorts, wiping his mouth and tossing the green linen napkin on top of his plate. "Fair enough. If that's what you have in mind, how about we do something delightfully London."

I'm intrigued, despite my best efforts, and tell myself my mother will be pleased. Well, as long as I don't tell her who accompanied me. "What do you have in mind?"

"Can it be a surprise?" He holds up his hands at my look. "I promise, no funny business. Just a lovely, Christmassy London afternoon."

"Somewhere people will leave you alone?" The skepticism in my voice makes him reconsider.

"I don't think it'll be too bad during the day. Kids are still in school, too." He gives me the trademark Cary White smile, the one full of sly merriment and dimples that melts hearts all over the world, and I'll be damned if my knees don't go weak. "Are you going to let me get in the car this time?"

"I suppose. But you're going to have to stay on your side."

"As long as it's the side with the fun stuff, like the alcohol."

We duck into the backseat of BGG's car and Cary rolls

down the privacy partition separating us from the very affable, polite English driver.

"What's your name?" Cary asks the middle-aged man behind the wheel.

"Giles, sir."

"Right oh. Giles. Lovely to meet you."

"And you, sir."

"Tell you what. You don't have to call me sir if you'll give us a lift to Somerset House."

Giles's gaze trails from Cary to me, then back again, making me wonder whether he's going to call the local tabloids as soon as we're out of earshot. "Ice skating this afternoon, eh?"

"That's the plan."

"I'll get you there straightaway. Have no fear about that."

"Thank you, my good man!"

He rolls the partition up again, which might seem rude if someone else did it, but Cary's one of those people who can tell you to sod off and you'd smile and nod, and probably thank him on the way out the door.

"What's Somerset House?"

"It's so easy to forget that even though you've spent time in England, you're basically a London virgin." He taps the window as we turn toward the historic area and the river.

Geography has always been a thing for me—I have an odd sense of direction. I can always face myself north no matter whether I'm in a totally new place or not. It's a fun party trick.

235

"It's a fancy museum, kind of by the opera house. You'll love it. Very cheesy."

I flick his bicep, impressively hard through his leather jacket. I try in vain to stop my mind from remembering how those arms feel around me, what his skin feels like under my fingernails.

"You can ice skate?" I ask, anything to move my train of thought onto more appropriate tracks.

"Sure. Can't you?"

"It's been years, but yeah. I played hockey once upon a time."

"Really? Hockey?" His blue eyes are wide, as though he's seeing me in a whole new light. "Like, with pads and fistfights and hair pulling and everything?"

"Whoa, whoa. You can just stop imagining me in some kind of underwear tickle fight on the ice right now."

"Never gonna happen, love."

My cheeks get hot and I look away, pretending to take in the scenery outside the window. "Anyway, I'm from Seattle, which is basically Canada. Hockey is our religion."

"You keep surprising me."

We lapse into silence, Cary fingering the bottles in the minibar before deciding against it, apparently, and the sights and sounds of London proper sliding by outside the car's tinted windows. My mind wanders back to the morning we met for the first time.

The whole coast looks like it's about to burst into flames with the sunrise. I've been out most of the night, alone and freezing on the beach but the chill is more than worth the worry it will have caused my father. My stomach is tight with the indignity of being forced to spend the summer with him while Tim stays home the first month, of being eighteen and being forced to do anything, really.

A boy jogs along the water, sun streaming through his dark waves, and to my eyes he's some kind of fairy—unreal in his beauty and the way he just appears, as though someone sent him to me.

He stops and I scramble up, swatting soggy sand from my butt and arms and legs. The flurry of movement makes him grin, and he swipes sticky beads of sweat from his forehead. "Are you a mermaid? Washed up on the shore?"

I frown at him. Typical boy, thinking girls are just there for the saving. "No. And if I were, I would only be here to trick you into coming into the water with me so I could drown you."

He laughs, a lovely, full sound that stretches out over the waves until it tumbles over the horizon. "Bloody brilliant. So what are you doing out here, human girl?"

I shrug, not inclined to fight my smile. "Hiding from my dad."

"Really? Why would you do that?" He plops down and pats the sand next to him, squinting up at me with the strangest expression of contentment and awe. "Sit down and tell me the story of your life."

For some reason, I do. "I'm Christina."

"Cary."

We talk all morning, until my father's housekeeper finds

*me and drags me back home. The strange thing is, after a couple
of hours with Cary, going back to the house and my father and
my summer in Cornwall didn't bother me at all.*

The Thames sparkles under the December sunshine,
blinding but pretty in the same way the summer sunshine had
been all those years ago. It takes me a moment to figure out
which scene I'm in.

"Where'd you go?" Cary asks softly, his gaze intense
on my face.

I shake my head, manage a smile that feels reflective of my
memory—both happy and sad. "Another universe."

"It looks familiar," he replies, not taking his eyes from
my face.

I turn away, feeling exposed under his scrutiny, and
look out the window. We've pulled up in front of a beautiful
building. The thing is massive, with more of a palatial feel
about it as opposed to a museum, which is what the signs
promise it is, and the entire neoclassical courtyard is covered
in ice. A giant Christmas tree lights up the sidelines as a few
couples, some lone skaters, and a handful of small children
glide over the smooth ice that seems to stretch forever. The
scene reminds me of Rockefeller Center in New York City,
but grander and with more old-world charm.

"Wow," is the profound comment that comes from my
brain as we step out into the bright, chilly afternoon.

"I know. It's kind of dorky and honestly, I haven't been
here in years, but it's beautiful. Want to skate or just hit the
bar?"

"Let's skate for a bit, then I'd be up for some hot chocolate if we have time."

"As you wish, love."

I follow him around to the skate rental counter and bite my tongue to keep from arguing as he pays, not needing to ask my size. After my skates are laced up and our shoes are stowed in a locker, I pull thick mittens out of my coat pockets and jam a stocking cap on my head. Cary dons a woolen gray one and wraps a matching scarf around his neck. With his trademark dark waves hidden and the winter gear obscuring a little of his face, he's at least harder to recognize.

Not for me. Never for me, but aside from a few curious glances in the locker room, no one pays us much mind.

He's right about the rink and grounds not being too busy—there are younger kids, those not subjected to school hours just yet, but I can see that when the holiday beings in a few days that Somerset House will be packed with teenagers and families alike.

Today, there's plenty of room to spread out, and I take advantage, dusting off my old skills and enjoying the cut of my blades on the fresh ice, lapping Cary a few times before slowing down to glide at his side. My face feels flushed from the cold and the exhilaration of exercise, and happiness like I haven't felt in years outside of work trickles in steady streams through my blood. It's so perfect, this place. Like it's part of a movie set or a play, something apart from reality.

It makes anything seem possible, and as I sneak a look at Cary's face to find him watching me with a rapt, adoring expression, the toe pick on my skate catches an uneven spot in the ice.

My arms flail as my legs work to keep me upright, all of which is a fruitless battle. I land on my butt, one leg flying up in the air to catch Cary's calf, a motion that sends him tumbling toward the ice, too. He lands on top of my left half, squishing all of the air from one lung.

I lay on my back, forgetting trying to get up while I struggle to breathe, and feel Cary lean into my side.

"Are you okay?" He reaches up and tucks an escaped strand of blond hair back under my cap. Mirth dances behind the concern in his dark-blue eyes, begging for permission to be let loose, and the smile I manage sets it free.

Before long we're both on our backs, cackling as we stare up at the sky and try to catch our breath. Cary's fingers wrap around my mitten. I don't pull away, even though I know that I should—I've forgotten why it's so important, or let myself forget, at least for right now.

"You know, you always were such a graceful girl, Christina Lake. I'm glad to see that some things haven't changed."

I sit up, whacking him in the stomach and earning a groan. "You're not going to be joining the ballet anytime soon, you know."

He struggles to a sitting position, too, his eyes sparkling as he peers into my face. "We make quite a pair."

Cary reaches out again, smoothing back more of my stray hairs, his hands lingering on my cheeks. We're sitting so close together, near enough that the white clouds of our breath mingle before they dissipate, and I've been kissed by Cary White enough times to know what's going through his mind.

It was as simple as breathing that summer, and again the other night. Kissing him. As though I couldn't survive without my lips touching his at every opportunity. He's looking at me that way now, his gaze dropping to my mouth, tongue snaking out to wet his lips. My heart flings itself at my rib cage and all of a sudden my layers of clothes are suffocating me with heat. Tingles drop lower, between my thighs, and it takes every one of the memories of Cary leaving me, every one of Violet's threats to my future, to push me away.

I manage to climb to my feet on the sharp blades, breathing hard and trying to force my heart to slow down while Cary gets up, too, his smile turning a little sad. My chest tightens, because we're finally facing the truth—things will never be the way they were, and how we ended means that even the good memories are tarnished.

"Ready for that cocoa now?"

"Will they put peppermint schnapps in it?"

He snorts, leading me back to remove our skates. "How about we try something more traditional, like wassail."

"Like, 'here we come a-wassailing'?"

"I guess?" His good humor is back, but it's quieter now. Steady, as though no number of awkward moments can shake it.

The café area of Somerset House is as ethereal as the rest

of the place—like some kind of holiday fantasy inside a London souvenir snow globe. The steaming drink, which Cary delivers with a plateful of mini-scones, smells like heaven. It coats my tongue with honey and cloves, and a strong sprinkle of cinnamon, which is probably why he suggested we try it to begin with.

"It's like cider that dripped straight off Santa's beard," I breathe, licking my lips.

"You are so weird," Cary observes, eating the vanilla scone as crumbs fall to the napkin.

I shrug, sipping more of the drink and snatching the mini–cranberry scone off the plate. "It's better than being boring."

"I'll give you that."

We snack in silence for a while. I watch the people around us and out on the skating rink, the happiness from earlier still floating around us like little bubbles in a champagne glass.

"Tell me about what happened with your dad. You two were so . . . not close, maybe, but alike. Back then." His tone is careful on this subject, not assuming the way it is when he talks about the two of us.

It's not my favorite topic of conversation, but spilling my guts to Cary has never been hard. I let myself enjoy being in his company again, near someone who listens without judgment, who knows when to give advice and when to simply nod and grunt.

"He bailed after Tim died. Married Imogen, started

being Winnie and Eliza's dad, never called, never wrote. It's a story that would be familiar to you, I think." My comment comes out harsh, but there's no other way to draw the comparison. They had both been awful to me.

For his part, Cary winces. "I deserve that. Did he tell you why?"

"At dinner last night. He was depressed, and by the time he was better he figured I hated him. Which was true."

Cary's hand snakes out, warm from being wrapped around his mug, and covers mine. "True, but the same thing you accused me of at lunch applies to him, too. It should have been up to you whether to let him back into your life."

My throat burns at his comment, and the frank comparison to my father. It's a reminder that even though they hurt me, it's within my power to be the bigger person and accept apologies all around. "Thank you."

"I think you do want him in your life. He's your dad, love. You don't have to forgive and forget all at once, but don't you want to be part of his life?"

"You mean embrace the whole stepfamily thing?" I frown, still inclined to blame Imogen and her girls even though they had nothing to do with it. Even though, to hear my dad tell it, she had saved his life and even my mom wants me to meet them.

"They might not be all that bad. Or maybe they're awful witches, but either way, you'll have a story to tell." Cary winks and pulls his hand back, sipping more of his drink.

It's as though we've come full circle, him and me. That morning on the beach all of those years ago, he'd convinced me that my father wanting to spend one last summer with me only meant that he loved me. That he'd miss me, and knew things would be changing, and really, what was so bad about that?

I'd gone home with a different attitude, and I realized now that I would check out of the hotel and spend the next ten days with my father. Or, if Imogen and the girls are awful, maybe just a couple of nights.

Strange to realize, but I'm actually hoping they're not. Awful.

"You know what, Cary? I think you just might be right!"

"What?" The exaggerated shock on his handsome face makes me giggle.

"Don't let it go to your head."

There's a pause as we grin at each other, staring for a little too long, before he clears his throat and looks down at his hands for a couple of seconds.

"I've been trying to figure out how to start this conversation with you, and I don't think I've hit on the exact right way to put it just yet." Cary's statement, calm and curious, snags my attention. His expression is wide open, nothing to hide, and frankness hangs in his welcoming gaze.

Wariness dampens my illusion of bliss and freedom. "What conversation?"

"The one where I ask you to do something crazy."

"I'm not skinny-dipping again. Especially not in the

winter." He'd talked me into that once upon a time. The truth is, there's not a single day anywhere in England that's warm enough to get in the water without a wet suit, and the coast at Cornwall had nearly frozen us both in the middle of July.

"If I thought I could talk you into it, I'd have gone for it already." He laughs softly. "The thing is, the moment I saw your face in that recording studio the other day I knew that whatever was between us four years ago is still there. It never left; it's tied us together this whole time, but I'm not going to sit here and ask you to start over. We can't erase everything that happened. We can't pick up where we left off. So what do we do?"

I don't know how to answer that. The idea that Cary and I could ever be, well, *Cary and I* again is a dream I snuffed out long ago. It had hurt too much to believe in anything but letting him go.

Now he's sitting here, asking me to get out the key and open that box full of hope and heartache and the idea— buried deeper than the others—that I'll never find anyone else who makes me feel the way he does, not ever.

"I don't know." I swallow, determined not to cry. "It took me longer than I care to admit to get this far, Cary. Not to mention that I want this career and Violet will ruin me if she thinks I'm here for you."

"Let me worry about her. You might be surprised to learn that I have some pull at BGG."

I find the courage to meet his gaze. To open myself to

him, let him see the fear and the pain, the anxiety. "I don't want your help, just like I didn't want my father's. This is my dream job and I'm good at it."

"You are, love. You always were—hell, we wouldn't have gotten discovered if you weren't. I wouldn't be writing songs without your gorgeous bull head badgering me into giving it a go." He sighs, pain lacing the fine lines around his troubled eyes. "Can we just, I don't know, try again? Remember the versions of us that fell in love and why, deal with the versions of us we've become in the past four years, and see what happens between Cary and Christina now? Violet be damned? Because I can't be in the same room with you and pretend I don't want that. And I'm not going to."

Bravery has never been my strong suit. I barely made it through my brother's death. I've avoided my father and his new family, and would have kept doing that if this whole forced holiday hadn't come up. I never asked Cary why he left, or even did something simple like confronted whoever keeps using my shower shoes in the sorority house.

But now it comes from somewhere deep inside me, a place that's never healed, has always hoped, and knows that maybe all of the decisions in my life have led me here.

As though I never had a choice because there's only one right answer

"We can try being friends again, Cary. Get to know each other. Laugh, move on from . . . everything. But we're not advertising this. My job is important to me."

He grins like a little boy handed a large present on Christmas morning. "Deal."

I think he's smiling because I've gone and admitted that exploring the lingering feelings between us is important to me, too.

Chapter
8

I keep my eyes out the window on the way to my father's house even though there's not much to see except highway at first. The driver he sent—Alfred, again—gets creative as we wind through Wimbledon, which is the same moment that the familiar tingles of affection for England attack me in full force. It's been years since I've been back to the place I once would have referred to as home and I've never seen it in winter.

Wimbledon has always been a sleepy little place unless the tournament is going on, and with snow covering the streets and dusting the lampposts decked with greenery and red ribbons, it's pretty enough to make me forget that I'm still not sure going to my dad's is the right decision.

At least for a few minutes.

Then we cross the River Thames and head toward Hyde Park, the ritzy area of the city my father has lived in since he moved abroad after my parents' divorce. Everything about my father's life is extravagant. As long as he keeps churning out carbon copies of his first bestselling novel, published twenty years ago now, there doesn't seem to be a reason to worry the money is ever going to dry up.

We pull up to the wrought iron gate. It opens after a quiet buzzing floats through the frosty windows and we pull around to the back of an imposing white three-story home with stark black shutters. Buttery light spills from the windows on the ground floor, illuminating snow that looks dusted with glitter and decorations that have to have been professionally done.

"Home sweet home," I mutter, getting out before Alfred unbuckles his seat belt.

It's familiar but strange, because it looks so much different in the winter. The stately, classic English home is always impressive and lovely, but among the drifting snowflakes it appears magical. Like something out of a Bridget Jones movie or the postcards Dad used to stick in my Christmas gifts every year.

I hate that the sight of it makes my chest ache. Hate that I've missed being here after all.

My dad meets me at the front door, stepping out into the cold and casting a glance behind him into the glowing house. A shaggy, golden ball of fur slips out before he can close the door, hurling itself at me. Despite all of my twisted feelings over being here, a delighted squeal pops straight out of my mouth.

"Baxter!"

I drop to my knees, ignoring the wet chill that soaks the knees of my jeans to wrap my arms around the old dog. His fur is soft and familiar under my palms and my cheeks feel as though they'll split from my grin. Baxter's whole body wags as he frolics around me, too excited to settle down.

He runs off after a moment, lifting a leg to pee on a bush. I stand up, shaking my head. "I think I was afraid to ask if he was still . . . around."

"Old Baxter? He's got more than a decade under his belt now but he's going strong." A hesitant smile twitches my dad's lips. "I'm so glad you're here, bud. And I know we agreed to work on things, but in the meantime . . . I wanted to ask you not to take my failings out on Imogen and the girls. It's Christmas in a few days; everyone's here. It would be nice to enjoy it."

"So, you want me to act like everything's back to normal? I'm not sure I can do that."

"You don't have to be fake. Just . . . polite."

Irritation stirs in my gut, swirling up clouds of impatience. "I'm not going to get inside and start throwing furniture through the windows and slamming beers. I just work in publicity; I'm not a rock star."

"Thank you." Dad chuckles, amusement dancing in his dark eyes as he pushes open the door. A wash of freezing-cold air sweeps into the cozy interior, inspiring me to follow him and Baxter quickly.

I follow my dad over the threshold and through into a

bright, warm kitchen. He's remodeled since I was here last, and all of the appliances are stainless steel. The countertops are some sort of expensive marble and the cabinets are cherry instead of blond. The effect is beautiful and inviting. I hate that it makes me feel that way.

Despite my attitude, the smell of spices and smoked poultry makes my mouth water—it's been too long since Cary and I noshed that Indian food.

"Everyone's probably in the sitting room. May I take your coat?"

I hand over the black-and-white herringbone and run my hands through my pale tangles. Years of successfully avoiding my evil stepmother are about to come to an end. Not that I've been invited to meet her before now. That last summer in Cornwall they had just met, and I'd made no secret of the fact that if she made an appearance at our house that summer, I'd be gone.

He hangs my coat up in a hall closet as we drift past, then leads me over polished oak floors into the living room. Nothing has been remodeled in here; flames crackle in a massive stone fireplace and the off-white, overstuffed furniture remains miraculously clean. A pretty woman who's probably in her early forties sits with a cross-stitch in her lap and her feet tucked underneath her. Two girls splay on the couch, their backs to me so that all I can see is ash-blond hair that matches their mother's.

The woman looks up, and when her eyes find me lurking in the doorway, she lights up with a smile. Imogen—despite my snarking with Jessica, I could never forget her name—gets to her feet and glides across the room in a series of graceful movements, snapping her fingers at her daughters on her way.

Their heads swivel to glimpse me, then they make eye contact with each other before following their mother's lead. She's in front of me, her hand extended. "You must be Christina. Your father has told us so much about you and I can't tell you how excited we were to hear you'd be joining us for the holiday."

"It's a surprise to me," I respond, feeling the heat of my father's gaze on the side of my face. I grit my teeth. "A good surprise."

"I'm Imogen," she continues, smoothing over the tension that bubbled up with my awkward non-intro. "These are my daughters, Winnie and Eliza."

She nods to the taller one first, then the shorter. Other than height, it's almost impossible to tell the two of them apart. I'm guessing the shorter one is older, since she's got a Cambridge sweatshirt on. That must make her Eliza.

"Winnie is just sixteen and Eliza goes to university, like you."

They both smile and shake my hand, adding their own quiet exclamations about being happy to finally meet me, and that it's crazy that it's been so long. It takes all of my self-control not to look toward my father—not to ask whether they know I've never been invited or if this is all part of some elaborate show.

"Why don't I take you upstairs and help you get settled," Imogen says. "I'm afraid we've had to rearrange a few things since this visit was last minute. We've got you in a different room than the one you're used to."

"It's fine. I never really had a room here. We were always on our way to or from Cornwall when I visited."

She smiles again. It's big and her teeth are white and straight—not very British of her, even if her accent is stronger than my dad's. "I love the house in Cornwall, but I'm sure it was boring for you as a girl."

"Most of the time," I murmur, my mind leapfrogging without permission through the decade of boring summers to the one that was the exact opposite.

Imogen leads me up the back staircase, our footsteps silenced by the thick carpet running up the center of the steps. The banister, trim, and doors have been painted ivory, and the color instead of the former pockmarked oak brightens every space more than I would have thought possible. It looks good, her touch on the house. It's not as though my mother ever lived here, or Imogen replaced her in that way. All of those years after he and mom divorced and he moved back to London, I was the girl in his house. In his life.

And it's not as though I was redecorating.

As much as I want Imogen to be as easy to hate as every Disney stepmother ever, she's not the one I'm pissed at—in fact, if she had saved my dad the way he described, I'm grudgingly thankful for her.

She pushes open the door at the end of the hallway, holding it to let me pass. Like the rest of the house, the guest room is lush and decorated with excellent taste. I bite my tongue to stop from asking whether she did it all herself or they hired someone. I might be playing nice but I don't have to be friendly.

"Can I get you anything, dear? This room has its own *en suite* and there are towels and toiletries under the sink in case you forgot anything. If you want to get settled and maybe slip into some more comfortable clothes, we'd love to get acquainted downstairs."

"I don't know, Imogen. I'm pretty tired." It's a bogus answer, since it's only nine o'clock and my minimal jet lag has passed, but getting here and meeting them is enough for one night.

"I'm sure this is all a little overwhelming for you." Her smile falters. "I told Gerard it would be best to warn you as opposed to simply showing up at the inn, but he worried you'd just avoid him."

"Honestly, I might have. I guess not seeing me for four years doesn't mean he doesn't know me."

This time, my awkwardness is too much for even Imogen's easy hospitality to overcome. She twists her fingers together, looking toward the door with a longing that's almost comical.

"I'll come down for a bit," I amend, guilt tickling the back of my throat. Stupid manners. "I'm a little hungry and whatever you were cooking smells great."

"Lovely." Imogen turns to go, tucking stray blond strands back into her hairpins. She pauses in the doorway, the hesitance in her gaze making me sure I'm not going to want to hear what's next. "Christina . . . your father is a man. I don't know much about your experience with the opposite sex, but even though they act like nothing bothers them, they have as many emotions as we do."

I give her a weak smile, feeling my resistance to this experience fade a little more. "You guys are British. I didn't know any of you had emotions to begin with."

She laughs, a little louder than the joke warrants, and reaches out to pat the back of my hand. Her skin is warm and dry, pleasant the way her touch feels on the house, and then she's gone.

I blow out my breath and spin around, unzipping my suitcase before giving up on pretending everything is fine. The bed is soft, sinking under my weight, and I lay flat on my back. The ceiling is painted white; a blank slate like my life after that summer I turned eighteen.

Before, I had a dad who loved me, even if we didn't see each other all that often. I had an older brother who was more like a best friend, a boy who made my world spin around and turn my knees into pudding, and a future that was so close and so big I could touch it.

Then Dad met Imogen, Cary left me, and Tim died.

Blank slate.

Nothing will ever bring back Tim, which means that life is gone forever. But Cary wants to . . . what? Get reacquainted? And my dad is here. He's downstairs, and even if he's doing all of this because my mother guilted him into it, he didn't have to. He could have blown it off.

But he came. He laid out an explanation and apologized and I believe him. My mind and my heart aren't better, aren't healed or ready to trust him, but we're here. My dad was my hero until his career took off, then things went south with my mom and he left, but we managed to bandage those hurts with summers at the shore and letters and phone calls in between. If he's trying, if he wants to try, I know Cary is right.

I have to, as well.

There's a good chance my heart won't survive another failure, but finding the strength to keep pushing him away if he's really looking for a way in isn't going to be easy.

A knock on the door reminds me I'm supposed to be freshening up and rejoining the ragtag bunch downstairs. Except they're not ragtag at all. They make *me* feel that way, with all of their English put-togetherness.

I might be half English but it's not the half that's proper and organized and well groomed.

"Come in."

The blond head that pokes into my space doesn't belong to Imogen. It's the taller one. Winnie.

"Hello," she starts, glancing around nervously, as though she's worried she's interrupted some sort of private or nefarious act. Baxter noses in behind her and leaps up onto my bed, leaving wet footprints on the comforter. "I just

256

wanted to check on you. And bring you a plate of biscuits. Mum says they're your favorite."

Winnie glances down at the plate in her hands and my gaze follows, landing on a pile of powdered-sugar-dusted chocolate crinkles. My mouth waters and my eyes try to do the same—my dad remembered.

"Thank you," I croak, my fingers closing around a cookie.

She slides the plate onto the white-painted desk against one wall and then perches in the chair, frowning at Baxter when he jumps down and trots over to look up at her with big, begging eyes.

The fact that she assumes she's welcome in my room makes it clear she's young and well loved. Two things I'm familiar with.

"Must be pretty weird, having a whole new family."

I cringe at her choice of words. "I have a family. You guys are . . . new. But not family."

That seems to take her aback, like I pinched her harder than necessary under the table, but like all confident teenagers, she shakes it off fast. "What did you ask Father Christmas for?"

"Excuse me?"

"You know, pressies? A present?" Winnie squints at me, maybe wondering if her new stepsister is daft.

"Oh. I don't know. I guess I don't really need anything."

"Are you really going to the Pursuant concert on New Year's Eve?" Her grayish eyes shine.

"Yeah."

"You don't sound very excited about it."

"I'm not, really."

"Why not? Because you work with bands all the time and you're all jaded and too cool?"

That makes me snort. I'm getting dangerously close to liking this girl. "No. It's just more of a job, I guess."

"Yeah, but this is *Pursuant*. Why? I mean Cary White's dreamy and the rest of the guys aren't far behind." She wrinkles her nose. "Except Simon. The drummer."

"I know who he is." In spite of myself, a smile finds my lips at the memory of Simon trying to talk to girls on the beach—his unruly, Howard Stern–like hair flopping in his eyes and his almost translucent skin blinding everyone in a ten-mile radius. According to Cary he's not having those problems now that the band's got a couple of Grammys on their studio wall, but that's not exactly appropriate conversation. "He's a nice guy, though."

"You *know* them?"

I swallow hard, not smiling now. Not wanting to remember right now, not able to force away the images with the sound of our endless laughter ringing in my ears. Simon, David, Alfie, Cedric, and of course, Cary. Guys I considered friends at one time. There's no easy way to explain what changed to a starstruck, pushy sixteen-year-old girl.

"I think we should go downstairs. I'm pretty hungry and I don't think cookies are going to cut it." Her face falls. "Thank you for bringing them up, though. I'll take them with me to the studio tomorrow. Maybe give one to Simon."

That makes her smile, and she bounces out of the chair and ahead of me down the hallway, Baxter on her heels. A feeling starts in the pit of my stomach, sort of like dread mixed with uncertainty. These people seem determined to be not awful, which is really going to screw with my plans to hate them all forever.

The kitchen smells even better since Imogen warmed up leftover chunks of roasted game hen and potatoes, and everyone sits with me around the table. Imogen and my father have tea, while Winnie snacks on sugar cookies and Eliza picks at what looks like a leftover breakfast pastry. They ask about things like my flight, about what my duties will be and when there might be free time for us to hang out, and I answer as best I can while my head fills up with emotions that are just impossible to fight all at once.

"Christina, the girls and I were thinking perhaps a lunch and spa day is in order before the holiday—let us know when you'll have the time so you can join us."

I give her a noncommittal nod and mumble something about checking my schedule.

Then Winnie shrieks and jumps up, babbling something about Cary White and Somerset House as she shoves her phone in my face. My father peers over my shoulder as Winnie flips through an article—if you can call it that—on one of Great Britain's more disgusting gossip sites. Which is saying something.

There are pictures of Cary and me.

The site uploaded a whole album of them, starting with

us lacing up our skates, going through our day, and ending with us gazing at each other over the café table. There are some close-ups of the moment we almost kissed, sitting on the ice. There is speculation over who I am and what exactly we might be talking about over the wassail, when my face squinches up in a terrible, unattractive grimace that's pretty standard when I'm trying not to cry.

"You're famous!" Winnie squeals. "Why didn't you tell me!"

I push the phone away, nervous again although it's hard to put my finger on why. This is normal. It's the kind of thing that happened a lot with my dad when we were younger and his books were being turned into movies every other year. The paparazzi had always been sniffing around. It had sucked. I had worried about my romance ending up the same way when I was eighteen and could see that Pursuant really had something special.

Except this time I'm not a kid, and it's not just annoying.

It's going to get me fired.

"Yeah, well, the life of fame and fortune isn't all it's cracked up to be, as most people who have actually lived it can attest."

When Cary and I had been falling in love, it had made me feel immense guilt, hoping he and Pursuant wouldn't make it big. I didn't want to be the girlfriend of a rock star. Never had.

But I had wanted him.

"Well, *I* think you're crazy," Winnie pouts, perching on the edge of the couch.

Eliza gives up trying to read, since her sister's butt is blocking her light, and puts down her book. She peers at me around Winnie's vibrating form. "So, what's up with you two, anyway?"

I shrug, avoiding my father's gaze, which feels hot on the back of my neck. He'd been tolerant of my affair with Cary that summer, at least as first. The more serious things got, the less excited he seemed to be about the whole thing, and no one had witnessed more of my heartbreak than him.

"We're . . . I don't know. Working together. Trying to figure it out." I risk a glance at my dad, whose lips are pressed together. "I guess it's the trip for asking Christina's forgiveness."

He pales slightly. "I'm surprised, honestly, that you even agreed to this trip knowing you'd have to see him. Now these photos . . . This is going to sound hypocritical, but be careful, Chrissie."

Worry wrinkles the skin on his forehead. It makes sense that he'd be wary of my getting tangled up with Cary again, given that he witnessed the aftermath of my losing him the first time.

This feels like something more than that, though. Like he hoped for some reason of his own that Cary's and my paths would stay divergent.

Before I figure out how to ask him about it, my phone

dings with a text message. It's from Jessica, and just seeing her tiny thumbnail face floods me with potent relief. It also pinches me with the need to hear her voice, to talk to someone at least a little removed from all of this emotion.

Dude. Pics are everywhere. WHAT THE FUCK IS HAPPENING? CALL ME!

"Um, can we talk about this later? My roommate needs me."

I race out of the room before anyone can argue, the phone already ringing in my ear.

"Hello, Jessie's phone," a lilting, sexy Irish accent greets me. "How may I direct your call?"

Despite the events of the past ten minutes, a smile twitches the corners of my lips. "Is Jessica available?"

"There's no Jessica here, I'm afraid, just a gorgeous, half-naked Jessie who's hot for me—ow!"

A rustling, then a clatter, force me to pull the phone away from my ear before my roommate's slightly breathless voice comes on the line. "Chris?"

"Yeah," I laugh. "Did I interrupt something?"

"No, no. I'm just changing clothes so we can go tend the horses. Anytime I take off my shirt Grady assumes it's for his benefit."

I giggle harder, temporarily forgetting that all of my professional dreams are about to be shattered. "Give the guy a break, Jess. He only gets to see you every couple of months."

"Yeah, yeah. Enough about Grady and his needy nether regions."

"Hey!" Comes the muffled protest from the background. "I can hear you, you know."

"I know that," Jessica hisses. "I'm not daft. Chris?"

"I'm still here."

"What is happening with you and the sexy singer? Because those photos make it seem like . . . something. Definitely something more than casual for-old-times'-sake sex."

I pause, unsure how to answer. "We just went ice skating together. I fell down. He fell down. We had wassail and talked."

"What in God's name is wassail?"

I think Grady's muffled voice explains that it's spiced cider, so I skip that response.

"What did you talk about? Did you ask him what happened before and everything?"

"Yeah. He apologized the first time we were alone together and not, you know, naked. Blamed it on being scared of our connection, then feeling like it was too late to apologize." I hesitate, thinking of those pictures. Of my face on the Internet even though I didn't say it was okay, or put it there. "But he wants to try again. His words."

She pauses. "What do you want?"

It's not the first time today that I've wondered just that, but it is the first time anyone else has bothered to ask in so many words. "What do I *want* or what's not going to get me fired?"

"I know you're going to say the smart thing to do is to

fortify the little stone castle you live in, Chris—the one that I'm just barely close enough to that I can shout through the windows. Maybe you're right. He hurt you. He made you this way, and now he wants another chance." She pauses. "But the job thing, that's complicated. Surely there's a way around it."

"To be fair, he's only part of what made me this way." I hesitate, searching my soul. "But my boss is the queen of the harpies, and there are rules about dating in the workplace for a reason."

"This is, like, a onetime thing, though, you working in London. You're just on loan." The hopeful tinge to her voice tries to trigger the same response in me.

The thought of Violet's scowl squashes it. "Maybe, but I'm still representing BGG. It's an issue."

"But you're thinking about it, I can tell. Seeing him again?"

I bite my lip, my heart struggling to ask for what it wants. "I want this job, you know that. But I also want to be brave, Jess. Like you."

That makes her snort. "I'm happy to hear I'm such an inspiration. And for the record, I think if you really want to do this, the job thing will sort itself out. You're a genius at music publicity, and your bosses in the States love you. You're never going to be able to get over this guy if you don't feel like the two of you saw this thing through to the end."

"You think it's going to end?" Some of the knots in my belly pull tight again at the mere suggestion.

"I don't think anything except that I love you and I want you to be able to live a good life, with actual human beings in it who are close to you. So do what you have to do, babe." She sucks in a deep breath, as though gathering oxygen in case she needs to argue with me. "How's life in the hotel? Are you using your meal allowance to order decadent room service and wander around in a thick robe?"

"I'm not Julia Roberts in *Pretty Woman*. And I'm not staying at the hotel. My dad asked me to come meet the stepfamily and everything and I sort of agreed."

"Okaaaaaay, I would have thought a text was in order about that, but fine. How's it going? You're going to stay for Christmas?"

"I think so." It surprises me to find out I'm no longer anxious to get away. It's nice enough here, and everyone's doing a decent job of respecting my privacy. Winnie's questions are annoying, but also charming in their way. "It's not as bad as I thought it would be. At least not so far."

"Hmm. You've had quite a big trip, huh?"

"You might say that. How's Ireland?"

"Gorgeous and mysterious and, you know, it has Grady." The smile comes through in her voice. "But we were thinking a little trip to London might be in order. You know, if you want company on New Year's Eve."

Excitement lifts my spirits. "You can totally come for the fund-raiser and concert. We can go out afterward. That would be fun."

"If you really want me, we'd love to come."

"Yes. No doubt."

That settled, we sign off pretty quickly. She and Grady have chores to do and I'm about to fall asleep with my phone in my hand. Once Jess and I say good-bye, I do as abbreviated a bedtime routine as possible before climbing back under the covers. My mind starts working again after the lights are off and I'm snuggled up, and the first thing that comes to mind is that now that Christmas includes other people, presents are going to be in order.

Without thinking too hard about it, I pick up my phone and find the entry Cary programmed with his number before we parted ways earlier. I key in a text message and hit send before my courage can fail me.

Hey. We have a couple of days off. If you're not busy, want to help me buy gifts?

He responds quickly. In my mind, he's lying in bed trying to sleep, too, and the image of Cary in bed floods me with heat and desire and a million mental pictures that, now that we've broken the floodgates, I suspect will never go away.

For your dad's fam? So you're staying?

Yes. Nosy.

I think about adding a smiley face but figure he knows me well enough to figure that out.

Glad. German market or Oxford Street?

We can decide later. See you Tues.

Good night, love.

Good night.

The three little dots that promise he's typing pop up,

then disappear, then repeat the process three or four times. I doze off, my phone clutched in my hand, wondering whether he's wishing—like I am—that we were together right now.

The message is there when I wake up.

I'm glad you're here.

Chapter
9

The next morning finds me in Violet's office, called on the carpet over the photos on that website. They're all over the place and speculation is everywhere as far as who I am, whether I'm Cary's muse, and a million other less appropriate wonderings, all of which apparently piss off my boss.

I mean, they piss me off, too. But it's sort of my business.

Violet, though, looks as if her head might actually pop off. She paces in front of the large window in her office, the thick carpet muting the *click-clack* of her stilettos. When she pauses, she crosses her arms over her chest and raises her manicured eyebrows. "Well? Do you have one single reason that I shouldn't send you packing right now?"

I swallow down my fears over her doing just that and try to formulate a response. Even though she had given me the no-hanky-panky speech, dating the talent isn't against any kind of *official* policy that I know of—in fact, I wouldn't be anywhere near the first person at BGG to do it.

The snarky reply of *because then you'd have to do all of this yourself* probably won't do me any favors, so I dismiss it and go with something more placating. "I can't change the fact that Cary and I have a past, and my bosses at home were made aware of it before they sent me here."

Granted, I hadn't gone into gory detail, but I had let them know we were acquainted.

"That's doesn't make me feel better," she snarls. "You're supposed to be in charge of publicity for the band, not getting your own stupid face in the papers."

That makes me bristle. "I grew *up* in the papers, which you'd know if you bothered to learn a single thing about me, and I have no desire to be back there. Nothing that's going on or not going on between Cary and me is impacting my job, which just two days ago, by the way, you—rather grudgingly—told my bosses in Dallas I was doing well. This doesn't change anything."

Her face is white, her hands fisted so tight her knuckles are, too. She wants to fire me. It's written all over her face but she's not going to. Jessica was right about me being good at this job. Those two things are going to get me through another day, but who knows what will happen if things move forward between us.

"Get the hell out of my office. And stay out of the fucking papers."

Violet turns her back on me and I don't have to be dismissed twice. The people in the hallway and outer office do poor impressions of people who weren't eavesdropping, and if my name and full history aren't splashed on the front page of every gossip site by tomorrow morning I'll eat my hat. And not a little one, either. A giant British one that someone would wear to a polo match.

I think about how I'm supposed to go shopping with Cary in public, and how easy it will be for us to have a repeat performance of this whole stupid thing—one that might not end up in my favor. In the backseat of the car, my fingers hover over the keyboard on my phone. My brain urges them to cancel, to put my future above my past, but every time Cary's face pops into my mind, I can't help but think maybe he can be both.

So, I don't cancel. But I don't stop worrying, either.

The days fly by, and the band's schedule keeps all of us too busy to worry too much about developing personal relationships. That doesn't stop my whole body from flushing anytime Cary's within touching distance, or his eyes from lingering on me when he should be watching his music or answering a question.

It certainly doesn't discourage David from interrupting us whenever we have a moment alone or making snide comments with every other breath. None of them had been too happy about our reconnection, to be honest, though the others had been quieter about it.

"So this is happening again?" Cedric asked at rehearsal, eyebrows raised in an expression that makes it hard to decipher his thoughts. "You two?"

I looked at Cary and he looked at me, a softness to his lips and eyes that made me hot. I shrugged and tried not to smile. "We're exploring our options."

"Bollocks. Cary's done writing decent tunes, I can see it now." Simon shakes his head, but he's not really upset.

"I think . . . I hope the two of you know what you're doing." Cedric reaches out and squeezes my hand. "Because I love you both."

"Sod off, wanker. I told you I don't swing that way." Cary grinned, and he and Cedric got into a childish shoving match that knocked over some of Simon's drums, at which point the grouchy producer shouted at them to settle the fuck down.

Violet's ignored me, but we've been busy in the office, too—filling out questionnaires and insurance paperwork, booking ads, and approving artwork. It's exhilarating and reminds me of all the reasons that pushed me into the world of PR and music. The fast pace, the in-the-moment decisions, thinking on my feet, creating a public image, and helping talent live up to it . . . I love it all. Every minute.

Tuesday morning, the day of my shopping date with Cary, starts later than usual. Sunlight streaks through the window but it's weak, obscured by clouds as they roll and thicken. The news said we might be getting some snow before midnight, and with Christmas days away, it seems like perfect timing.

Cary's supposed to pop by and pick me up around ten. We're going to do some shopping, have an early dinner, maybe see a film if we feel like it. I kind of want to force him to show me more of London at Christmas, not sit in a dark theater, but if the places will be too packed maybe it'll be too much for him. For both of us, really.

Everyone's in the kitchen when I shuffle down, intent on using tea or coffee to shock my system awake. After working a million hours recently it's weird to not have anywhere to be early this morning. My body struggles to understand why we're awake and moving if we don't have to be, and three and a half years of college have proved that caffeine is the only cure for that sort of lethargy.

Dad looks up from his notebook, the pages covered with his looping, indecipherable scrawl and blue ink smeared across the heel of his hand. He's pushed away a plate of half-eaten eggs and ham, a stray potato perched on the edge, ready to leap and leave a greasy smudge on the holiday-red tablecloth.

Eliza has her nose in a book as Winnie natters on about what presents she expects her sister to have bought her and Imogen piles dishes in the sink even though a housekeeper comes in every day except Sundays to tidy up. Living here for even a brief time has made me realize that she takes a lot of pride in the house. *She's* the reason it feels like a home, and even though my father has the kind of money that would allow her to never lift a single finger, she enjoys the ownership.

"Good morning, daughter," my father mumbles, managing to tear his eyes away from his thoughts. Once he gets going on a new book idea there's no stopping him.

"Christina." Imogen turns from the sink with a smile. "Would you like some eggs? I've kept some warm for you."

"That'd be great." I slide into the chair on my father's left, with Eliza to *my* left.

She closes her book and picks up her fork, watching me with interest. "You're up late. No work today?"

"Nothing scheduled. Cary's coming to pick me up in an hour or so. Shopping."

Winnie's mouth drops open. "Cary White's coming *here? To our house?*"

"Well, yeah." I can't help but smile at the amazement on her face. "Do you want to meet him?"

"Are you kidding?" Eliza's the one who answers, her gray eyes shining. "I mean, I'd rather it was Alfie, but maybe next time."

"Alfie?" Her sister screeches. "You are seriously the only girl in the entire world who fancies him."

"Winifred, mind the volume, please." Imogen wrinkles her nose as she slides a warm plate of eggs, bread, potatoes, and ham onto the table. "And be nice to your sister."

Winnie makes a face at me. After her mother turns her back, of course, although the slight smile on my father's lips suggests he doesn't miss it.

I spoon eggs into my mouth, grabbing hungrily for a steaming cup of tea when Imogen sets it down, and listen to the long-forgotten sounds of sibling squabbles around the table. It doesn't make me as sad as expected—maybe because Winnie and Eliza are sisters, not brothers, or maybe because I've been imagining things will be worse than they are—but it's not hard being here, now.

"Do you want to come to the Christmas concert, too, Eliza?"

"Why don't we all go?" My father's deep baritone cuts through the chattering and squeals at the table.

My mouth falls a bit slack. "You want to come see Pursuant?"

"It's Christmas." He meets my gaze. "And this is important to you. We should all be there, as support."

Imogen walks up behind him, putting a hand on his shoulder. "I think it's a lovely idea. Girls?"

They're both grinning, no response needed.

"And Christina, we were hoping you'd want to join us for that little girls' day out tomorrow. Manicures, maybe a facial, and lunch? We plan to finish up a little last-minute shopping, too."

"I could do that in the morning, I think. The guys have early staging at the venue in the evening."

"Wonderful." She beams, convincing me she's excited to spend the day with all three of us. The woman has made it impossible for me to find one single thing to dislike about her.

Baxter noses my hand, looking for handouts. I oblige with a few pieces of potato, scratching him behind the ears and thinking how I've forgotten the magic of having a dog around. My dad's had Baxter since I was a kid and even though he was only my summer dog, I love him.

I glance at my watch and stand up, carrying my dishes to the sink and looking longingly at the pot of tea. One more cup would be magic but I don't think leaving Cary alone with my stepsisters will be a positive experience for anyone.

I rush through a shower, dust on a light layer of makeup, and throw on jeans, a sweater, and my favorite pair of boots before blow-drying my long hair. I leave it in loose waves, since it looks good straight from the shower, and remember to swipe on some red lipstick just as the bell rings downstairs.

No matter how quickly I hustle into my coat, dump necessities into my purse, and clamor for the foyer, there's no hope of beating my stepsisters to the punch. Even Eliza, who has been bookish and soft-spoken, loiters in the entry-way.

My father is nowhere to be found, which I think odd, and Imogen, too, makes herself scarce.

Cary's eyes meet mine over Winnie's bouncing head. They brighten and he smiles, and both girls turn to search for the source of his distraction. "You look smashing, love."

"I took a shower."

"Celebrate small accomplishments, I always say." He turns his velvety eyes on the girls. "And who are these ravishing young ladies?"

275

"These are my stepsisters, Winnie and Eliza." I motion to them in turn and the girls grin and nod. "They're going to come to the Christmas show."

"Great! It's going to be righteous."

"I think it's great you guys are donating all of the proceeds on New Year's Eve," Eliza says, softly.

"Thank you."

Winnie pouts at the attention Eliza's getting, sidling closer to Cary. "Is Cedric seeing anyone?"

"Okay, it's time to go." I move, nudging my date toward the door, unable to stop smiling. "He's way too old for you, Winnie."

He winks. "I would never let anyone I like go out with that rogue, anyway."

"Great, Cary. Make him the bad boy. That'll deter her." I roll my eyes. "I'll see you girls later. Tell Dad to text me if he gets worried. I'm not sure how late we'll be out."

They giggle behind my back as we step out into the blustery morning and I snap my head around, catching Cary making a funny, cross-eyed face over my shoulder. I swat him. "Stop that."

"What? One of us has to be the cool one."

"They actually seem to like me, thank you very much."

He snags my waist, pulling me tight against his chest and breathing deep against my ear. "God, you smell like heaven."

I relax against him, just for a moment, and inhale. "You smell like cinnamon."

We pull apart, my whole body reluctant to do so, already cold and aching for more of his touch. I'm like a drug addict that's been going through withdrawal.

"Well, have you decided where we should go today? The German market is quaint, but I'd hate for you to miss the shopping on Oxford Street."

"Do we have time to do both?"

"I don't have a single thing on my schedule today but you, love. We can do whatever you want." The mischievous glint in his eyes says he can read my mind, and the direction it's going as far as what I really want to do with him today.

We've only just started this thing again. It would be stupid, and dangerous, to fall back into old patterns and easiness too fast. I'm not sure why. Maybe I'm trying to convince myself we should get to know each other again even though it feels as if we never stopped.

"Are you worried about more tabloid stuff?" He squints at me, reading my mind.

I haven't told him how close Violet had come to firing me, but he must have guessed we had a tussle. Things have been tense. "Yes. You don't have to worry about BGG cutting *you* loose, given that you help them earn half their yearly income. I'm expendable."

The look he gives me is affronted. "You are nothing of the sort, and Violet knows it. I knew when we met that you would kick ass at this job, and you do. You're competent, organized, eloquent, and even better than that, sober. She's not going to fire you."

"She hates me," I lament, more bothered by the fact than I want to be.

The tips of his ears go red and he avoids my gaze as we ramble down the street a bit. "She sort of fancies me. It's probably not easy for her, having you here."

There's more left unsaid, I sense—tales of sex, probably more casual on his part than hers, and my stomach gets greasy, queasy, at the thought even though it's not like I've been celibate. It's been four years, and my ex-boyfriend is an international sensation.

I suck in a deep breath, choosing to let the Violet revelation roll off my back. "Okay, where to first? I mean, I kind of want to take a ride on the London Eye but I'm guessing there aren't good shops up there."

"That might be a little *too* touristy for me." He shrugs. "I vote for the market first and Oxford Street later, since the Christmas lights won't be on until nightfall."

"I had no idea you were such a holiday expert, Cary White. Are you a secret Christmas lover?"

He opens the passenger door to a classic black Audi, his ears still flushed as he slams the door and runs around to get behind the wheel. "It's not much of a secret. My mum is kind of a nut about it."

Cary's parents are the most proper British people I've ever met. His father is a banker, his mother stays home and does charity work. She greets her husband every afternoon with a kiss and a cup of tea and they discuss things like world events and books in front of the fireplace after dinner. They're so normal that it's not normal.

"So she took you to do all of these things as a kid?" The London streets slip by outside, the sky darkening with every block we put behind us. "Which was your favorite?"

"As a kid, definitely the Winter Wonderland. It's part of the German markets—like a little carnival. The slapped-together rides nearly gave my father a stroke but mum always let me ride. She even went with me."

"The life of an only child." Even though I don't mean to, my voice is sad. I didn't grow up an only child, but it's been my life over the past four years. It kind of sucks.

"Your stepsisters seem nice," Cary comments, as though reading my mind. "Squealy, but nice."

"They're big fans."

"Yeah, of Ced. What's that about?" he asks, trying his best to sound insulted.

"Oh, don't worry. Eliza actually fancies Alfie."

"Really? How old is she?"

"I don't know. A year younger than me, maybe? Nineteen or twenty? She goes to university." I shake my head, my own wide smile a surprise. "I think I could like them. They're friendly and open and interested in my life. They make my dad happy."

"How's all that going? Your dad."

"I don't know. We had a good talk the other night and we've been trying. It's not as hard in some ways, being around him again, and in others it's harder." I twist my lips, trying to make my thoughts make sense. "Being with him reminds me of Tim, and it hurts. It hurts a lot."

Cary's left hand leaves the stick shift and drifts toward mine. He laces our fingers together and gives me an encouraging squeeze, but doesn't interject. He's always had this way about him of just being with me, on my side, with having to say anything.

It's rare, to find a person who can sense when there isn't a single sentence that could help.

We pass the rest of the drive in companionable silence, Cary directing my attention to points of interest here and there. A love of travel, a touch of wanderlust, has infected me since childhood, and being here in essentially a new place, excitement starts to overtake my emotional quagmire for the first time.

The Winter Wonderland is exactly as promised—quaint little carnival, complete with booths full of cheap prizes, a lit up Ferris wheel and other rides run by suspect looking folks, and stands selling delicious smelling things like currywurst and pastries.

I make Cary buy me a sweet chocolate pretzel before we head to the market. There are so many beautiful handmade items, some more food, woodcarvings, cheap souvenirs that will fall apart in less than a week, and about a million beer steins.

There's not much here that would make a gift worthy of my dad or his family, but I do pick up bags of kettlecorn, some caramel fudge, and three handmade notebooks for my father. He collects them. They lay all over the house, some empty, others with two or three pages scribbled on, others so full they're falling apart. He's a squirrel and inside the notebooks are his hidden nuts—pieces of ideas, sketches of characters, random scenes that don't belong to any specific story, as far as I can tell—and he'll never have enough of them.

"Do you want to eat here?"

"I'm not too hungry. Maybe just grab some currywurst?"

Cary shakes his head, a smile playing on his full lips as he gazes down at me. Our shoulders brush and electricity zaps me. "You eat worse than I do. That's saying something."

"Ugh, I hate it when you get in parental mode," I tease, crossing my eyes at him and guiding us toward the food. Even though Cary's a musician, he's never been a stereotype. Between the two of us, I've always been the broody one, the dreamer, the risk taker. He's the voice of reason, the hand pulling me back from the edge.

Except for the skinny-dipping, but he had ulterior motives for that.

Ten minutes later we've got our paper tubs full of currywurst and settle where we can watch people ice-skate while we eat. "This is freaking delicious." Cary's watching me eat, a funny expression of loss on his face. "What? Am I eating too much of your share?"

"No. It's just . . . I've missed so much. Tell me everything,

Chris. What you've been up to, how you've changed. I feel as though I still know you, but what kind of presumptuous ass does that make me?"

"Oh." I chew and swallow, then pop another bite in my mouth, trying to decide where to start. This day is fun, it's lighthearted, and I don't want to ruin it by talking about anything too deep and depressing. "Well, you knew I was going to TCU. It was an . . . interesting adjustment, going to Texas from the West Coast, but I'm not sorry. I love my sorority and my roommate and I feel like it helped me find the best fit for me, careerwise."

"And you never changed your mind about working in the music industry, or in PR." He gives me a faint smile. "Inspired any other artists to write songs lately?"

It's on the tip of my tongue to ask the question that's been rattling around in my brain for years—whether his songs are about us. I don't. Maybe because there's a smidge of jealously on his face, as though it would kill him to think my pushing him into songwriting hadn't been because I loved him, but because I sensed it would be a good fit and maybe I'd done it for others.

There's a little bit of deliciousness to it, thinking Cary White might be jealous. And more than a little satisfaction, because no matter how he's making me feel today, he's made me feel awful, too.

We toss our trash and amble to the car, our hands finding each other's like they're magnets. I've launched into the story of how Jessica and I met and became friends when

Cary finally scores a parking spot near Oxford Street. We spend hours wandering through the high-end stores, the shops offering local fare that's at least as expensive, if not more, and then have soup and sandwiches as an early dinner as the lights start to turn on up and down the street.

Packages are heavy on my arms as we step out to look, even though Cary's carrying more than half of them. A girl who spent the better half of her dinner staring at us gets up the nerve to come over as we're leaving.

"Are you Cary White?" She slides an envious glance toward me.

"I'm afraid so," Cary replies, quirking a handsome but put-on smile for her.

"Could you sign my iPod for me?"

"Sure." He pulls a Sharpie from his pocket and takes the silver device from her, flipping it over to scrawl his name on the back. The girl can't decide whether she's happier to stare at him or more curious to stare at me. In the end, she looks more than a little put out that he didn't introduce me—she probably thought she'd get a couple hundred pounds for that information.

"Sorry," he murmurs, picking up my hand.

"It's fine." And it is. This is Cary's life, and I realize that we've been talking about me most of the day. "Tell me about your life the last four years. It must have been an amazing ride."

He answers, talking about recording and weeks on tour, his first appearance on a talk show and hitting the charts, as we stroll down a street that's more magical than it was an hour ago. Lanterns bob on wires strung across the blocks and designs made out of strings and strings of Christmas lights enchant the evening, All of the storefronts are lit up and the street ends with a dazzling Christmas tree and a giant sign wishing patrons a Merry Christmas.

"It's been lonely. That's been the biggest surprise." Cary finishes his recap, pulling to the side by the tree. The glow from the colored lights, the huge glass ornaments, illuminates pain in his face, and longing, and something that looks very much like regret.

"Lonely?" I ask, short of breath. It hurts to think of him hurting. Like he's a part of me. The revelation is shocking after months and months of hoping he was hurting as much as I was.

"You know, the different cities, new hotel rooms. The guys are there, and we're real friends. You know that. But everyone else is just along for the ride for one reason or another." He doesn't look away even though raw emotions flicker over his face. "I've missed having someone to talk to the way I could talk to you. And there have been girls who've tried, but . . . they weren't you, love."

My stomach clenches at the thought of all of the dates I've been on with perfectly nice boys, and how many of the potential relationships just died away. I take a step toward Cary, then another, pulled by those magnets again. My palms land on his chest, the beat of his heart coming through his sweater and coat to thud against my skin.

I tilt my face up to see him better, craving those blue eyes like they can save my life. "I haven't met another you, either, for the record."

The honesty is hard. To admit that there hasn't been anyone else makes me ashamed all over again, like the loser who got kicked to the curb and was still waiting there, ready to leap, four years later.

He reaches down and pulls my chin up when I try to look away. The touch of his skin against mine lights a fire in my blood and I lean into it, hungry for more as tears prick my eyes. "No. Chris, *I* don't deserve *you*. I don't deserve this try again, but I will not be the one to muck it up this time. I promise you that."

The world stops moving around us. The smell of cinnamon and boy, of Cary, wraps me like a warm cloak and desire starts to devour me from the inside out. He licks his lips, eyes fastened to my mouth, and no amount of good sense will allow me to put a stop to this before it starts.

His fingertips, calloused from years of strumming one instrument or another, graze my jaw as he fits his lips against mine. My hands curl into his coat, hanging on for dear life as he opens me up again, tongue searching for mine until they connect in a shared gasp that makes me want to cry.

His other hand finds the small of my back, pressing me tight against him, as his mouth moves against mine. He tastes like summer and love, like cinnamon and heartbreak, and like a million other things I want to devour for the rest of my life.

The world comes back with strange flashes of light, and as Cary eases away, his forehead resting against mine, my heart pounds from the kiss, slamming around in my chest so hard it's difficult to breathe and the short puffs of air leaving Cary's lips betray his own reaction to our official reconnection.

The pad of his thumb still strokes my jaw, his gaze locked on mine. "Do you want to get out of here?"

I am desperate for some privacy. Need to get my hands on all of him again, to be able to believe this is real, we're real, and all of this is happening not just in a dream. It doesn't occur to me that he might have another reason for the suggestion until he tips his head to one side and I notice that we've attracted a small audience with cell phone cameras.

I am so fired.

We kiss all the way up to Cary's penthouse apartment, the elevator moving too fast for us to do anything else and agonizingly slow at the same time. It's dark when we crash through his door, except for the lights of London shining from below, and neither one of us wastes time turning them on.

Cary's lips are hot on mine, demanding and sensual as he toys with my tongue, sucks on my lower lip, and delivers a nip here and there. The preview of what's to come has me soaked and shaking with need, hungry for him, before he pushes me backward into his bedroom. It's not like the last time, when I wanted to have him but not feel anything but the physical. We're needy but not rushing, not scared of what happens when it's over.

The bed is huge and soft when I land on it, kicking off my boots and undoing the buckle on Cary's belt as he tears his shirt off, then lifts my sweater and tank top over my head. I take a moment to stare at him—same defined pecs, same washboard abs, and all the pale skin that comes with the English-boy package.

Then my pants are gone, and his shoes and jeans, until hot skin touches hot skin atop the fluffy navy blue covers. His hands roam from my neck over my chest, down to my hip, and his mouth abandons mine to follow the path of his fingers. I fist my hands in his hair, dragging his lips back to mine when I can't stand it another moment.

"God, I have missed you, love. It hurts, I've missed you so much." There's a catch in his throat that stings in mine, and in his eyes hangs a plain truth that neither of us has ever been able to deny.

We need this. Need each other in a way that's unexplainable. Undeniable and terrifying in its intensity, in how it engulfs us, and even in this moment it baffles me all over again that he'd found the strength to walk away.

"I want this, Cary. Immediately, if you don't mind."

"You're so bossy." He leans down, kissing me until I forget my name or what I said, then reaches over to his nightstand and pulls out a condom.

"You like it," I tease back, my eyes on his progress while

waves of heat keep coming from my middle, spilling down my legs and into my breasts like they're anxious for his touch. "Now come here."

Cary hovers over me, knee spreading my thighs, and tangles his hands in my hair as he pushes inside me. We stay there, perfectly still, staring at each other for what might be forever, or might be half a breath.

It's all the time it takes to crack me open, to really, finally admit that this "try again" means everything to me. To blow up the walls, let light and warmth and need back in after four years of darkness, and the pain surprises me. My arms circle his neck and pull him to me as we move together, the feeling of his skin against mine, familiar but still thrilling, applies salve to the raw sensation of being opened up again.

If the other night taught me anything, it's that our bodies have forgotten nothing about pleasing the other. Tonight is no different, and we take our time stumbling up a familiar hill and falling off a well-worn cliff together. Cary's arms are around me, my cheek pressed into his shoulder as we get our breath. I, for one, am a little dumbfounded at how our day of Christmas shopping turned out.

"What's wrong?" His brow furrows, mounds of concern edging out the contentment in his eyes.

"Yes. I just . . . I can't help but feel stupid. You left me and here I am falling back in your bed not once, but twice, without even making you work for it properly."

He laughs, the sound vibrating my palm on his chest as

he swipes a kiss over my temple. When he pulls away to look me in the face, his expression has turned serious. "Oh, love. I should be the one who feels stupid. I am dumb, and I am lucky. I am so goddamn lucky, Christina. No matter what happens next."

"I hope it's more sex," I say, wanting to lighten the mood.

"On that, I think I can oblige," he replies, copying my tone even though his gaze stays earnest as it searches mine. "For as long as you'll let me."

There's something about the way he says it, as though he expects another shoe to drop at some point, seizes my heart with fear. It's almost as though Cary knows something I don't, because right now, lying in his arms again, I have zero fight left in me.

I give him my most serious, appraising expression. "Mr. Big Time, and I'm just getting started. I hope you're up for it."

Chapter
10

The morning of my outing with the Evil Stepmother and her spawn dawns *really* early, as though maybe they're starting to take their roles seriously and are going to demand I bring them tea and biscuits in bed.

Only one eye answers the demand to open, and it obliges with the tiniest possible crack to find Winnie bouncing on the edge of my bed in her pajamas. "What are you doing, psycho? It's the middle of the night."

"No, you got *home* in the middle of the night. It's almost eight, and mum made appointments for nine, so it's time to rise and shine."

"You are not a normal teenager."

She beams. "Thank you."

My eye drops closed again but Winnie doesn't leave. There's no beating her, apparently, so I roll over and stretch, then dump myself out of bed and stumble toward the bathroom.

Water on my face helps with the eye crusties and the murderous urges, though a shower would really be best.

It was like nothing had changed, except everything was different. We have an appreciation for each other now, for the rarity of what we have, that we never would have thought to have four years ago. I felt precious in Cary's arms in a way I never had before and instead of giving me a breakable tint, it made me strong.

"Why are you smiling at yourself like a daft cow?" Winnie frowns from the doorway into the bedroom.

I frown back and shut the door in her face, amused but also in need of some privacy.

"Were you with Cary all night? What happened?" Her muffled voice carries through the wood.

I sigh and lean my head against the door, unable to stop my smile. "Winnie, let me get a shower and get ready and I promise I'll give you a report during our day, okay?"

"Fine," she says, grumpily.

Her feet shuffle on the thick carpet toward the door and I turn on the shower. I have to get ready too fast to let my thoughts linger or drift, thought I've caught sight of my own expression in the mirror a half dozen times and it does indeed look dazed.

My father and Imogen for sure are going to know what's up if I can't get it under control, and fast.

"Good morning!" Imogen sings from the laundry room, shrugging into her coat. "I'm sorry it's so early. I didn't realize you would be out so late."

My gaze snaps up and I search her face for any sign that she's reprimanding me, but find nothing. If anything, she looks genuinely sorry to have woken me after a late night.

"It's okay. I'm not much for sleeping late, anyway." I give her a smile so she knows I'm telling the truth. "You know what dad says—every hour before noon is worth two after."

"I hate that saying," Eliza mumbles as she joins us, hitching a pretty designer purse up on her shoulder.

"Where's your sister?" Imogen blows her dark-blond bangs out of her eyes.

Eliza rolls her eyes. "On the Internet looking at pictures of Cary and Christina making out by the tree on Oxford Street."

I choke on the to-go tea I grabbed from the kitchen, my cheeks as hot as the liquid that sloshes onto my hand. Imogen's gray eyes are huge and full of sparkling laughter as she watches me try to compose myself, and even Eliza seems pleased with being the one to break the gossip first, for once.

"I can see we're going to have an interesting conversation on our outing today."

"Can we please not talk about it until we get to lunch?" I ask, face still aflame as Winnie bounces in from the kitchen. "I don't want anyone to overhear and give the papers anything to talk about."

"Oh, they've already got plenty to talk about but you're right, they don't know who you are." Winnie snatches her coat and puts it on, shoving her cell phone in the pocket before grabbing the door handle. "Are we going or what?"

Imogen shakes her head, following her daughters out into the chilly morning. The sky remains gray, even though we didn't get any snow yesterday like I'd hoped. Maybe today.

"I swear, that girl cannot be British; she's far too demonstrative," Imogen jokes. "She must be a fairy changeling."

"I don't think she's dainty enough to be a fairy."

My joke makes my stepmother laugh, the sound as pleasing and well-designed as everything else that comes out of her. Alfred has the day off and the salon is in the neighborhood, so we decide to walk, despite the low temperature. Cold air fills my lungs, bracing me for the day and all of the questions, but it turns out even Winnie respects my wishes once our feet are soaking in hot, fragrant tubs of water.

"Eliza, what are you studying at Cambridge?" I ask, trying to pull her out of her shell. She reminds me a bit of Tim, because back in the days when we were small, I was more like Winnie.

Tim was quiet. He tended to get shoved into the background, labeled as shy or uninteresting but really I was just an obnoxious attention whore.

Her soft eyes light up. "Literature. I'd like to be a writer like your father. I mean, not *like* your father because I'm not interested in writing bestsellers, really, but you . . . you know what I mean."

"I think so. You want to be a serious writer."

Her gaze flits to mine, unsure as she bites her lower lip. "I don't mean it like that."

"Trust me, I am the last person to defend my father's work as worthy of awards. I should warn you, though, that there's no money in serious writing."

"Well, I suppose I'll just have to marry well. You'll introduce me to Alfie in a few days."

Imogen's eyes fly open wide and she sets down the magazine she was reading in her lap. "Eliza!"

Winnie and I are already lost to giggles, my gyrations making the woman trying to scrub my feet frown in protest. I wave a hand toward Imogen. "It's fine. I won't allow any stepsisters of mine to get involved with musicians, trust me. Besides, bands come and go. If you want to find a rich husband, best go with a physician or someone in finance."

She nods, as though she already had her sights set on someone more practical, anyway.

We finish up our manicures and pedicures and head for lunch at a small but fancy café down the street toward our house. It's a tearoom of sorts, which delights me to no end, and we let Imogen order an array of teas and sandwiches and pastries from the pretty white menus on the table.

Once the waitress is gone and Winnie gives the room a not-so-subtle once-over for anyone who might be listening in, she turns her accusing gaze on me. "Okay, Christina, spill. Are you and Cary dating?"

I pick at the tablecloth, but there's a smile in my heart that won't stay off my face. "*Dating* is a weird word."

It is, because dating is something people do to get to know each other. To decide whether they want to know each other better, to go to bed together, to meet each other's families and go on holiday, but Cary and I don't need to go through any of that.

Except maybe, as he pointed out, we do. Maybe we have been. We're not strangers, but we're also not the same people who fell in love at the beach four years ago.

"Why?" Winnie asks, ready with her next eighteen questions.

"I don't know. Probably because we had a summer romance when we were kids." The phrase *we were in love before* dances on the tip of my tongue. I don't say it because that truth is for me. I've held on to it so tight for the past four years; letting go of it isn't something I'm ready to do.

"Good thing we've got a long lunch, because I have a feeling this is a bang-up story." Eliza's interested now, bored of our talk of majors and careers and husbands. It's fun to see her loosen up, even if it is at the prospect of my bared soul.

Imogen doesn't say anything, and the curious but not surprised expression on her pretty face makes me positive my father already filled her in on the events of my last summer in England. Maybe it's creepy, to imagine them going to bed and discussing their kids' lives, but my heart swells at the idea that I'm one of those kids. That I have been, even during the years we've been separated.

"There's nothing too interesting to tell," I start, drawing it out for suspense. The whole thing is so much easier to talk about now that Cary's back in my life. "We met in Cornwall and we just clicked. We spent all our time together—the band was already playing gigs, which is how I know them so well. I did a lot of work promoting them even then, at the restaurant where I worked and other local places."

"So, what happened?" Winnie's eyes are huge, her tea getting cold on the table in front of her.

I shrug. "I'm sorry to be the bearer of bad news, but summer romances are defined by the season they're named for, and they usually only last as long. People go home, back to their lives, drift apart."

It's not what happened with us, not truly, and the sharp way Imogen's watching me suggests she knows that. There's no way I'm coughing up all the grisly details about being left in the dust and letting them judge me for giving him another chance so readily. Nothing any of them has said or done suggests they would do any such thing, which leaves me with only one conclusion—*I'm* judging me for letting Cary back into my life with so little regard for my own well-being.

"That's so sad." Winnie's voice quiets to a previously unheard level. Then she brightens. "But, like, *destiny* brought you back together. The band got famous, you got a job at BGG, they sent you to London. Gosh. It really is like a movie or something."

Imogen's hand covers mine, surprising me. "I'm glad that you've gotten some closure as far as that relationship that obviously played such a role in your life, but personally, my favorite thing about this whole destiny thing is that it brought you into our lives for the first time."

"Me, too," Eliza slips in, her cheeks red. "I wish you could stay longer."

Now that I've gotten to know them, that my father has admitted his mistakes and promised that he wants me to be a part of his life, I can't imagine at least not giving this whole expanded family thing a go. "I'm sure we'll be making plans to visit much more often now that we've gotten acquainted."

That makes them all happy, and the sandwiches and cakes arrive with more tea. We spend the rest of the afternoon in giggles and wide eyes, and arrive home just as the first snowflakes start to drift from the thickening evening clouds.

My father's in the living room with Baxter, staring at a roaring fire that's pouring so much heat into the room he must have started it awhile ago, and he turns with a happy smile at the sight of the four of us together. They drop their packages and Winnie runs to the restroom. Imogen gathers the bags and goes to tuck them away while Eliza disappears without telling us where she's headed.

"Did you have a good day, bud?"

"I did. They're lovely girls, Dad. I'm not sure it would have been possible to hate them no matter how hard I tried."

"They are. *You* are a lovely girl, too, which is why I knew you would all get on." He kisses the top of my head, an arm tight around my shoulder. "It's my fault, things getting this far gone. I'm glad you decided not to punish them for my foul-ups, because you'd all miss out on some great friendships, I think."

Eliza slips back into the room, a DVD clutched between her fingers. My gaze falls on the familiar case, nostalgia and grief welling up like a fountain.

"Your dad said it was your favorite."

It's a Wonderful Life had been my brother's favorite, and we'd watched it every holiday for that reason. I used to pretend it bored me to tears but really, it had become my favorite, too.

"It's a great film," I manage to choke out.

"Do you want to watch it?"

I nod, and Imogen pops in to ask if anyone wants cocoa before we get started. My mind wanders to what Imogen said in the tearoom, thinking perhaps there's some truth to it.

If some unseen force or hand guided me back to England this holiday, or if my path had always been meant to wind back here, maybe it's not for Cary at all. Or at least, not *just* for him.

So much of the woman I've become has been formed out of loss. Cary left me without a word. Tim disappeared, again without a good-bye. He never knew about the epilepsy. The seizures had always been small, they said. Missing time, nothing more. Then one day he'd been driving, had his first grand mal, and that was it.

My father's abandonment had been the last straw in a very, very flimsy house that fell and left me with nothing but a soul stripped bare to the wind.

I built those walls again, high and tight, and on them I

painted smiling faces that promised the world and all of my new friends at school that Christina Lake was a happy girl. She's had some hardships but she's fine. Not fucked up at all, nope, not her.

It had all been a lie, and the worst part is until I faced them—Cary and my dad—I hadn't even been able to face the truth of how they'd broken me. Now that all of us are struggling toward honesty and maybe, in time, true forgiveness, it seems possible that I could put all the pieces of me back together again after all.

Possible. I think I like that word.

Imogen returns with her hands full of steaming mugs and as we settle around the television, George Bailey's life just beginning on the screen, a warmth fills the room that has nothing to do with the roaring fire or mugs of hot chocolate.

Chapter

11

As sure as I'd been the other night about my feelings for Cary, part of me struggled on the way home to shake the fear that I would regret it. After spending the next several days in his unbelievably comfortable penthouse apartment, most of those worries are wiped away.

Cary lies on his side, facing me, and smiles. "I think we're going to have to leave the house later."

I heave a theatrical, pouty sigh. "I know. You guys have sound check."

"I thought maybe we could grab something to eat before we go. Otherwise it's going to be stale craft services for the next six or seven hours."

"Hmm." I reach out a hand and rest it on his bare hip, letting my fingers dangle teasingly. "How much time do you suppose we need for eating dinner?"

It's about two in the afternoon, I think. I came over

around nine, as early as I could reasonably leave my dad's, and we've been in bed, dozing off between hours of not being able to keep our hands off each other. This already might be one of the best days of my life, even if it doesn't include watching a band I've worked with pull off an amazing interview or put on a dynamite show, which have been the things to make me happy most often over the past couple of years.

His body responds to my soft touch and he eases closer, dipping his lips to mine. They're soft, plying as he opens me wide and I melt into him, our skin already hot when it meets. Our kiss deepens on instinct, through practice, and I don't know how I've managed to survive so long without it. He's teasing me, going slowly and pulling away at the exact moment he knows I want him to press harder, so I hook a leg over him and roll until I'm in control.

I give him a wicked grin and reach for the condoms on the nightstand before taking care of business, and getting him right where I want him.

"I have to say, there are some things about grown-up Christina I rather fancy," he murmurs, hands tight on my thighs.

"Is that right?" I start to move, relishing the way his eyes roll back in his head, the way his teeth sneak out to bite his lip while he struggles for self-control. "Such as?"

"Your confidence. Not that you didn't have it before, but this girl? Knows she's sexy."

I bend over, moving against him while we kiss, our

tongues playing lazily for as long as our bodies will accept the slower pace. His hands move higher, one on my breast and one in between my legs, my palms flat against his chest as I give in to the pleasure, to the emotions wrangling for prominence as the room falls away to darkness that makes me forget everything but the way we feel.

When the world comes back I'm clinging to his sweaty chest and his muscles are flexed as he holds me tight. His gaze sweeps my face, hungry and sort of enchanted. We collapse together, a tangle of slick limbs and heaving torsos, twisted hair and grinning faces.

"I think we might want to call Guinness. This must be some kind of record."

Cary tucks me close against him, his chin resting on top of my head. "*Hmm.* Maybe we should wait a day or two, just to really make sure we've got it locked up."

I get a case of the giggles, pressing a kiss to his shoulder before making a run for the bathroom. He's getting dressed when I emerge, and as much as I don't want to, I follow suit. We've got to be at the Grouse in a few hours. We shouldn't be late, especially when David still acts like the two of us being happy together is some kind of affront to the world at large. There's also Violet, who's still looking for any excuse to fire me even after the Dallas office e-mailed to tell me not to worry about the tabloids. And cc'd her.

The first thought worries me more than the second, and I frown as my sweater comes down over my head. "Why does David hate me so much?"

"What? He doesn't."

It's hard to tell, since Cary's got his toothbrush in his mouth, but the answer comes awfully quick. I roll my eyes and pull on my jeans and boots, choosing not to argue at the moment. He probably doesn't want me to think that his friends don't like me, which is silly considering that David never made a secret of thinking I was nothing more than something that would hold them all back once they got their shot.

I put paste on the second toothbrush and watch us in the mirror, letting Cary think he's making me feel better by sweeping the whole oddity under the rug. Some people just don't get on with other people, I suppose, and it's nothing to spend too much time fretting over.

David is the farthest thing from my mind as we throw on coats and take a car service to a private restaurant near the Grouse. Our dinner is quiet and expensive, and Cary pays again. No one bothers us. We're trapped in a bubble that distorts reality, one that makes the idea of problems more of a concept. Life can't go on this uninterrupted and lovely for very long. I'm not naive enough to think it can but what's the harm in encouraging it to last as long as possible?

That thought arrives the same time as the bread pudding we're sharing for dessert, and it spikes a strange kind of fear in my middle. I have the strangest feeling there's not a natural end to our blissful bubble, but something sinister waiting to burst it, lurking just out of my line of sight.

It's weird, but I have the feeling that if I opened my

eyes long enough, it would be easy enough to see what's waiting for us.

"What are you thinking about?"

"I don't know. Just . . . I'm scared, I guess. Things are so good."

Fear flickers in his blue eyes before he gives me a smile that's meant to be reassuring but doesn't quite make it. "You are such a worrier, love."

"Maybe. But our lives are still so different. What's really changed from four years ago?" The question I don't ask, but the one he hears anyway, is what's going to stop him from deciding his life would be simpler without me? Again?

It surprises me that somehow, through Cary and my father both reentering my life, I've realized that even though things haven't been perfect, I built a life on my own. I have Jessica. I have my mother and my sorority sisters and my career.

My world is brighter, better with them in it, but it's made me see that it wasn't empty before. Will I have to start all over if I lose them again?

"I'm not going anywhere, that's what's different. I'm not scared, Chris, at least not of this amazing thing you and I have. I'm scared of living without it." Despite his words, he *is* scared. It's all over his face, in the desperate edge to his tone. "No matter what happens this time, I'm not running from you."

Before I can get him to clarify what he means by *this time*, my cell phone dings with a message from Cedric.

Sound check starts in fifteen. Let Cary put his willy away and get your asses over here.

I snort. "We'd better get going. The guys are already there."

Cary nods, pressing his lips into a line that makes him look older than twenty-one. But then he helps me into my coat, tucks my arm through his, leans in to take a deep breath against the soft skin underneath my ear, and everything is back to good.

The guys are waiting on the small, worn wooden stage, tuning their instruments and working with techs to insert the right in-ear microphones and arrange the speakers. Cary steps away from me with a kiss on the cheek, goes through some laughing, shoving, punch on the arm ritual with his friends, and slings his guitar over his shoulder. Seeing him like this, onstage, is like watching a dolphin glide through the water. He's meant to be here, to sing and entertain and tuck his hair behind his ear while he concentrates on serenading the masses with his gorgeous music. There's a beauty about him that takes my breath away. It's a gift, one I would never ask him to give up or put away no matter how much the life puts me off.

The rehearsal and sound check drone on, the same snippets of songs, same riffs, being played over and over again until they sound right. I pull a book out of my messenger bag and read, getting through the better part of two hundred pages before I realize the room has gone silent and look up to find them packing things away for the night.

"You ready?" Cary uses a towel to wipe sweat off his forehead, his thin T-shirt clinging to his damp frame in a way that makes me want to rip it off him.

What is wrong with me? We had sex like, four times today already.

It's the light inside his eyes, under his skin, in his smile, present so much more here tonight than any other place we've been together. But my eyes are heavy, my body desperately needs a wash, and there's something fragile about him tonight, ever since dinner. Something fragile about us.

Cary drives me home, kisses me good night, and promises to see me for Christmas Eve. His parents have gone on holiday with his mother's family, so my father insisted we invite him. The stepsisters were ecstatic, although they'd still rather the whole band be popping by as well.

I slam the door and watch him drive away, feeling like some strange apparition on the porch. Snowflakes drift down, illuminated by the streetlamps and muffling the sounds of the world. The neighboring homes have the same tasteful decorations as my father's, with strings of different-colored lights lending a festive mood to the evening that can't quite soothe my nerves. I tell myself not to give in to the worry thickening in my blood. That it doesn't have to be too good to be true.

Whatever's bothering me, whatever's on his mind, we'll figure it out together. We just have to.

Everything about Christmas Eve goes off without a hitch, largely due to Imogen's tireless efforts. It's as though she's trying to win some kind of award for a magazine. Or maybe she has some inside knowledge that Saint Peter is really impressed by excellent holiday meals and is angling for a smooth path through the pearly gates.

The only thing that's strange is how my father and Cary keep eyeing each other. Like each is trying to guess the next move in a game that no one is playing. It's especially odd given that they've both encouraged me to mend fences with the other . . . well, Cary more than my dad. But now they act like being in the same room together is some form of silent torture.

Or like they know something I don't.

I push away my lingering unease before it can ruin my Christmas.

Now we're in the living room with the fire roaring again, and we're all too full of guinea fowl and pudding to talk, never mind use our brains for things like thinking. I feel heavy all over, as though my body has sunk so deep into the sectional that it's being absorbed.

"How about a game? We could play cards. Or something else." Imogen remains upbeat, but she's alone in that feat.

Eliza waves a listless hand, too tired to even open the book that rests on the end table at her side. Winnie's curled up in a recliner, her glassy gaze on *Miracle on 34th Street* as it flickers across the big screen. My father's watching, too, aside from the glances he keeps sneaking at Cary and me, snuggled together against the other arm of the couch.

"So, Cary, Gerard tells me that you're very close to your family. Where are they tonight?" Imogen picks up her needlepoint and settles a pair of reading glasses onto her nose.

"My mum's family takes a Christmas holiday every five years. Somewhere warm, usually—they're in Bali right now. I typically go, but when the double opportunity of the Christmas concert and then the telethon came up, the band couldn't say no."

"I think it's lovely. Especially that you chose the C.U.R.E. Epilepsy foundation. Was that your idea?"

His cheeks go pink. "It was, yes. I didn't know Chris would be here, but she . . . the family . . . they've never been far from my thoughts."

"That's lovely of you, dear." Imogen smiles gently, seemingly aware of his discomfort at being put on the spot. "So many people forget to give back."

My father grunts. "I've always been good about it, myself, but since I married Imogen there have been years we've given away more than we've kept."

"And still had more than enough to go around," she reminds him gently.

Dad *is* socially conscious, and has always been good about charity donations. He's also financially savvy, so the fact that donating it means not having to pay taxes on it probably plays into his level of generosity, too.

"I grew up without wanting anything but honestly, the

amount of money we make now is insane. There's no way I could spend it, not if I lived to be two hundred. Why stuff it in my mattress when it could be doing good?" Cary looks down at his hands, avoiding the intense gaze my father has him pinned with, and again it seems as though the two of them know something the rest of us don't.

I cuddle closer to him, reaching for his hand and sighing when his fingers close around mine. Imogen smiles faintly and my father looks back to the television.

"What kind of game did you have in mind, Mrs. Lake?" Cary asks, looking a bit restless. Or perhaps tired of being the one answering all of the questions.

She brightens. "Oh, I don't know, dear. Cards? Pinochle?"

"I think that sounds like fun." He squeezes my hand, looking down into my face. "Be my partner?"

"Duh," I reply, even though I have my doubts about being able to get off the couch.

"I'll play with you, Mom," Eliza volunteers. "That'll save you twenty minutes of trying to cajole Gerard into it."

"I appreciate that, Eliza. Winnie and I will just finish the movie."

"We'll try to pretend we don't hear the snores." Imogen puts her knitting aside and gets to her feet, pausing on her way to the china hutch to put her arms around my father's neck and press a kiss to his cheek.

It's weird, being happy that my dad found someone nice and devoted. Sort of like a betrayal of my mother, but it's not,

309

really. The two of them were ill suited, not built to last. No way they would have survived Tim's death, even if they had lasted that long.

Cary stands up and reaches back for me, and I struggle free from the couch's clutches. We follow Imogen and Eliza into the dining room, where my stepsister switches on some Christmas music and Imogen deals the cards. It's cozy, with the low hum of the music and the *swish* of the cards interspersed with some trash talk across the table. The sound of my father's impressive snores makes its way across the threshold and makes us all laugh, and after a couple of rounds of cards we cut the pies. Winnie and Dad join us in the kitchen and all I can think is how easy this is. How simple it would be to include Cary in this world—how simple it has been for me to slip into this household.

When I found out I was going to spend the holiday away from my mom, nothing could have convinced me that I'd be sitting here, surrounded by strangers and the estranged, and feel perfectly at home.

Chapter 12

I only get to spend a few hours of Christmas morning with my dad and his family before it's time to run out the door to the Grouse. The concert doesn't start until seven, but I have to be there by noon in order to make sure all of the equipment, craft services, and interview rooms are set up. I check the list of complimentary tickets against the ones left at the box office to make sure no one was forgotten. The leadership from the nonprofit group that's going to be handling the distribution of gifts and money, this year and next, arrives, and I escort them to their green room and go over their schedules with them.

There isn't much time to pause but when there is, all I can think about is how much I love this life. My job. Working with talent, being the person pulling the strings to a perfect production from behind the scenes . . . if Cary was born to be onstage, I was born to do this, and it feels pretty damn amazing to be trusted to do it at my age and with my still limited experience.

By the time Cary and the guys show up at five, it doesn't seem as though it could possibly be two hours until showtime. I get them settled, make sure they don't need anything, and keep running around like a chicken without a head until everyone has fulfilled their pre-show obligations and the guys are all present and accounted for, ready to go on after the opening act. This is a small venue, a private show for donors and families with buckets of money, and not the massive public event the concert will be at the O2 next week.

Just thinking about running a show at one of the biggest venues in the world thrills me, even if Violet will be back to help.

The guys are great, as usual—all of them really came through, and the pregame interviews were smart and sweet, just funny enough and with drops of good cheer that will have people snatching up Pursuant records when the new one drops next month.

I've just herded them to their final wardrobe check when Winnie sprints to my side, throwing her arms around my neck. She's wearing a sequined red top, black leggings, and flats—sparkling from head to toe. "Oh my Lord, Christina, you're sweaty. But this is seriously the most amazing thing that has ever happened to me in my entire life. Thank you, thank you, thank you!"

I pry her arms off my neck so I can breathe. "You're welcome. And you look fabulous, by the way."

"Of course I do." She peers around me, fluffing her hair as she looks for the guys. "Where's the band?"

"They're ready to go on." I hide my smile and accept a side hug from my dad. "Hey. I'm glad you came."

"Thank you for leaving the tickets. They're in the third row. We just wanted to come say hi," Imogen says, flushed and wild-eyed. Apparently she's at least 10 percent as excited as Winnie.

Eliza adds a thank-you, her eyes wide as she takes it all in.

"You've been busy, bud? You are sort of damp." My dad wrinkles his nose in mock seriousness. *"Ew."*

"Whatever. I *have* been busy, as it happens. If this was a regular road show there would be even more to do, but a one-off isn't so bad."

He hands me a to-go cup of tea. "Eliza's idea, but we thought it was a good one. We'll see you after, yeah?"

I nod and shoo them off, smiling as the scent of the lemon and honey helps unwind the knots in the back of my neck and between my shoulders. A few minutes later the opening act, an up-and-coming teenage girl with a folksy voice, steps onstage with her acoustic guitar. Polite applause fills the small venue and she performs her steady, sweet songs to increasing delight.

Then the lights go down, the first strains of Pursuant's

opening number fill the air, and I collapse into a chair in the green room.

I stay there for the first three-quarters of the set, enjoying my tea and watching the concert on the monitor. It feels so amazingly good to sit down and let my mind blank out for a little bit. I'm ready for relaxing and a few celebratory drinks after this thing is over.

The last set begins and I drain the rest of my tea, drop it in the receptacle, and wander out to stand in the wings. There's no comparing the sound on the monitors to the real thing; from the sidelines I can see the passion in their eyes, the mischievous smiles on their faces, the sweat dropping onto their instruments from their shaggy hair. They sound fantastic, everything coming together in the best way possible for the last song on the set list. My heart swells with pride—for them, for me, for how far all of us have come, apart and together.

The guys run off the stage, panting and chugging bottles of water in the opposite wing as the crowd screams and claps in the darkness, begging for just a couple more songs. Pursuant waits a couple of minutes and then reemerges and starts one of their earlier and biggest hits.

Cary pauses after two songs, putting the microphone back on it's stand and running his fingers through his damp hair as he waits for the crowd to quiet. When they do, he winks and then has to repeat the entire process.

A wry smile twists my lips. My guy, the lady-killer.

"First off, we just want to thank you all again for coming

out and sharing part of your Christmas with us. It means a lot, and it means even more to all of the kids who, because of your generosity, will have better quality holidays in the years to come. You're lovely!" The audience applauds, rapt. "You might have heard that we have a new album coming out!" Another pause, more clapping. "We're going to end the night with what will be our first single, and I'd like to dedicate the song to the very special girl who inspired it. She knows who she is."

He winks a second time amid disappointed groans from the people who obviously expected to be let in on our little secret, but everyone stops to listen as they break into the song that stopped my heart that first day in the studio, and again at the radio station.

The refrain, as haunting and beautiful as ever, rings in my ears:

I never told you about the mistake I made
But you could never have forgiven me, anyway.
I walked away, I couldn't stay
Now you're my secret mistake.

It brings back so many memories, and with them that strange, increasingly persistent idea that I still don't know the whole story about that summer. The song makes it sound like a whole lot more than a stupid kid scared off by the intensity of his own feelings.

But then the show is over and Cary's stinky, sweaty

arms are around me. He's heavy, as though he left every last ounce of energy out on the stage and now needs me to hold him up. I swat him away, wrinkling my nose.

"Gross. They have showers here, you know."

"Are you offering to scrub me down?"

I laugh, happiness flooding me. My body is like an overfilled balloon, full of light and air and maybe something that doesn't even have a word to describe it. Cary's eyes sparkle with the same incredulous thrill fizzing in my blood and he leans down, kissing me like the entire band, half the crew, and a bunch of people who with working cell phones aren't watching.

By the time he pulls away most people are talking, pretending not to see us, but the band is still gathered. They're swigging more water, dissecting what they think went well, what they think can be improved upon, and generally celebrating a super job.

"Hey, White, were you thinking we'd all do something after the telethon on New Year's Eve or what?" Alfie asks the question, his pale cheeks bright spots of color, like a Raggedy Andy doll. "I've got to see about an invitation for a lady friend, if so."

"Like he cares if you bring a girl. Look at the dolt. He barely knows anyone else is in the room." Simon rolls his eyes, using a towel to wipe his face for the sixth time since they exited the stage.

Cary turns back to me. He leaves a little space between us, seeming to realize that he does actually smell, but keeps his

316

hands on my biceps. "What do you say, love? Want to spend New Year's Eve with me and this lot?"

I'd rather spend it with just the two of us, but given he's still going to be onstage when the clock strikes twelve, that seems a bit unlikely. "You're there, I'm there."

"Righto." He turns back to his friends. "We're in."

"Just fucking stop." David's gaze is on fire, impatience and rage emanating from every pore in his body as he stares at Cary, totally ignoring me. "Cut this bullshit, man."

"David, don't." Cary's teeth are clenched, his face white. "Let it go. This isn't the same fight it was four years ago."

Confusion rips through me, stumbling on the heels of fear and dread so potent I taste metal on my tongue. Realize I've bitten my cheek. The look on Cary's face does nothing to reassure me, because he's terrified. Sick. Not looking at me, but staring back at his second guitarist with a desperation that takes my breath away.

"It *is* the same fight. You have been a complete tool ever since she walked into that studio the other day, and I'm not having it. We have a good thing going. A new album coming out and plenty of money in the bank. We can't have you chucking it all to follow her home this time, either."

This time?

"Cary, what's he talking about?" My blood feels cold, my lips frozen, as though trying to protect me from what's coming.

He looks at me then, sorrow and regret wrestling with fear on his face. "Chris, I—"

317

"You still haven't told her? God, you really are such a tosser." He steps toward us, threatening enough that I take a step or two back.

It doesn't take long to realize he's planning a verbal attack, not another kind.

"Cary only started seeing you all those years ago because your father paid him off, and promised to get us a meeting with a decent label besides. Twisted, right? He made you think he was in love and all of that to make sure he got a leg up and a fat wallet but then the summer was over, and so were you." He crosses his arms. "I'm guessing that answers a lot of your questions."

Pain tears me in half. My heart feels as though it's in tatters and the world is on mute. My ears are ringing with the silence because, based on the shamed expression on Cary's face, David's words must be true.

The second guitarist's features twist with perverse pleasure, a power-drenched smile on his thin lips. "Violet says you're untouchable because you probably blew half of corporate back in the States, but if you don't sod off and leave this band be after New Year's, we'll find out whether my happiness or your skills as a publicist mean more to this label."

He turns and stalks away, each and every word leaving a hole in me the size of a grapefruit. I turn a gaze on Cary, who knows better than to touch me right now. He stands quietly within arms reach, his expression a mixture of devastation and guilt that leaves me cold from the inside out.

"You went out with me for money? To get you the fame you knew I would hate? Took my virginity for cash? What kind of person are you?" My words gets softer, fade with each syllable until I wonder if he can even hear me. Wonder if it even matters. "How could you lie to me like this?"

"Chris, wait. It's . . . it's not like he says, not really—"

"Save it. I'm done listening to the freaking bollocks that spills out of your mouth. Just leave me alone unless you have a PR-related crisis." I spin around and run smack into my father. My stepsisters are staring, their jaws slack, and Imogen's soft features are painted with horror.

The look on my dad's face, stuck somewhere between panic and regret, tells me everything I need to know.

"*Et tu,* Father?" I whisper before shouldering past him.

My feet get me the hell out of this shitty, backwoods theater, headed for the tube station down the street when I realize I don't have a way to get home. Alfred brought me this morning, but then he went home and gathered the girls and my father. It's freezing, the snow having piled up a couple of inches and soaking into my tights. I'd worn a dress and flats, thinking I'd be inside the whole time.

"Need a ride?" Eliza's soft voice brushes my shoulders.

"Yes."

All of the strength bleeds out of me in a sob that feels as though it tears something loose. Cary lied to me—from the very beginning, but the second betrayal stings so much more.

What's in it for him now?

319

I shake off the question.

It doesn't matter. I don't care.

Her arm goes around my shoulder and she hugs me tight for a second, then leads me around to the front of the building. I don't have my coat and shivers set in, but they only have a little to do with the cold.

My stepsister hands over her hat and scarf, insisting when I refuse. "Come on. You're snookered, and my car's a couple blocks away. The last thing we need is someone to recognize you from the websites."

She's right. I jam the hat on and wind the scarf so it covers my mouth and jaw. "Why do you have your car?"

"I was going out afterward." She holds up a hand. "It's fine. I don't mind taking you home."

"Can we maybe take a drive first? I don't want to go back there until my dad's asleep."

"Sure. I've even got a bag in my trunk with spare clothes in it." She shrugs at my questioning look. "I'm kind of messy and it drives my mother nuts, so I've been hiding dirty laundry and the fact that I didn't fold anything before coming home from school."

Her car is a dark-blue mini thing that vaguely resembles a vehicle but it warms up fast. I hold my hands in front of the heat, hot tears leaking down my cheeks. I can't make sense of anything. Can't face the truth, can't deny that the past week has been a worthless, heartbreaking lie.

"Do you fancy a beer?"

"Hmm?"

320

"I was thinking that you haven't really gotten to see much of London, and one of my favorite pubs is right on the river near the London Bridge." She pauses. "Or we can just walk along the river if you prefer."

"Beer sounds fine."

She drives in silence, leaving me to my thoughts and the pretty holiday view outside the window. The restaurant is closed when we get there—most things are closed, actually, since it's pretty late on Christmas night—but there's a place called The Scoop that has tables and chairs by the river. We use towels from Eliza's trunk to clear the snow, then sit down on them, shivering even wrapped in layers of clothes.

"It's usually bustling here—lots of markets and food. You should really come back in a couple of days."

The disappointment in her voice tugs at my conscience and I give her a smile, nodding toward the London Bridge, all lit up. "It's very beautiful. And peaceful, this way."

Tears burn the back of my throat and pool in my eyes, blurring the beauty of the strange country. I look away, but Eliza reaches over, her gloved fingers grasping mine.

"I'm sorry that happened to you back there," Eliza starts. "Total bollocks."

"Thanks," I whisper, hugging myself in an attempt to hold it together. "I should have known."

We sit for a long time, not moving, just watching the water. While Winnie's energy and light have made me love her, Eliza's ability—and willingness—to sit with me in freezing-cold silence endears her to me just as much. The idea of getting up, of going home, feels like admitting what happened at the event actually happened. Right now I still feel as though I could walk backward and change it all.

"Christina?"

"Hmm?"

"I know this is none of my business, and I don't know you that well, but . . . it's just that there's no way Cary is this good a liar. The way he looks at you, he's never content unless he's with you or making plans to be with you. He doesn't care if the wankers in the press know it, either. He loves you so much he can barely figure out how to handle it. So, I don't know what happened four years ago or what's happened since, or whether you should forgive him. I just thought you should know."

Her words have the stink of truth on them, but my damaged, ravaged soul isn't ready to hear it. I don't say anything, my gaze trained on the city's oldest bridge, letting my heart harden again in all the old places.

Chapter
13

Bud, would you please open the door. We need to talk about this."

The music blaring from my headphones can't quite block out his voice. Nothing can stop Cary's daily text messages. They're not frequent enough to be annoying, just once in the morning, once at night, always the same thing. There's one sitting on my phone now, and I click it to make it go away and *I'm sorry. I want to explain, if you'll let me. I miss you* disappears.

There's another text, from Jessica, too.

Are you still in bed? You have to go talk to him. This is crazy!!!!!!!!!!!!!

I flick it away, too, way too exhausted to deal with so many exclamation points. I tried to go back to the inn but they don't have any rooms, and neither did the other three hotels near the O2 that I called on our way home the other night. It's frustrating, being stuck in here like a pouting teenager, but it's only a couple more days and I can get back to the States and my real life.

My father's footsteps shuffle away, replaced by quiet padding and an insistent scratch. I open the door just wide enough to admit Baxter, letting him jump up on the bed even though his feet are muddy again. I scratch his belly and he smells like the outdoors so I bury my face in his scruff to stop my mind from trying to make me think about all of the things I'd rather forget.

I *want* to talk to my father, and Cary, or maybe even David because there's pieces of this story that are still missing, truths only they can supply but the idea of facing any of them makes me want to disappear.

There's another knock about an hour later, and I ignore that one, too.

"It's just me," Eliza's voice promises. "I come bearing food."

My stomach rumbles at the mention of breakfast, even though it's nearly lunchtime, and I swing open the door to find the older of my stepsisters with a tray of scones and tea. "You're a lifesaver."

She steps past me when I try to take the tray, sliding it onto my desk and going over to the dresser to pop a DVD into the player. I raise an eyebrow as she flops belly first onto the mussed bed.

I close the door and try to decide whether to argue with her, but it's not worth it when there are scones in the vicinity.

The first one I grab is cinnamon, and the smell of it reminds me of Cary with such force that I drop it into the trash like it's on fire.

"You have got to scrub these sheets. It smells like dirty body and dog." Eliza wrinkles her nose, but pinches off a corner of her pastry for Baxter, anyway.

"I know. I'm wallowing. Give me a break." The opening credits to what looks like a cheesy movie pop up on the television. "What's that?"

"*Another Cinderella Story.* The superior of the Cinderella Stories. Ask anyone. It's a widely known fact."

"The one with Selena Gomez?" My tone conveys my dubiousness. "Really?"

"Really. Shut up and watch. You need a distraction, and so do I. No more job, and university doesn't resume for another couple of weeks. It's weird living at home again after being away."

"Agreed." I settle next to her with a plate of strawberry scones, a cup of tea balanced on my knee, surprised to find myself grateful for the company. Jessica and I have been texting this whole mess to death, but there's nothing to solve and through the phone just isn't the same.

The pastry settles in my belly as the first part of the movie plays—Selena Gomez is a maid-stepdaughter that lives in the crappiest room in the house, but she goes to a dance and seduces a real-life pop star, of course in disguise. We're to the point where he's using her mp3 player in lieu of a glass slipper when Winnie hops through the door, not bothering to knock, reminding me too late that I didn't lock the door. She plops between us on the bed, knocking my empty dishes to the floor. "Hey, what are you watching on the telly?"

"Another Cinderella Story?"

"Ugh, and Eliza tried to tell you it's the best, right? The third one is obviously better. The guy in that one is hot. And British."

"I guess we'll just have to watch both so she can be the tie breaker."

I shake my head, wondering how I got involved in this and how on earth I'm going to get out of watching another one of these movies today.

The movie plays for another forty-five minutes, through her real identity being revealed, him liking her anyway, then some horrible bitch from her school trying to break them up. It's the most ridiculous thing in the world, but it almost makes me cry. What if that's what's going on with Cary?

"Look, Christina." Winnie snaps her fingers, earning my attention. "You have got to stop moping. Take a shower. Get dressed and go face this shite head on. Take Cary back or don't, but do something instead of sitting here doing Sweet Fanny Adams."

"What?" Even I've never heard that one.

She waves her hand. "The point is, I've always wanted an older sister to look up to, and you're really disappointing me."

"Hey, sitting right here," Eliza mutters, glaring at her younger sister.

"I mean, Eliza's good for books and academic and

326

moral-type stuff, but you're different. You're brave and exciting and you have, like, cool friends. I want to be like *that* Christina. This one smells funny."

"Again, I am sitting right here, and my friends are plenty cool." Eliza blows her bangs out of her face. "That said, she's not wrong. This isn't you, hiding in your room. You've got to face it."

"I was over it, you know. Over *him*. Moved on. Accepted I'd never know what happened. Then I came here and he lied right to my face about why we didn't last."

"Did he?"

Eliza's question is smart. She must have been giving this whole situation quite a bit of thought, because she's come up with a question I can't answer. Just because Cary took money to befriend me, even though my dad promised him everything he ever wanted if he'd stop me from going home, it still doesn't explain why he left the way he did, without so much as a good-bye.

It doesn't explain why he would leave that note, the one telling me I'm the one, or why all of his lyrics talk about regret. Maybe he did leave that way because he was scared of what was between us, just not for the reasons I thought.

The mood in my room shifts. I look up to find my dad in the doorway, since Winnie left it open. The girls scurry out without having to be asked, Eliza shooting me an apologetic look before she shuts the door, leaving me alone with my dad.

I fold my arms over my chest. "I don't want to talk to you."

"Well, that's okay because I'm going to talk. All you have to do is listen."

It's clear from the set of his jaw and the way he's blocking my escape that he isn't going to give me a choice. I think briefly about making a run for it but Winnie's words shame me into facing him without running away.

"I guess I can't stop you." I scrunch my fingers in Baxter's blond curls but even he deserts me, hopping down to follow Eliza and her plate of food.

"Right." He clears his throat, expression changing from stern to guilty. "I paid Cary to take you out when you first arrived in Cornwall that summer, and made the promises David described regarding a label meeting. I realize now that it was insulting and horrible, but you didn't want to come and without your brother, I worried you'd spend the whole summer locked inside and end up hating me for making you come."

"That's mature."

He winces. "I deserve that. It was self-serving, but, Chrissie, I couldn't have foreseen what would happen between the two of you. That you'd fall in love with him, that it would sweep you up the way it did. That it would change your life."

Tears gather in my eyes despite my best efforts. "How could you let me start seeing him again when I came back here? You let me look like a fool, chasing after him when he never wanted me in the first place."

My dad steps toward me, close enough to touch, and

reaches out to brush away my tears. His fingers are useless against them, which makes me think of Cary and his grandmother's hankies, which makes me cry harder.

"Chrissie, you're not right about that. I didn't say anything, even though I was worried, because that boy is mad about you. He's been in love with you since that summer, which I think is evident." He puts a finger under my chin, lifting my face until our eyes meet. "He gave the money back at the end of the summer. Before he left. Said he couldn't possibly take it. That he should be paying for your company, not the other way around, and I know it tore him up to think that you'd find out."

"He didn't give back the meeting that launched his band, though, did he?" Even knowing that fame would be the one thing that would make a reconciliation even more impossible.

"He did, in a way. I have connections at Sony. BGG contacted them before I could set up a meeting, and I think time has proved that a stroke of luck on Pursuant's part. They got their first record deal on their own and their talent took them the rest of the way." He cocks his head at me, his smile sad. "You knew them better than anyone, Chrissie. You must have known they would make it."

"I don't know what to say." Not only that, I don't know what to *feel*. Part of me rejoices at the news that, at the very least, our beginning wasn't a lie. The relief doesn't stem my embarrassment over being a charity case, or that obviously the entire band knew the whole time.

But it does change *some*thing.

"I can't tell you how to feel about Cary hiding all of this from you. I can't tell you what to do, or whether you'll regret walking away or not. I just thought you should know that he cares about you, Chrissie. He always has." He gives me a sad smile. "You know I've never been crazy about the idea of you getting involved with someone who lives his kind of life, *my* kind of life, but despite everything that's happened, he's not a bad guy. He's handling the fame better than I could have at his age. What I will tell you is that, if you don't hear him out . . . *that*, I think you'll regret."

My dad presses a kiss to my forehead. Tears flow like they're coming from a natural spring that will never run out of water. They don't stop when he leaves me alone with my thoughts.

Can I forgive him?

Will he ask me to?

Or is this thing between us finally over for good?

The one thing I do know is that my stepsisters don't have to worry about my wallowing in this room for much longer, because I have to work tomorrow. Which means facing Cary, even if I don't have a clue how to answer any of the questions rattling around in my head.

If I thought my nerves were bad walking into BGG my first day in London, they're nothing compared to walking into the O2 to start the New Year's Eve setup. I beat Violet to the venue, a small victory in itself, but I'm determined to have more of them throughout the day. Despite my heart being broken, despite my deep fear of abandonment being awoken just two days before, I'm not giving up my job. I'm here to work, and work I shall, even if the thought of spending the day with Cary and not talking about the things rattling around in my soul makes me want to die a bit.

"You're early," Violet comments, dark circles around her luminous green eyes. Unlike all normal bosses, she doesn't seem pleased by my consistent punctuality. I'm starting to think she might be part woman, part horrible beast.

"Yes, well. If you're not ten minutes early, you're late," I quip, then clear my throat after realizing I just intimated that she was late. "Um, you look ill. Are you well?"

"I am not, in fact, well. My parents' house is hosting the plague for the holidays. Tell me where we are on New Year's."

I clear my throat and start talking about members of the press who have requested access, how many volunteers were credentialed to answer the phones, how many comped tickets had been asked for up until this point, and a million other details. I get her a cup of tea in the process, which she takes with greedy hands and an actual thank-you.

The band shows up toward the end of my debrief and start unpacking their instruments while their roadies—I'm not sure if they're called something different when a band isn't actually on the road—start setting things up for sound check. Cary tries to catch my eye several times but I ignore him, thinking up more things to tell Violet. She and the other guys glance between the two of us, clearly unsure how to handle this second change to the status quo, but I ignore it all until the band has gone out onto the stage to start warming up.

I take a deep breath, focusing on the fact that I'm backstage, about to run a massive concert and charity event at the freaking O2, but the beast portion of Violet won't let me get away with that.

"Trouble in paradise?" She raises her eyebrows at me.

"I don't want to talk about it. It has nothing to do with why we're here."

"Fair enough." She watches them play for a while, making notes in a little book, then cocks her head at me to follow her back away from the music. "I need you to spend the next couple of days following up with the interviews that haven't been confirmed, and then getting everything scheduled on the day. We also need to confirm with all of the telethon presenters—the other acts for that night. Oh. And the guys have a wardrobe fitting on Monday. Other than that, and one final sound check on the thirtieth, that's it."

"Oh, that's it?" I smile, softening my sarcasm. It will take hours and hours to get in touch with everyone and get a schedule down, but it means I'll be spending most of my time in the office between now and the concert, and that makes me happy.

"Chris, can I talk to you?"

I freeze at the sound of Cary's voice and turn to find him

in the doorway of the green room. We've been here for hours and he's damp all over, his face pale as he waits for my response. My heart thuds in my chest and my stomach threatens to hurl up everything I've eaten today—which isn't much—but I do my best to keep all of that off my face.

"I don't think now's the best time. In fact, if you guys are done, I think I'll get started on that to-do list, Violet."

My boss nods, a very unprofessional look of satisfaction on her pretty face as she agrees to let me get the hell out of here. I grab my coat and push past Cary, trying to ignore the way my body is aware of his in the split second they're near enough to touch.

The expression of determination on my ex-boyfriend's face when I glance up convinces me that home is the last place I should go. He's determined to force me into a conversation I'm not ready to have, and like my father earlier, if he can find me, we'll have it.

Instead of going back to Hyde Park in my father's car, I ask Alfred to tell the family I'm doing some sightseeing and take a taxi to the London Eye.

Chapter
14

I buy my ticket to go around the bizarrely huge circle of cages, then check my watch. It's after four, and the plaque on the wall says the place closes at eight thirty, so I turn back to the woman behind the counter. "How long does it take to go around on this thing?"

It's probably like a Ferris wheel, with the whole thing stopping every ten seconds for the next car to load and unload, which means a trip around on this massive thing could take at least half an hour.

"Twenty to thirty minutes. Do you not have time?"

"No, I'd like . . ." My mind struggles with the math. "Eight tickets."

"Excuse me?"

"Yeah, I'm just going to ride it until you close."

"I'm not sure . . ." She's stuttering, flustered, and my desire to be away from her grows.

"I have the money. You can either sell me eight tickets now or look at my face every thirty minutes for the rest of the day. What's it going to be?"

She purses her lips, clearly pissed about being spoken to in such a manner, but sells me the tickets. I wait in line, then tell the ticket taker my plan when I get to the front. He's less concerned, just shrugging and tearing all eight of my tickets at once, then looking closely at my face, maybe to memorize it.

The older man gives the back of my hand a pat. "Can't forget a pretty face like yours. Take all the time you need."

I board with my group, maybe fifteen others, and find that the wheel doesn't stop moving. People depart from one side, we board into the other, while our pod drags slowly next to the platform. The first trip around takes a little less than thirty minutes, and I stare out the window, properly stunned by the gorgeous, sweeping views of the Tower, Parliament, Westminster Abbey, and all the rest. By my third trip around I've sat away from the windows, cross-legged and lost in my own thoughts.

Time gets away from me as I circle the sky above London, and the sun has long set by the time the rest of the Eye's patrons dwindle. In fact, I'm alone in the pod now, the last couple having given me the side eye and deciding to wait for the next one the last time the doors opened at the bottom. A glance at my watch says it's just before eight, which means I've got only one more lap around before I'm going to have to go back to my father's house or somewhere else. It's not that I've solved the world's problems in here—or even my own—but in a funny way it's allowed me to step away from them. As though this isn't just a pod on a giant Ferris wheel but a dimension separate from reality.

That is, of course, until the doors open one last time and Cary steps off the platform and into my pod. I almost get up, almost run away, but then I think of Winnie and Eliza and my own pride, and stand my ground.

"How did you find me?"

Cary shakes his head, slumping against one of the windows and onto his butt a few feet away from me. "I know you, Christina. You should get that through your thick head."

I suppose I *had* mentioned wanting to ride on the London Eye the other day, and I had sent the message home that I would be sightseeing. Still. How many places had he tried first?

He looks up, running his hands through his hair. It's devastating, how handsome he is. How broken he looks, how my soul hurts at the knowledge that I've done this to him.

But he's done it to me. We've torn each other apart, and what kind of love is that?

"Well, you've obviously decided we need to talk. So, let's talk," I say, trying to be brave. To summon the girl who survived on her own, who landed this coveted internship, who Winnie wants to look up to. I've never had a little sister, or a little sibling, and find that being a role model brings a strange sort of pleasure along with responsibility.

"I'm sorry to push this on you, but keeping these words bottled up inside is killing me. And I'm tired of writing songs about it, Chris. I want to tell you things, real things, straight to your face. First off, it's true that your dad asked me to . . . befriend you when you came to Cornwall. He was worried you would turn right back around and go home, and I was saving for a car and Pursuant was desperate for a break. But all of that went right out the window when I met you." His hands clench into fists as he steps closer, close enough for the smell of cinnamon and fear to wind their way into my nose. "God, Chris. I fell in love with you on the beach that first day. Your feistiness, the way you gave me lip. How you listened to me, and thought what I said might be worthwhile."

"You have more to offer than music, Cary. I didn't fall in love with a rock star." I don't know what makes me say that, makes me want to soothe away his long-hidden fears that he's some kind of lesser being because he plays a guitar instead of curing diseases or saving starving kids.

"I know. You never took my shit, you're smarter than me, and you make me think about what's important." His smile wobbles. "You encouraged me. Made me feel like I could do anything and I gave that money back to your dad because it made me feel slimy. Terrible. If you ever found out, I knew you'd dump me and nothing scared me more."

None of this makes sense in light of the way things turned out but I don't ask again why he left. I'm afraid he'll tell another lie. Or maybe I'm afraid he'll tell the truth.

"I wanted to apply to university in America to be closer to you. Even when BGG showed up and wanted to sign us, I thought we could wait. Go to the States and launch from there." The tips of his ears turn red and he unclenches his fingers only to squeeze them shut again, as though he doesn't know what to do with them. "David threw a fit. Threatened to tell you everything and make it sound horrible. Pretty much how he did the other night. I figured . . . I don't know what I figured. That you were better off without a jerk who would take money to spend time with a girl. That it would hurt you so badly to know how we got started, that knowing would tarnish everything that happened between us—everything beautiful—and I couldn't stand that."

My heart aches so badly I want to rip it out of my chest. All of this is so unfair. "It hurt me just as badly to have you walk away and never know why."

"I know. I know that now, and I wish that I would have told you the truth and accepted your judgment like a man. I can't go back and change things, love. I can't put eighteen-year-old us back together again, but now that everything's out in the open, I can do this. I can tell you that I love you. I've always loved you, and getting a second chance to hold you and be with you and laugh with you this past week is the most amazing thing that's ever happened to me." His eyes catch mine, holding on for dear life. "We have some-thing *now*, Chris. Forget then. Forget David's wanker ass and your dad's insecurity and whether or not you want a high-profile boyfriend—none of that matters as much as the fact that we're goddamn *right* for each other. We're never going to find anyone else."

His words flutter around me, brush my cheeks and run fingers through my hair that are almost soothing. They prick my skin like bee stings, sharp and brief, opening my eyes wide to the truth of it all—of us. He's being honest. None of the hesitation or fear of another shoe to drop flicker in his face. He's determined. Hurting.

But not lying.

"I don't . . . I don't know what to say." I whisper for the second time today. It's too much to deal with all at once, with him sitting there looking like Cary and breaking my heart all over again.

He watches me, his gaze still burning like it's the sun. The Eye stops, our cage opening for the last time, and the elderly ticket taker peers inside as though he's worried. "Are you okay, Miss? We're closing up for the night."

"I'm fine," I tell him, exiting onto the other side of the platform. Cary follows me, silent, his hands stuck in the pockets of his tight jeans.

"I'll give you some time with those thoughts rattling around in that beautiful brain. But this? Isn't over."

I don't know whether he's talking about us or the conversation, but as I let him put me into a taxi back to my dad's, I have a sneaking feeling he's right. Especially since I'll have to face him again in a few days.

And if I know Cary—and I do—he's not going away without an answer. Not this time.

Chapter

15

"You realize what's happened here, right?" Jessie looks at me in the bathroom mirror, her eyes open wide as she applies a second layer of mascara.

Confusion wrinkles my brow. "I must have blacked out while you were talking again."

"You've ruined everything. You've ruined Disney!"

"What's that, now?" I squint at her. "Have you been, like, hexed by a fairy in Ireland or something?"

She shakes her head. "Fairies do not use hexes. I just mean that your stepmother and stepsisters are kind of awesome."

"Yeah . . ."

"So, Disney could be lying about all of it. *All* of it! Just let that sink in for a minute."

"I don't think disproving one assumption disproves them all. You might need to retake statistics."

"No fucking way. I got my one math requirement out of the way freshman year and never looked back." She finishes primping and sits on the counter to watch me. "Anyway, I'm not saying they're for sure liars about all of it, just that your family makes me wonder."

I give her the smile she wants. "They're not bad."

The perkiness falls away from her posture and expression as she stares at me over the next couple of minutes. "Are you really going to tell Cary to piss up a rope?"

My shoulders slump. "I don't know, Jess. All that stuff he said makes it seem like I should forgive him but I don't think I can spend the rest of my life feeling like the idiot who got duped by the same guy *three* times. Fool me once and all of that."

"I really don't think he's trying to dupe you. You might want to consider that possibility before you walk away."

Walk away. Can I really walk away from Cary? From the only relationship I've ever had that's made me feel like I could have it and bring the world to my feet, besides?

"What are you scared of?"

"*Everything.* I'm scared of not having him. I'm scared of being taken advantage of—of giving him the idea that he can just do whatever he wants and I'll be waiting to take him back. Of being the dumbass who went ahead and fell in love with the guy paid to take her out." I shake my head, swallowing hard. "I'm the butt of everyone's joke. How can I even face the rest of the guys? And there's the small matter of my job."

I hadn't forgotten David's threat, nor the reality that he would and could make good on it. No matter how good I am as a publicist, no matter how much confidence the brass have in me, they aren't going to hire someone who makes even one member of their hottest act uncomfortable.

"Christina, listen to me." Jessica waits until my eyes raise to meet hers. "You cannot worry about what other people think. There will be other jobs, but there might not be other loves like this one. You can't change what's already happened in your life but you can take control of what happens next. It's a waste of time, trying to figure out anything other than what you want. What will make you happy, what you can live with and what you can't. That's all."

"Oh, that's all? No pressure."

She shrugs and hops down, heading into the bedroom. "I didn't say it was easy. But you'd better think fast because we need to go. It's after ten."

The guys are hosting the telethon for twelve of its twenty-four hours, beginning at noon today and ending at midnight, with the concert playing the last two hours. We're supposed to be in the studio by eleven, which means it's definitely time to get going.

My phone buzzes, but it's not my morning text from Cary. It's from Violet.

I'm assuming you're on your way and that everything is set.

Yes. On my way now.

342

"You ready?" Jessica asks.

I don't know if she's talking about leaving or facing Cary, but either way, it's too late to say no.

Traffic is terrible, a seven-car pileup turning Alfred into a basket case and making me late. Jessica isn't with me—she and Grady went to visit a few of his friends and then have a New Year's Eve dinner before meeting me at the studio later. We're all supposed to go out for a few drinks after the telethon ends but I'm trying to come up with a good excuse not to, because who wants to lug a broken heart out with a happy couple?

Not this girl.

I run into the studio, flashing credentials at the guard and scribbling my name on the sign-in sheet before finding the green room where the band is waiting.

They're all calm, perched on couches and already dressed in an array of hipster garb, when I burst through the door. I do a quick inventory to make sure they all look acceptable, my gaze landing on Cary for the briefest possible moment and never meeting his eyes.

"I'm sorry I'm late. You guys look good. Any problems? Questions? Are you ready?"

"We're fine, calm down." Cedric straightens the cuffs on his shirt. "We've all got our scripts and we've been over them with Vi. We're ready."

"Good. Okay, good." I hate not feeling prepared. I hate

that I bailed on them, on my responsibilities, like a big fat baby. "I'm sorry."

"Stop saying that. It's annoying." Simon looks pointedly at Cary when our eyes meet, and when my gaze slides toward my . . . whatever he is now, he's staring at me.

The jagged edge of pain in his blue eyes takes my breath away. It's like someone punched all of the air out of my lungs and it takes long moments for me to pull my gaze away. Nothing has really changed since I first landed and promised Violet that none of this would affect my performance—Cary and I just took a small detour into Happy Land. Small, and over.

"So, we've got less than five minutes. Maybe we should get out there."

"You do that. I'm going to get all of your interviews and acts lined up and ready—there are some nonprofits here that want some blurbs, maybe some face time if you have a lull."

They rouse themselves, tossing bottles of water into the trash and grabbing rumpled scripts. They file out past me, Simon and Alfie first. David freezes when the words I don't want to hear come from behind him in line.

"Can I talk to you for a minute?" Cary asks, his voice as raw as his expression. "Please."

"You guys need to get out there," I reply without looking at him. I can't look at him or I'll fall apart, and now isn't the time. I still don't know if I can do this again—open up. Forgive.

"I don't give a single shite about being out there on time right now. I care about you."

"Come on, man. You're being a todger. Let's go." David reaches back and pushes Cary in front of him. When I don't object, he shoves him right out the door and into the hallway.

Cedric pauses in front of me, folding his arms and tapping his foot until I look up. My throat is on fire but my eyes are dry. Progress.

The disappointment on Ced's handsome face sets my jaw. "What?"

"Don't do this to him, Chris. Whatever the answer, just tell him, because not knowing is killing him. No matter what he's done, I know you care." He pauses, glaring. "Fucking act like it."

The amount of shame and sorrow that flood me at his angry accusation makes it hard to see as I follow them down the hall to the soundstage where the telethon is being taped. There are bleachers set up for an audience that will switch out every two hours, and the requisite phone bank operators—about two dozen. Another five dozen are back-stage so that no one who calls to donate to the same children's charity gets a busy signal.

The guys take over, introducing themselves and engaging in some funny banter before settling down and talking about what a great opportunity they have to help raise money for such a worth cause. Standard fare, but they pull it off with the characteristic honesty and earnestness that has earned them a million fans.

Cary watches me with a thoughtful expression during commercial breaks, and with each one that passes, my anxiety ramps up. He doesn't come over to where I'm standing in the wings, and he doesn't chase me down when I move a little farther back and settle into a chair. But something's coming. I'm pushing him, letting him stew, and anyone can see that he's about to explode.

There's no way to talk to him now, though, even if I knew what I wanted to say, and I'm starting to worry that he's going to lose it on live television and BGG is going to fire me anyway for breaking their biggest cash cow.

They play a couple of songs. Each guy takes a turn, talking about their childhood holidays and how they can't imagine growing up without memories like those, without being healthy, then they play another song.

The day ticks away. It's during the eight o'clock hour that Cary takes the mike to host for ten minutes. The sound of his voice makes my heart ache. The stories about his childhood, about his perfect parents, bring a smile to my face. Then he glances back toward me, and my stomach seizes.

"I have a special incentive to announce for all of you viewers. I know there's been some speculation over the last couple weeks as to the identity of the mystery woman in my life. What I can tell you is that she's an amazing woman who changes my world for the better every time she steps into it, and being without her makes me realize what's really important in this life." He pauses, swallowing hard. "Our goal for our twelve hours on this program is five hundred thousand pounds. If you all make it a hundred thousand above that—so, six hundred thousand pounds before midnight—not only will I personally donate another hundred thousand, I'll also kiss the love of my life at midnight, right on this spot."

My phone rings before the last words leave his lips. It's Jessica, but I don't answer it because I can't breathe. I can't move. I have no idea what possessed him to do that, but by the way he marches toward me once the cameras cut to commercial break indicates I'm about to find out.

This time I do run away—straight to the green room, where I stay for a long time. Not hiding, because they can find me if they need me, but thinking. Processing. Gathering the scraps of my courage and my heart and my dignity, which I find to not be quite as scattered as I thought.

Cary's words—the truth about us—started to heal them.

Cary wants to kiss me in front of millions of people later tonight.

The thought makes me want to throw up. The knowledge is there, deep and true, that I want to kiss him, too. I want to stake my claim on him, show what we have to the world and not look back, but can I do it? Am I just scared, or is there some other, more founded reason for my hesitance?

"Oh my God, Christina. I swear, I have never seen more drama in my entire life." Jessica shoves her way into the green room, visitor badge swinging around her neck. A tall, handsome guy with killer dimples follows her, his hands stuffed deep in his jeans. "Oh, this is Grady."

I shake his hand. "I'm sure you would have gotten a better introduction if it weren't for Cary's impromptu television announcement. Sorry."

He quirks a smile and slips a long arm around my roommate's waist. "I'm getting used to it. And enjoying every minute."

She swats him, pretending to be embarrassed but lighting up until his gaze. "Stop being adorable. Christina doesn't want to see that right now."

"No, it's fine."

"What are you going to do?"

"I don't know. I'm thinking about it."

"Guy makes a declaration like that on national television, he's serious," Grady observes, then holds up his hands. "I'm just saying."

It's pretty much the same observation Eliza made in the car the other night, and for what it's worth, there's not a doubt in my mind that Cary's being honest. That he believes the same thing I do about us being meant for one another and I'm already regretting not running into his arms the moment he said it on the Eye the other night. Because the longer I wait the more time I have to think, and the more doubts start to creep in as far as whether I'm going to look like an idiot. On live television.

If *I'm* being honest, I agree with him. Our summer

romance was great and sweet but what we've rediscovered and nurtured over the past couple of weeks is even better. Stronger. We're not figuring out who we are anymore, but we're still pushing each other to move and grow and achieve.

And if *that's* true, it shouldn't matter what anyone thinks. Are you going to be eighty years old regretting what people thought of you for five minutes or regretting never having real love again?

It's an easy enough question to answer.

I hug Jessica, my heart full. "Thanks for being here. And for calling me on my bullshit."

"Someone has to," she says into my ear. "Thanks for letting me."

We smile, a little goofily, and Grady shakes his head. "I swear, women have some weird kind of silent language. What does this mean?"

"It means she's going to stop worrying and start doing," my roommate replies.

"Doing Cary?" he asks slyly.

I can't help but laugh at how much of a guy he is—the total opposite of Brennan, who Jessie dated for the first half of our junior year. "I like you, Grady. The two of you really suit each other."

"We think so." He grins down at Jess in a way that makes me think Cary and I aren't the only two people who've managed to find that perfect person halfway around the world.

"Do you guys want some dinner?" My stomach is tied

up in a thousand knots. There's no way I could eat, but that doesn't mean they shouldn't. "There's all kinds of crap in the room next door."

"We've eaten."

Time passes in the most agonizingly slow manner ever known to man for the next couple of hours. The three of us watch the concert from the green room, our feet up as we try not to notice the ticker creep higher and higher. It's almost midnight when it slides over six hundred thousand pounds.

Every blood cell in my body comes to a stop as Cary faces the camera. "You did it, Great Britain! This is amazing, and I'm following through on my promise to increase your giving by another hundred thousand pounds as we speak."

Someone shouts from the audience, the words inaudible, but the red tinge to Cary's ears says he made them out. "I'm not sure if I'm going to be able to follow through on the first part of my promise . . ." He trails off to a chorus of boos.

"Get off your ass, Lake. Go big or go home."

"Around here, I believe they call that a full monty," Grady interjects. "What? I'm trying to be helpful."

"Well, in America our only full monty references a British movie about male strippers." Jessica raises her eyebrows in the form of a challenge.

"That show's only for you, Jessie."

"Now I'm definitely getting out of here," I mumble, attempting to joke myself out of wanting to toss my cookies.

"Go."

My roommate doesn't have to tell me again; I'm halfway

350

out the door by the time the one syllable command leaves her lips. I make my way down the maze of hallways to the stage again and stand behind one of the curtains. The pained, embarrassed expression on Cary's face tickles my conscience. My stomach hurts, but the longer I look at him, the surer I feel that this is the right thing.

When I first saw him again, there was hesitance between us. As though it was too good to be true, our coming back together, and now I know why. Now, we've crashed. Bottomed out, all the way back to where this whole thing started, but instead of falling into nothing, we've hit the bedrock of our relationship.

I'm awed to find that first layer, laid that day we met, has never shaken. We might be at the bottom, but the footing is surprisingly solid.

The crowd starts counting at ten, their voices chanting backward. Cary drops the microphone to his side, not bothering to hide his wrecked expression. Tears shine in his eyes, but I'm euphoric as I step out onto the stage.

The crowd pauses at number seven to cheer. Cary turns to see me coming toward him at a brisk pace and he lights up from the inside, rushing to meet me.

Five . . . four . . .

We crash into each other, his arms lifting me against his chest as I laugh at the unbelievable high of this . . . thing. This us.

"Do you want to start with what in the hell you think you're doing, promising people we'll kiss on camera at midnight? Did it occur to you that I might not want to do any such thing?"

"It's for a good cause," he says, plying me with those pleading eyes.

"You're an ass," is all I can think to say. He knows me too well. There are no cards up my sleeve. No tricks that he hasn't seen. It's liberating to have someone know you that well but it's bad for keeping secrets.

"I know. But I'm *your* ass, if you'll have me."

I swallow hard, taking courage from the adoration in his eyes, then give him what he wants. "I love you, Cary White. Mistakes and all."

"Since I am an utter fuck-up, I'm probably going to make a few more. So you have no idea how happy I am to hear you say that."

His lips meet mine as the clock chimes midnight. They're soft and salty, sweet and hungry as we cling to each other. The audience hoots and hollers and the world watches as confetti rains down on us from above, but the only thing that matters is Cary, and me, and the fact that we're finally back where we belong.

Epilogue

Cary's lips linger against mine. I roll closer to him, reveling in his warmth even as the buzzer rings from his doorman's desk for the third time.

"You know that's your friends, right?" he murmurs against my mouth. "We're supposed to be ready to go."

I groan, twisting my lips into a pout. "But I don't want to go anywhere."

"I'd love to oblige, as ever, but you're the one who made plans, remember? Plus, I have a surprise for you."

My eyes fly open to take in his sparkling blue eyes, the way his dark hair flops down onto his forehead, and my skin starts to tingle. "Tell me."

"Oh no. You have to get up and get dressed first. We don't have time for showers, which is good and bad. Good, because I'm going to smell your naked skin on me all day and bad because everyone else is probably going to, as well."

I shake my head. "You say the weirdest shit and make it sexy."

"It's a gift." He swats my ass as I roll to my feet and dig clean clothes out of my messenger bag. "I'll get the door."

"You might want to put some pants on, first."

"Noted." He struts over to the closet, his hard, angular body on display for my eyes only.

It's not so bad, being with a rock star. I get to see what everyone else wants to see, and there's something secretly delicious about that.

Of course, I only get to see it for one more day. Then he goes back to his world, and I go back to mine. We haven't talked much about it yet, and I've tried to console myself with the promise that I'm almost done with school. What are a few more months when we've been apart for years?

By the time I get dressed and swipe on some makeup in an attempt to look like I haven't been getting ravaged all day, Jessie and Grady are sitting on the couch in the living room, chatting with Cary.

"Hey. Sorry."

"No worries. I mean, we've been there." My roommate casts a sly, slightly lustful look at her boyfriend, who turns red.

"Where are we going again?" I accept the hot cup of tea Cary offers, smiling at the dusting of cinnamon on the rim.

"It's the last day of decorations and that sort of thing, and your roommate has never been to London. I'm thinking the grotto or Covent Garden, then a nice dinner." He smiles at my friends. "I'd be stoked to get to know you both better. I've not met anyone from Christina's new life."

"We're stoked to spend the day with you!" Jessie exclaims. "I mean, I've never met a real live rock star."

"Rock is a relative term," he explains.

"So is star," I quip, ducking his elbow.

"Well, at least you two will get to see more of each other next summer, right? With the tour?" Grady's bright gaze slides from Cary to me, and his face falls. "What? Did I read that wrong?"

"What's that?" I look at my boyfriend. "We've been, um, not watching the news."

"I guess your surprise is out of the bag," Cary sighs. "But I suppose you did get dressed. Pursuant just booked a US summer tour."

A grin stretches my lips. Not that I wouldn't have gone anywhere to see him, but this is great news. "That's fantastic!"

"It is, but you should know that BGG already assigned our staff, including interns."

My heart sinks, even though the fact that David hasn't gotten me fired yet is some kind of miracle. "Oh."

"We had a long conference call two days ago, talking about who we want on the road with us and what kind of promotion we're expected to do." He stops, shooting a glance toward Grady. "Can we meet you guys downstairs in a few minutes?"

"Sure. Absolutely, mate."

"Take your time," Jessie adds, giving my hand a squeeze on her way out.

"So, your good news is also bad news?"

"No, it's all good news. I'm just fucking with you."

"What?"

"Of course I told them you were the only intern I wanted on the tour." He holds up his hands, cutting off my reply. "David agreed, that wanker. He thinks you'll be less of a distraction if you're there and I'm not always thinking about you. He's daft, obviously, since I'm always thinking about you."

He puts his arms around me and nuzzles my neck. I struggle against him for a moment in an attempt to punish him for being awful, then give in. "You are a sick bastard. Totally lost the plot, you know that?"

"I know. It's this girl that I just can't get out of my head."

I pull back so I can look him in the face, unable to get enough of just watching him. I hope that never changes. "You really are a charmer, Cary White. But what makes you think I'm going to spend my summer following you around? I'm up for the golden goose of internships in the New York office, and I'm hoping to get a full-time position there after graduation."

"So, you're saying you don't want to tour with us?" The sorrow on his face makes me giggle, which makes him snatch me against him, fingers digging into my ribs.

I wriggle loose, putting some distance between us and

my hands on my hips. "I'm saying there's nothing I want more than to see you every day for the rest of my life, but I'm not going to throw away everything I've worked for over the past four years, either. So, I'll take the job on Pursuant's tour, but only if nothing better comes along first."

He smiles, the room getting brighter. "I think that's fair. Maybe after the tour I'll follow *you* around instead."

"You just want to look at my ass."

"I'll never deny it." He pulls me close, brushing a kiss across my lips that leaves me hungry for more. "You're not getting rid of me this time, Bug. Not ever."

Cary catches my lips more roughly this time, all earnest sweetness and heat as my heart stutters, tickling my chest with fluttering wings. I look deep into his eyes, and then gaze out across the gorgeous London skyline as he goes to get ready for our next adventure. A light lace of snow flutters down, dusting the twilight with a sparkling blanket, leaving the city looking magical at the start of a blank slate.

It's a brand new year, and I'm not scared anymore—not of our past, not of our future, and not of the girl I've managed to become along this path littered with heartbreak and abandonment and ambition and love and forgiveness.

I think I like her. I think I like her a lot.

Acknowledgments

I am so grateful to everyone who helped these novellas become a reality in a very short period of time—starting with County Clare, Ireland, itself for the inspiration. The people there (particularly the McCormacks, who hosted us at their B&B, the Donour Lodge) run a close second. Everyone was friendly, quick with a smile, and so proud to share facts and secrets about the land they call home. I'll never forget it.

Second, my agent, Kathleen Rushall, who fleshed out more than one little idea with me before we landed on a few that might work. She's fast—her mind, her e-mail responses, her wit—and I stop on a regular basis to appreciate how much she's brought to both my writing and my career. Thank you for taking a chance on us a year and a half ago.

Meredith Rich, my editor at Bloomsbury Spark—this is our first project together and we already know it won't be our last(!). After seeing how your notes and thoughts and improvements turned these novellas into something more than they could have been without you, I couldn't be happier about that fact. Thank you for believing in me!

I also want to thank everyone else at Bloomsbury whom I have yet to "meet" but know worked hard to put this book into reader's hands—cover designers, assistants, formatters, editors—thank you for your hard work. As someone who has done it all herself for over two years, I know how much of your precious time has been given to me.

Thank you to my family, as always, for asking when my next book is coming out, and for wanting to know how things are going even when all I do is mumble at you from behind dirty curtains of hair while not looking up from my laptop—even on vacation. Thanks also to my dear, dear friends and critique partners, Leigh Ann Kopans and Denise Grover Swank, who are involved and much loved, even when they're not so involved or much loved.

Last but never least, thank you, Paul, for cleaning the kitchen when I've let it sit, for making me dinners (that you've sometimes foraged for yourself), and for your ever-so-polite reminders that perhaps a shower might be in order. Even I have to admit that you're sometimes right about that.